The Demon's Fog

By Christine Soltis

Copyright © 2010

Original inception 2003
First publication July 2010
Copyright © July 2010
ISBN number: 978-0-557-63188-9

Other novels by this author:
In A Land Of Hatred, July 2008
In A Land Of Change, April 2009
In A Land Of Destruction, November 2009

Poetry compilations:
Pathways to the Maze, December 2008
The Perils of Melancholy, August 2009

Short Story Book:
A Dark Kaleidoscope, August 2009

Combined Edition:
A Dark Kaleidoscope-The Perils of Melancholy, August 2009

Visit http://darkwriters.tripod.com
or email at: inalandofhatred@gmail.com

In Association With
www.enertiaglobal.com
and Veltri Talent Management

Edited By Christie Johnson

In
Association
With

e-nertia global systems

E-nertia Global Systems, LLC.
and Veltri Talent Management

Christine Soltis

.

4

CONTENTS

Christine Soltis

INTRODUCTION

Three males and one female.

Not your typical circle of friends. But some might say four boys hung together, since the girl was your typical tomboy.

Mina Clyne, Jesse Webber, Ryan Fisher and Scott Wood have shared 13 years of friendship. Through those years, from science fiction to the seemingly simpler events of the world and science- such as the evolution of a caterpillar into a butterfly, a tadpole into a frog; this adventure-seeking team has watched in their explorations.

Like detectives, the four have competed with their intelligence, seeing whose hypothesis or idea could explain matters best by checking facts to prove it. As friends, of course, they have disagreed constantly, agreeing nearly as much. It is a friendship based upon the rebuttal of differing ideas and opinions.

Intellectually challenging of themselves, together they attended the same college with scholarships based on their high school academic performance. Together, they graduated the same year. Even the expected wild life of dorm living could not deter their pursuit of intellectual matters.

On this particular day, back in the small town of Joseph City, Arizona, the four gathered at Scott's house. Searching the Internet for disgusting, horrible or just plain unexplainable events was typical behavior for them. Each had their own belief in the supernatural, though it listed lower on the level of possibilities for some, particularly since science explained a great deal of the workings of the universe.

And so, yes, this is how it all began…

Christine Soltis

CHAPTER 1:
COMMON INTERESTS

"Check out this one. Wow," Jesse said.

Ryan looked up from his book at the half naked brunette sprawled across the screen.

"Yeah, she's attractive," he replied.

But his voice lacked the interest Jesse's had. Without another word, Ryan looked back at his book and began to read.

Jesse scoffed and shook his head. His face was mired with sarcasm. He started to turn towards Ryan but was stopped by his reflected mirror image, seduced by himself. His skin glowed a shiny bronze regularly enhanced by the Arizona sun. For a moment, he thought of how attractive he was.

"I am really sexy," he said.

At 21, with tamed, sandy blonde hair and entrancing brown eyes, Jesse spent the most time entertaining his perversions. He had always been more attractive to the opposite sex, though his interest did not lie in one for very long. He flexed a muscle to his reflection. The flattened doppelganger moved with him, causing him to smile amongst his vanity. His fine athletic build gave him the strong, sexy appearance he needed to downplay his intelligence.

Finally, he turned fully, facing Ryan. But Ryan didn't look up to acknowledge him. He kept his nose in the book.

"Put the book down and check this one out," Jesse said.

Ryan shook his head, still not looking up.

"No thanks," he replied.

Ryan appreciated a woman's beauty, but did not like to see them on a sleazy, pornographic sight. He was 21 as well; though much more mentally mature than Jesse. Considered a dweeb, or dork most of his life, he took his role proudly, never attempting to fit into the image of beauty in society.

Jesse turned away from Ryan, clicking away at a different site. His eyes widened. Jesse shrieked in excitement.

"Oh man! Look at this. Bet you don't know what they call that," he said, laughing in his obnoxious way.

Ryan looked up.

"Ha, ha, ha. Very funny. I've had a girlfriend before. Thanks," Ryan defended himself.

Continuing on his newest crusade, Jesse typed in the web address to find disgusting sexual fetishes. Watching as the screen popped up, he was always baffled at the sickening sights he found.

Jesse began whimpering like a dog. Ryan ignored him.

Instead, he reached into his small black book bag and retrieved a notebook. Scribbling on the paper, he took notes from his latest book on fascinating aspects of the meteor. He planned on finding out the sizes of the largest meteor, the heaviest, the smallest, where they had fallen and more. It was endless how many facts were in existence for only one topic. After viewing a shooting star in the sky just a few nights ago, he became obsessed with the universe above.

"Man, look!"

Jesse's voice intruded again over Ryan's studies.

Ryan scoffed.

"I don't want to watch you watch disgusting sexual fetishes. Just shut up and leave me alone. Can't you see I'm busy?" Ryan said, without looking up.

He didn't want his mind polluted. More than that, his book was more interesting than Jesse and his fantasies could ever be.

"You're a dork," Jesse replied.

Before Ryan could counter, Mina and Scott walked through the bedroom door with snacks in hand.

Jesse hurriedly clicked the exit icon, so that they wouldn't see what he was looking at on Scott's computer.

"What took you guys so long? I'm hungry," Jesse asked, lingering in his obnoxious tone.

Moving towards Jesse, Mina's dark eyes widened at his bossiness. Her tall, thin figure stopped, towering over him from his sitting position. Short, almond colored hair hung straight and fine around her face, without a bit of frizz. Her stunning, natural beauty and nearly flawless complexion never matched her voice or physique.

Jesse's eyes focused on her face, a look of arrogance still draped upon his.

Obnoxiously, she dropped a bag of chips onto his lap.

"Next time you go if you're so hungry," she said.

Abruptly she turned away with a misanthropic air following behind her. Jesse smiled sarcastically though his voice softened as he plowed into the bag.

"Thank you," he replied.

"So what did you guys do while we were gone?" Scott asked.

"Nothing," Jesse hurriedly replied, with the guilty look of a weasel spreading across his face.

Ryan scoffed.

"This moron was looking up porn again," Ryan spouted out.

"Again?" Scott asked.

Jesse's face flushed red in embarrassment.

"Sorry," he said to Scott.

Jesse turned to Ryan, changing his tone, "Thanks a lot asshole, for telling him."

Ryan smirked.

Jesse's embarrassment lingered inside of him. It wasn't that he thought Scott would be mad; it was just that he had a lot of respect for him. Of the group, Scott wore the nice guy title. He would not tell Scott, of course, but deep down, he admired him.

Mina rolled her eyes, uninterested in their fetishes.

"So what's the subject for the day?" she asked.

She was already bored.

"Meteors," Ryan responded of his own topic in a quiet, contemplative voice.

"I meant for us, what can we find to debate about?" she asked.

She was in the mood for some fun, stimulating conversation.

Jesse's eyes lit up.

"We should find something on the Internet," Jesse added.

"We don't want to talk about sex with you," Ryan said, his face draped with disgust.

"Shut up man, I meant real topics. Maybe missing person reports again," Jesse said.

He looked around at the rest of the group. A tone of seriousness crept into his voice, "We haven't studied those in a long time. And they're always happening."

"That is actually a good idea," Mina said.

"Sounds good to me," Scott agreed, nodding his head.

Jesse jumped back onto the computer, finding the proper search engine. Searching, he pulled up a website for cases of missing persons. Mina, Scott and Ryan eagerly gathered behind him, watching over his shoulder for anything interesting. Several minutes later, Jesse pulled up a news article and began to read.

"Joanie Milkin, kidnapped from a grocery store in Milwaukee, age 13," Jesse read, "Sound like a good one?" he asked, turning to face the rest of the group.

"Nah, too common," Mina replied, "We have to find something more unique."

"Okay."

He turned back to his search.

"How about John Kingloy, kidnapped in California while with his father on a fishing trip?" he tried again.

"Hmmm," Ryan muttered.

"Getting better," Scott replied, "Look up the details."

Jesse pulled up the screen and they began to read.

Apparently, the eight-year old boy had gone fishing with his father and his father's friend. Allegedly, while the father ran to a nearby store for drinks and snacks, the friend of the family disappeared with the son.

"Interesting," Jesse said.

Ryan pushed his glasses up his nose.

"Well what do you think? Do you think the father set it up?" he asked, "Maybe for money?"

Mina shook her head.

"Nah. What kind of father would do that? Of course, how could someone you are friends with just take your child like that?" she asked, "How could someone let them?"

"Probably was a set up," Jesse agreed, "By the father."

Now Scott shook his head.

"He had to trust the man to leave the boy with him though. I don't know, I don't think it was a set-up. I just think the friend must have planned it out really well," Scott added.

"How long ago did that happen?" Mina asked.

She wanted more details before making a decision.

"Two years ago," Jesse replied.

"And they still haven't found him?" Mina whispered.

"What would he do with a child?" Ryan wondered.

Mina blinked harshly.

"Well there are many things, he could have given him to another family, he could have molested him, he could have raised him as his own son if he loved the boy..." Mina offered, before Jesse interrupted.

"Or he could have killed the boy as some sort of sick, diluted experiment in his own desires to want to experience what it is like to inflict such a pain on another being," Jesse replied.

An odd look crossed Jesse's face.

Everyone quieted as the group looked at him suspiciously. Jesse always had the sickening aspect of people down, and they wondered at times if it was his own release of testing the waters of committing violent and explicit deeds.

Feeling their eyes on him, he realized that he had intermingled what he viewed as the sickening ways of all people into their current discussion.

Jesse shrugged his muscular shoulders, "It can happen, some people are sick," he said, trying to brush it off.

Instead of continuing to figure out what happened, Jesse dug deeper to find different cases. The rest of the group moved away from the computer as they contemplated and discussed the last case. But they didn't have long to consider it before Jesse waved them back. And this was a typical day for them.

"Hey, look at this. This is kind of odd," Jesse shrieked.

Ryan, Mina and Scott quickly returned to the computer. Jesse summarized the news article out loud.

"22-year old Carey Suttle was at a log cabin in Idaho, about seven years ago when the cabin caught fire. The dental records of her and her boyfriend were used to match the bodies but her younger sister, who was 18, just disappeared. There was no evidence of her body anywhere around," Jesse said.

Excitement rushed through his voice, matching the inner eagerness of the others.

"Fire starter," Ryan said.

But his voice was a whisper, lost in a movie of another time. The others ignored his film addiction.

"How did the fire start?" Mina asked.

"Did someone light it?" Scott asked.

Jesse read further.

"No," Jesse said.

Shock whisked across his face.

"It was due to faulty wiring in the cabin. The cabin was a vacation home that had just been worked on. The electrician did a half-assed job."

Scott stood back, his bright blue eyes aglow.

"What the hell happened to the other girl?" he asked.

Ryan shrugged, seeming to come back to reality.

"Maybe she woke up in the middle of the fire and escaped. Is there a lake close to the cabin?" Ryan asked.

Jesse read on, his eyes scanning as quickly as he could.

"It says search teams went out, but there was no sign of her. No, it says right here that there was no water source close to the fire. Nothing could explain the missing person," Jesse said.

Mina tapped her finger against her chin, thinking hard.

"Perhaps she became crazy because she couldn't save her sister and wandered into the woods, dying of exposure," Mina hypothesized.

Scott shook his head.

"They probably would have found her body though. She wouldn't have made it very far," Scott reasoned.

"That's true," Mina realized, though she knew that people in shock tended to have different reactions and sometimes, unexpected strength.

"But look here," Jesse pointed excitedly at the screen, "It says there was a pile of ashes a few feet from the cabin. It was several feet high, but they couldn't tell what burned at that part of the scene."

"Could she have run out of the cabin on fire then?" Mina offered.

"But look here," Jesse pointed again, "There were no teeth left over in the pile- nothing to decipher with dental records, no bones either, just ash. But if she were outside, she would have had a better chance of putting out the fire by rolling on the ground. It was just a pile of ashes."

Jesse's eyes opened wide, his voice incredulous now.

"That wasn't her body," Mina started, "I doubt that she would have burned completely to ash with no bodily remnants. Maybe she ran to the road, flagged someone down and was kidnapped from there."

"That's possible," Scott agreed.

Ryan shook his head.

"Depending on how far away the main road was and since it was a cabin, I'd imagine the road was quite a ways away," Ryan added.

"It was in the middle of the woods," Jesse finished.

Their debate continued until Mina had to leave for work. At the end of the day, they decided they didn't have anything extra to add to the missing cases report. There were just too many theories and possibilities to be picked apart.

They all parted ways. Jesse went home to look at some pornographic magazines he ordered, Ryan went to his house to read in the comfort of his room, while Scott surfed the Internet and emailed some of his other friends. None of them continued to mull over the case, except for Mina.

The case rang on her mind as she rang people's orders into the cash register. Although she had a Biology degree, Mina worked two unfulfilling jobs, one at a café and the other at the local library. Her brain needed the stimulation she lacked. And this case seemed like a good start.

The more she thought about the case, she realized that it was just one example of a sad occurrence, a tragedy of youth. But that was not what she focused on. Her mind wandered with the pile of ashes in the scene nearby.

How could this pile, this lone pile of ash several feet in height stand where nothing explainable had burned?

Of the group of friends she encircled herself with; she tended to take on more of an interest in the supernatural. To her, it just seemed strange that stories of monsters and ghosts could exist, without proper evidence of origins.

She believed they existed.

The evidence must be alive, though it is probably hidden well, she thought to herself.

When the workday ceased and she returned home that night, Mina immediately logged onto her computer. The others would have no interest in the case since it was so difficult, so she would research it on her own. Recently, she had not been able to find anything to drag her interest until now.

Hours passed until her eyestrain and stiff neck caused her to question her use of time. She blinked and looked away from the screen, still seeing the endless lines of sentences and paragraphs all tangled together in her vision.

Not even one more case.

She could not find another missing case with the same similarities. After hours of reading and researching with no new results, she gave up for the night. Her brain was spinning with the faces and words of lost people's stories. All those stories had no visible, shared ending with the rest of humanity. She tried to blink away the sadness, the sorrow buried in those faces and the faces of those who loved the missing. Together, they began to jumble in her tired mind.

She lay down and stared at the ceiling. Tomorrow, when she was not so tired, she would be able to do better research.

CHAPTER 2:
THE AWAKENING OF KNOWLEDGE

Though exhausted, Mina had difficulty sleeping. Awakening in the midst of the gloomy hours outside, around 4:40 AM, she thought of trying another search. It was just before the dawn of a new morning of sunshine, yet she felt so invigorated by her new case. Thoughts of this new research plagued her already, keeping her from the restful nights she had recently enjoyed.

She pulled herself out of bed and plopped down at her desk to begin her search. Surprisingly, this time, within 20 minutes, she located a story similar to the first one. Mina quietly read the details, summarizing them in her head.

Nearly 15 years ago, there was a family reunion held in one of the many wooded parks in Helena, Montana. By the end of the day, just before nightfall, most of the family members had gone home, leaving two middle-aged couples to clean up the mess. As dusk approached, and before finishing cleaning up, the couples indulged in roasting marshmallows. One of the couples left together for the restroom. When they came back, the other couple was gone. Their vehicle was still at the site of the reunion and the fire they built had been extinguished; only a large pile of ashes remained- more than three feet in height. The case remains a mystery to this day. Many wild animals roam the area and that is the suggested cause of the disappearance. All of it happened without a true, final explanation.

"Damn."

Mina's eyes were wide with wonder. Sitting back in her chair, she realized that if there were already two cases, then there must be many more. Two different states. Each of the two events she studied occurred in different states.

What did the two states have in common?

Montana and Idaho were the locations. She pulled a map out of her drawer and laid it across the desk. The two states bordered each other. And they were only a few states away from her. What else did these two places have in common?

She tapped her brain for answers.

In this article, the pile of ashes was there, as it had been in the last case. The strange part of this article was that the fire was extinguished before the pair disappeared.

Perhaps the couple was in the process of putting out the fire when someone came up behind them, Mina hypothesized. But where were the bodies? Who would kidnap a regular, middle-class and middle-aged couple? And who would put out a fire before a kidnapping? Maybe they were environmentally friendly kidnappers, Mina joked.

She scanned the article again. No one came forward to ask for ransom. They are still missing.

These have to be supernatural events. If ever there was one in existence, she thought to herself.

From the top drawer of her computer desk, Mina pulled out a small black notebook. She kept many of them, as did the others, just in case she needed to copy important information on a topic.

Along with her empty notebooks, there were many more in the lower drawers, filled with information that had sparked her interest in the past years. Some days, Mina went over her notebooks filled with dated info, just to brush up on her own personal experiments of the past. In this particular notebook, she recalled the details of last night's findings, along with the information she had just come across.

Just to be safe with her new case, she printed the information listed on her screen. If she figured the case out, she wanted proof with exact information from beginning to end. Unfortunately, she was missing the data they had found the night before.

Though Mina was ever more excited about the new discovery, she felt the effects of her lacking sleep. By 6 AM, the time when people were usually waking for work, she laid back down to rest.

After tossing, turning, thinking and staring off into the darkness of her room for the next 20 minutes, she finally drifted off into a much needed rest.

***

Mina awoke again around 1:00 in the afternoon, the typical life of a freshly post-college student.

Usually, on days not plagued by work, she met with Jesse, Ryan and Scott by two. Together, they kept each other on their toes with their competitive, intellectually stimulating friendship. At their jobs, they just seemed to be zombies; tools that just needed to make enough money to survive.

Mina hoped none of the group had dug into what they debated the other day, though she knew it was too unexplainable for them. This was her personal project. None of them were interested in the supernatural to the extent of Mina's interest.

Still lying in bed, Mina looked around her room. She gazed at several posters of wizards and magical lands, which framed her room's otherwise plain light blue walls. Each poster had a different wizard portrayed in it, one shrouded in blue, another in a morbid shade of red, while the last poster was shaded in a jade green.

Staring intently at the wizard in blue, directly in front of her, she thought of the hidden meaning of these posters. The red one symbolized an angry man, the green a kinder one, and to her, she considered blue as calmness.

Behind the wizard in the blue poster, there was a white and silver castle. A long dark path of stone led to it, separating the wizard in a three-dimensional image. Instead of following the path, he stood, waving a wand, as a stream of sparkly cloud began to unwind. The path was there and so was the power and from her point of view- the poster only lacked action.

In the right corner of her room, fictional figures of gargoyles, dragons and wizards were on display on special shelves she had built into the wall herself, specifically for them. Candles of many dark colors filled the spaces between those mystical figures. From the ceiling, glow in the dark stars and planets hung- still surviving from a much younger age. Towards the left side of the room, three large bookcases stood tall and made of a cheap wood, painted black.

The bookcase closest to her contained old horror movies on VHS tapes. Among them were many of her favorites; Creep Show, Fright Night, The Howling movies, Nightmare on Elm Street, The Exorcist and more.

The other two bookcases held novels of many different subjects ranging from astrology and fiction mysteries to psychology and much more. She had read them all, some even twice.

A few feet away but directly in front of her bed, a lone window graced the room, adding some small light through the blinds to brighten up her gloomy décor.

She continued to lay in bed until about 1:30, thinking about the supernatural and her case. Her eyes stared blankly at the ceiling now, uninterested in the contents of the room. Finally, she pulled herself out of bed to join the world of the living.

Once she finished getting ready, she leisurely walked to Ryan's. As she approached his home, she stared at the medium-sized yellow and white house. It was in desperate need of a paint job. Small amounts of cracked paint showed through from the front, though from her own experience, she knew that behind the house was the worst incidence of weathering. Short grass and shrubs framed the cracked, stone walkway in front, leading to a partially rotted, wooden porch.

The interior of Ryan's house had a lighthouse decorative style in shades of blue and sea green. Adjoined to the living room was a short staircase, which led Mina to Ryan's room. Ryan's mother was at work but Mina knew she was welcome.

Opening his bedroom door, Mina saw Ryan and Scott in front of Ryan's dated, dingy, yellow-colored computer monitor. They seemed deep into research.

"Hi," she said.

Neither one looked up from the screen. Usually, she would have startled them.

"Hello," Ryan replied, still without looking up.

"What are you guys into?" Mina inquired.

"We're just looking at job sites," Scott replied.

Ryan only had a part-time job at a bookstore in the mall. Scott, on the other hand, held a full-time job at a factory. Not one of them had landed good jobs after college, despite their intelligence.

"Anything good?" Mina wondered.

"There are a couple of jobs in different states," Ryan replied, still staring at the screen.

Mina walked over to the screen, looking at it.

"Ugh!" she gasped, "Why did you pick Florida, of all states?"

"We went through a lot of the hot states mostly," Scott answered.

Mina became bored and rolled her eyes.

"Where's Jesse?" she asked.

"Probably at home watching porn," Ryan replied, a hint of disgust in his voice.

Jesse and Ryan disliked each other more and more as the years passed. Mina and Scott noticed it before, but hoped it would somehow even itself out. Instead, it was only becoming worse, adding more tension to the two.

"What's the problem between you two?" Scott asked.

"We're just different," Ryan replied modestly.

"There's more to it than that," Scott pushed, "Come on, you can tell us."

Scott grinned, looking up at Mina. Ryan pursed his lips in contemplation before letting his thoughts slip free.

"He's an insensitive and uncontrollable being. He has no sense of when to draw the line and he grew up with everything he ever wanted so he takes advantage of an intelligence that others only wish they could have. The older he gets the more arrogant. It's always about Jesse- hey look what I'm doing, I'm Jesse, all eyes should be on me all the time," he mocked, "He doesn't care about anyone else and every time I see him, it makes me sick. There, that's how I feel."

Ryan looked away from them and pushed his glasses up his nose. Scott and Mina traded half smiles. Ryan's outburst left the two quiet for just a moment. Scott cleared his throat.

"Do you want my assessment of the situation?" Scott asked Ryan.

Plain and simply, they all wanted the tension to end. But neither ever dared ask for a solution. Ryan blinked, not knowing what to expect.

"Sure, if you think you can fix this," he said.

"You won't be offended by my honesty?" Scott asked.

Ryan was generally a defensive person.

"No," Ryan replied, curiously now.

Mina smiled from where she stood. She knew Scott wouldn't hold anything back.

"Ok, here it is," Scott said, looking at Mina with a small smile, "You feel frustrated with him, obviously, and he feels the same way about you. He just thinks that you should have more fun in your life, and you might need to, truly. Meanwhile, you think he is, of course, what you said. Now maybe the two of you should sit down and talk about this since you did become opposites. But don't forget, you were best friends at one time. You just have to learn to deal with each other's differing views about life and accept it rather than fighting over it. Respect each other for the way you are; be glad you are not the same. If you could just take the good parts of your friendship, then things will work out. Ignore any of his comments; allow him to say what he wants freely without becoming extremely defensive and ready to fight. I really do hate seeing you guys fight," Scott said.

Sincerity brimmed from his words.

Ryan sat there quietly, pondering the issue.

"Maybe I am defensive sometimes," he admitted.

Scott nodded.

"As intelligent as the two of you are, I'd think you wouldn't get to each other like you do. Just don't take things so seriously. It's like a never ending game of ping-pong, dashing comments back and forth for revenge," Scott continued.

Just then, Jesse walked in. Everyone quieted.

"What's up guys?" Jesse asked.

"Not much, they're looking for jobs," Mina replied.

"It's about time," Jesse said in his obnoxious voice.

Through his peripheral vision, Scott saw Ryan tense up in his seat. He knew that a retaliatory comment was about to be let loose from Ryan.

Scott and Mina waited for Ryan's comment. Surprisingly, Ryan said nothing. Jesse looked just as surprised as the others at Ryan's silence. His eyelashes seemed to flutter in confusion.

His tone of voice suddenly changed.

"Did you find any good ones?" Jesse asked.

Now he seemed curious, rather than cynical.

Scott and Mina looked at each other. This was the first time in a long time, as far as they could remember that those two had not continued an argument. Ryan ended a conflict before it started.

"Um, yeah, there are a couple," Scott replied.

Scott kept talking. He didn't want the mood of compromise to disintegrate.

"Around here?" Jesse questioned further.

"No, that's the part that sucks. They are all in other states," Scott explained.

"Well, I wouldn't mind moving to another state," Jesse continued.

A strange silence settled over the room.

Typically, Ryan might say, 'of course you wouldn't mind moving, you have plenty of mommy and daddy's money to help you out. Struggle, what would a struggle be to you?' then the argument might continue with the insults. But this time, nothing was said at all.

Scott blinked rapidly and then whisked his hands through his light red hair.

"Ok, um, yeah, I wouldn't mind moving either if I had the money to. It costs so much to find a place and drive a U-Haul or ship your stuff out. I'd have to save more for awhile before I could even consider moving," Scott said.

"Yeah, it would be expensive," Jesse followed, without bragging about his family's money this time.

Mina stood there, feeling as though she had just dropped into the Twilight Zone. This sudden attitude change for both Ryan and Jesse was a little creepy. It was for the better, and hopefully it would last, but for now, it was odd. It was very odd.

"Anyone need anything from the store?" Mina piped up.

Ever since she awakened, she wanted a Pepsi. She also needed to get out of the creepy mood in the room.

"Actually, I could use a Coke," Ryan said, digging into his pocket for money.

"If you want to pick me up a bag of barbeque chips and a Dr. Pepper, I would be very happy," Jesse said, reaching through the wad of money in his wallet.

"Scott, do you want to walk with me?" she asked, signaling for him to join her.

"Sure," he said.

Mina and Scott left for the store, while Jesse and Ryan searched the computer for jobs.

When they were a few feet away from the house, Mina looked over her shoulder before turning back to Scott. Excitedly, they took turns talking fast and nearly over each other.

"That was odd," she commented.

"You're telling me. I didn't expect that at all. I expected a bar room brawl," Scott said.

"Jesse acted like a real person for once. That's what confused me the most," she commented.

"And Ryan, he didn't let Jesse bug him at all. I guess I really am a strong influence," Scott said with a newfound pride.

"Oh, now I see where Jesse's ego went, straight to your head," she laughed, teasing him.

"And that's where Ryan's critical comments went- straight to your head," he laughed.

The small local store was within walking distance of all of their homes. It was the closest around, though there wasn't exactly a large selection in their small town.

The store was old and had glass doors that needed pulled open, unlike the modern automatic doors in larger stores and gas stations. Inside the store were old, beige shelves, which weren't quite as high as those in retail discount stores. That was the way Mina liked it. She preferred that profits go to small businesses rather than large corporations.

Mina gathered her items while Scott grabbed just about the same amount, though they were all for him.

"Are you going to eat all of that?" she asked, noticing his bag of Doritos, Pepsi, Cherry Coke, a bag of cinnamon rolls and a small package of powdered donuts.

"Don't I always?" he commented.

Scott was a nice height and build, composed mostly of muscle for his love of sports. It definitely didn't show how much junk food he ate.

After paying, they continued on their walk back to the house. They made a wager on the way back as to whether or not Jesse and Ryan would be fighting. Mina believed it was temporary and the fighting would begin at least within the week. Scott had more confidence in himself and his words, deciding it would be permanent.

When they arrived back to the house, they walked the stairs to his room very quietly; to make sure they would catch them, if the two were arguing. It was Mina's idea, since she suspected fighting.

Standing outside the door, Mina leaned her ear against it to catch any noise. She heard nothing.

She motioned for Scott to lean his ear against it as well. He did and was surprised at the quietness in the room.

After five more minutes, they finally heard a noise from within. Someone was standing and a chair was pushed back. Suddenly, the door opened inward, startling them. Jesse stood there, his eyes drifting suspiciously between the two of them.

"Were you guys kissing?" Jesse asked.

He noticed the look of surprise on their faces. Mina's face pulled into a grimace.

"No. Ew gross! How did you know we were out here?" Mina asked.

Jesse smiled wide.

"I've known you long enough that I could pick up the sound of your footsteps in the sands of the desert even if you were barefoot," Jesse replied.

Scott shook his head.

"Really? Your hearing is that good?" Scott joked.

It was almost as if there was some sort of connection between the four of them, that they could tell when one of them was near.

"Senses, it's the sense of intuition, my friend," Jesse replied, "Where's my food?"

Mina thrust the chips at him.

"Ah, so that's what it was, you smelled the chips," Mina joked.

"That too," Jesse said.

He moved back, giving the others space to come in. The two entered, handing Ryan his drink. Ryan paid no attention to them. He

25

was staring at the computer screen with great interest. Mina studied him.

"What are you into Ryan?" Mina asked, curious.

"Just browsing," he quietly replied.

Scott looked at Mina.

"What did you mean by ew, gross?" he interrupted, looking more intently at Mina, "Am I that unattractive?"

At first Mina was confused. Then she realized and laughed.

"Talk about a delayed reaction," she laughed, "No, not unattractive, you are just so much like a brother to me, it's gross."

"Okay, that's better," he joked.

Jesse watched them as he stuffed potato chips into his mouth.

"Aw, you guys are so sweet to each other," Jesse remarked, "Maybe some day you'll get married."

"Ha, ha. You're real funny," Scott said.

"Hey, I'm just saying what I've observed," Jesse said.

Mina rolled her eyes.

"So what do you guys want to do today?" Mina asked, trying to get them off of the stupid subject, "Anyone have any plans, thoughts, ideas?"

"Let's go back to missing cases, that was interesting," Ryan volunteered.

But he didn't look away from the screen as he spoke. Mina grew suspicious and immediately moved to the computer to see what he was doing. MISSING CASES lit up the top of the screen. Her heart rapidly raced.

"Find anything interesting?" she asked.

The nervousness was obvious in her voice. She wanted to work on this subject alone.

"No, not really. A few interesting cases here and there, but that's about it," he replied.

But his eyes never left the screen as he continued to search and read. Mina swallowed hard.

"Any cases with anything really just strange?" she asked.

Everyone else in the room watched Mina, wondering why she had taken a special interest in Ryan's researching. But Ryan himself was oblivious.

"Not really, but all unsolved cases seem strange," he replied. Mina continued.

"I mean, is there anything beyond the realm of human crime? Do any of them seem that way?" she interrogated.

An uneasy and even more desperate tone entered her voice. Her sudden change began to affect the others.

"What is this all about?" Jesse asked.

Mina quickly stood back.

"Nothing," she responded.

She looked away from the computer. Scott studied her.

"Seems like something," he said.

"I just thought there might be interesting things out there," Mina replied.

But her face gave her away. It was more than that. Jesse laughed.

"Like what, alien space ships?" he mocked.

"Shut up," Mina replied, her face reddening.

They all knew Mina constantly searched for evidence of the supernatural. It was the only thing that ever interested her for very long.

The room grew quiet. Even Ryan looked away from the computer. All eyes were staring at Mina. The way they were looking at her, it was as if she had parasitic worms crawling all over her body. The look in those eyes made her shiver with a coldness to her core. She blinked rapidly and broke the eerie silence.

"Well I gotta go," she said, "I have a lot of work to do...around the house."

She quickly exited with one fast wave. Once she was gone, Jesse turned to the remaining group.

"Why is she always searching for something she will never find?" Jesse asked.

Ryan pushed his glasses up his nose.

"Maybe she will find it," he said, "We don't know that she won't."

Seconds later, the argument Ryan and Jesse had so easily avoided now erupted full force. Scott shook his head, tuning them out. The arguing voices were natural background noise. When it didn't end several minutes later, Scott stood up, interrupting them.

"Guys, you don't want to fight. You haven't wanted to for such a long time, just stop. It really is pointless, you both have different opinions, just respect each other for that," he interjected.

"But..." Ryan and Jesse exclaimed in unison.

"But nothing," Scott interrupted before they could finish, "we don't always understand why the other one researches what they do, but we have to respect that as friends. Jesse, you always look up porn, Ryan, some of your subjects might seem boring and Mina, she searches for what she wants to."

"But the supernatural?" Jesse asked, "I like to watch the movies but does she really think it's real?"

His voice held incredulous disgust. Scott shook his head.

"Yes, we all believe it is interesting, we all just don't choose to hunt for it. Just respect her for searching what we don't, as she allows us respect for our own searches. There's no reason to look at her like she's weird all the time. It's just her thing," Scott reasoned.

The room became quiet again as the two pondered Scott's words.

"We've all been friends for so long," Scott finished, breaking into the silence.

All Scott knew now was that Mina had won the wager even if the fight started in her favor.

***

Outside, Mina walked briskly to her home. Her friends had looked at her like she was such a freak, as usual, for her quest.

How can I be the freak, I'm not looking up porn like Jesse, she thought to herself.

She studied the ground as she walked. The chipped cement of the holey sidewalk was a usual visual.

Looking up from the ground, she asked aloud to no one, "Is there something out there? Or am I wasting my time?"

The wind picked up, furiously whisking around the chimes of a neighbor's porch, creating an ominous clattering of bells in the night.

A brief chill shivered through Mina as her ears captured the continuing song, interpreting it as an answer to her question.

"If there is something I'll find it, and I'll show them there is such a thing as the supernatural. It's not just something for stories. It is real. They believe. They've always believed. They're just too scared to search," she said.

At least they wouldn't be searching for what she was searching for. One good thing came out of them looking at her like a freak.

CHAPTER 3:
QUESTIONABLE TOPICS

Now in her room, Mina immediately logged onto her computer.

I don't even know why I went over there. I have so much more to do here, she thought to herself.

But after an hour of researching the missing cases of lost faces, she could not find anything at all. There were plenty of missing cases, and there were plenty of fire stories in the news, but there weren't enough examples of both to make for strange occurrences.

Maybe she really was making something out of nothing. Perhaps she would never find evidence.

She shook her head, and then stretched her right hand back to rub her neck. It had become stiff from sitting in front of the computer for the last hour.

She shook her head, raising her left hand to help the other. Her eyes drifted to the ceiling, her mind lost in constant thought. Nothing really mattered to her, research-wise, that is, except finding examples of the supernatural. She couldn't fully understand why she was so caught up in it, why it was so important to make the discovery. She just knew that she wanted to. Her need, her urge to search had lain dormant for a while. In the past, she even read tabloids for ideas, though she definitely did not believe everything she read.

Mina went downstairs to the refrigerator for a glass of milk. She didn't really like milk; she just knew she should drink it. Carrying it back up the stairs, she could hear her mother opening the front door, coming home from work.

She hurried up the stairs to avoid conversation. She loved her parents but she was too caught up in her own world and felt isolation from most others, besides her three best friends. She felt guilty for not wanting to talk, but it was just how she felt.

Back in her room, she quietly shut the door. Mina set her milk down on the desk next to her computer. Logging back on, she decided to search even harder. Not even ten minutes into her search, the telephone rang.

Reluctantly, Mina answered. Scott's voice echoed her name.

"Hi," she said.

She used a semi-pleasant tone, trying to hide her annoyance at the interruption.

"What happened earlier?" he asked.

"What do you mean?"

"You left sort of quickly and you seemed weirded out," Scott replied.

"I just don't like being looked at like I'm a freak," she said.

"No one meant to look at you like that, they just think…" he started.

"Think what? That I'm always searching a hopeless case?" she asked.

Scott paused for a moment.

"Yeah, honestly they think that. But it's your thing and they realize that now," Scott tried to comfort her.

"Well thanks for your support," she said sarcastically.

"Mina…" Scott began.

"All of us believe in the supernatural, I'm the only one not scared to search, and that is how I see it," she interrupted him, "Now, I have some things to do."

She hung up the phone.

At his house, Scott looked at the home phone, still listening to the faint dial tone. He couldn't remember a time when she had hung up on him. He sighed and hung the phone back on the receiver. As he walked upstairs to his bedroom, he began to think of her dark ways. He believed in the existence of the supernatural, but like most people, he didn't care to encounter it. But he knew that Mina would do anything to discover it. There was something wrong with finding the intangible almost…romantically interesting. It was an obsession to her.

An obsession that developed ever since….

No. He didn't want to think about that; it was a long time ago that it happened.

***

Mina continued her search even harder now. She knew she was close to the evidence. But hours into her search, she still achieved nothing more besides a stiffer neck.

Her hands found their way to her head to support it, her elbows resting on her desk. She wrapped a handful of hair within her fingers, pulling lightly. She blinked away the flashes of endless lines she'd read and groaned a low mixture of anger and frustration.

"UGGHHH!"

Her frustration was paramount. Why were things always so damn hard to discover? Anger heated her inner core, threatening to bubble forth. She was about to punch something. She needed to release this tension. She needed to find something to vent her anger on.

There was a knock on the outside of her bedroom door.

"Mina," her mother called.

She tried hard to mask the irritation in her voice with a feigned pleasant tone but only partially succeeded.

"What?" she asked.

"Do you want some dinner?"

Mina looked at the dragon clock on the wall in front of her desk. It registered 5:30 PM.

Holy shit, how did it get so late?

Her stomach growled. She ignored it.

"No, I'm fine," she replied.

She was too disgusted to eat now. Her time, hours of her time was wasted researching without achieving results. She was beyond disgusted. Outside the door her mother persisted.

"Are you sure? You probably haven't eaten all day."

Mina grumbled but got up and walked to the door.

Slowly she opened it, looking at her mother's concerned face. Her rounded face allowed the creased lines of age to furrow deeper with the typical worry of a mother. Black, dyed hair partially concealed the gray of her age, as her grayish-green eyes studied Mina. Suddenly Mina felt ashamed, but declined anyway.

"Mom, I'm fine. Really I'm not hungry right now," she said again, quietly.

"Oh, I just worry about you," her mother continued.

"I'm fine, I just have a lot of work to do," she said.

Her mother tried to look behind her into the room.

"Anything I can help you with?" she asked.

Mina's voice dropped even lower.

"Thanks but no. I have to get back to it," she said, "Thanks anyway."

As her mother walked away, she slowly shut the door.

Mina sat back down at the computer. She didn't immediately begin her search again. She just sat there and stared. Thinking deeply, wracking her brain, she tried to figure out what it could have been. But without more cases of it, she would not have enough evidence.

A pile of ashes and a missing body, she wondered. What makes that occur?

Suddenly, the sharp ringing of the phone broke the silence of her thoughts, seeming to nearly cause her heart a sudden interior explosion.

"Jesus," she said.

She was spooked with surprise so deep it was as if a monster had jumped from her closet.

Answering the phone, she couldn't mask her irritation this time.

"Hello," she answered angrily.

"Um, hi," Scott's voice came from the other end, "Did I interrupt something again?"

"No," she said.

But her voice remained in its quiet, though slightly irritable tone.

"Well I was just calling to see if you wanted to go to the café and grab something to eat," Scott offered.

He loved to eat and it was definitely dinnertime.

Mina looked at the clock. It was close to six now and she hadn't eaten all day. Within her stomach, she could feel the emptiness and hear the gurgling noises.

"Sure," she said, rubbing her eyes.

She had been in front of the computer too long and felt the strain. It would be nice to get some air through her limbs.

"It's 5:45 now. Meet you there at six?" Scott asked, breaking her train of thought again.

"Sounds good," she finished, hanging up the phone.

Mina grabbed a light jacket and was on her way out the door of her room. Downstairs, she could hear her parents arguing in the living room. The two of them argued often, though usually got along together well. She hated when they argued, because it was usually over what she considered, stupid, trivial, unimportant subjects.

Ah, this is one reason I don't plan on getting married ever, she thought to herself as she had so many times before.

She slipped out the front door without her parents noticing or interrupting their argument. Sneaking out was the easiest way to avoid conversation. Besides, her mother would want to know what she was up to, and would feel offended that she hadn't eaten at home.

She leisurely walked towards the café/diner. It was so close to home that she would have ten minutes to spare. It was hot out today. She definitely didn't need the jacket. The air blew dryly upon her face. When the wind blew, she enjoyed the breeze upon her.

As she walked, deep in thought again, she wondered of easier ways to find information. If only there was a list of odd cases, separate from all the others. But maybe they were classified. Perhaps she could access it…

"Booo!"

Mina jumped awkwardly into the air and out of her thoughts.

"Holy shit!" she shrieked.

Her heart fluttered precariously, almost in tune with Scott's laughter.

"That's the second time you did that to me today," Mina said, smacking Scott on the arm.

Scott laughed even harder.

"For someone who loves everything supernatural, you sure do scare easily. I could tell you were in another world. I figured it was the perfect time for a scare," Scott laughed.

"What are you doing here near my house? I thought we were meeting there," Mina said.

She hadn't really traveled far from home before running into him.

"I know how slow you are to get moving. I thought I'd just meet you at your house, but you were quicker than usual. Then I saw you, and the thought occurred to me that you were deep in thought, so I thought I'd pull you out of it," he said, still laughing.

"Well, if I would have fallen over from heart attack, I'm sure it wouldn't have been funny anymore," she said, holding her chest.

She was still irritated by her lack of progress in her research and weakened by lack of food.

"Someone's cranky," Scott remarked.

"And someone is just a little too happy," she remarked.

"With a friend like you, how could I not be happy?" he commented, trying to cheer her up with flattery.

Mina finally broke into a smile.

"Just shut up," she said.

"No problem," he said, punching her lightly on the shoulder.

They walked the rest of the way, chatting about the weather and any other topic Scott could think of. He wanted to get her out of the mood she had taken on earlier that day.

When they arrived at the cafe, they immediately took a seat at a booth by the window. They ordered their drinks first as is typical. The server came back to take their order. Mina went first.

"I'll take a grilled chicken sandwich, Colby cheese, grilled onions and mushrooms on it, with barbeque sauce, a side of onion rings and French fries," she said.

Scott looked at her with a funny expression.

"What?" she asked him, "I didn't eat all day, except for the brownie I bought at the store earlier."

Mina's height of about 5'7 with a weight of 125 pounds could fool anyone with her appetite.

"I just wondered where you will put all of that," Scott said, "It never ceases to amaze me how much you can eat without gaining weight."

Scott shook his head.

"I'll just have a burger, well done and French fries," Scott said.

After the server left, their conversation began again. For the next fifteen minutes, they talked about mundane, unimportant subjects.

"I'm starving," Mina finally said.

Now she could feel the bubbling emptiness within her stomach again.

"Me too," he remarked, looking around, "oh, here comes our food."

Mina ate her food faster than Scott. He couldn't help but watch her in amazement. Finishing before him, she browsed the dessert menu while he finished. Scott shook his head.

"I can't believe you can look at that after all you just ate," Scott remarked.

Mina looked at him, smiling indignantly.

"I didn't say I was going to order dessert. You're just so slow I have to find something to do. Besides, I have a fast metabolism," Mina smiled.

He shook his head in agreement.

Scott finished eating and the two talked until the server brought their check. After paying, they walked outside into the briskness of the night.

The night was quiet besides their footsteps and the rustling wind. The sky was clear of clouds as stars stood out amongst the entrenching blackness. Mina loved the stars, the night, and the lack of people clamoring around, just about every experience of being outside in the evening.

Watching Mina, Scott noticed her staring at the sky as they walked. He too looked up with admiration at the darkened sky. He wondered if now was a good time to ask her. Then again, maybe it wasn't.

"Sure is a beautiful sky," Scott remarked.

"Yeah," Mina replied quietly, "It's always that way, the sky, it's always that way."

Scott furrowed his eyebrows and looked at her.

"What do you mean? Of course it is," Scott said.

Mina shook her head.

"I mean, that even when the clouds are hovering above, the stars are still there. We just can't see them, that's all. And no one thinks that way. Everyone thinks that the stars are away when the clouds are out, that they just disappear. But they're there, just hidden, waiting for us to see through the fogginess, which is in the way of us knowing what is really there," Mina babbled.

Scott felt uneasiness arise in him.

"Mina. What is this all about?" he asked.

Snapping out of her daze, she replied, "Nothing."

"Mina, I know it's more than nothing. Something has sparked your interest and it has left you in a daze," Scott observed.

Her voice changed into a quiet monotone.

"Scott, we all have research on our own. We always have. There is nothing new here," she said.

Scott shrugged his shoulders.

"Yes, but we eventually share the subject with each other and usually it does not become a problem. What is so different about your new topic?" Scott wanted to know.

"It...is a secret this time," she said quietly.

She continued to stare up at the sky. Mina trusted Scott more than the others, but feared he would find her research impossible and ridiculous.

Standing directly in front of her, Scott stopped her in the middle of the dark sidewalk, forcing her eyes directly to his face.

"Mina, we have been friends forever, and as far back as I can remember, you have never kept these types of secrets. No research is that important," Scott reasoned.

"Scott, when I'm ready and confident, you will be the first to know," she said.

Scott studied her for a moment, deciding that she was sincere. He moved beside her again.

"I guess I can be satisfied for now, but no dissociating yourself from us, or rants about goofy subjects. I'll have to worry about sending you to a padded room," he joked.

Mina smiled, "No padded room here. I'd prefer to die a fiery death before living in solitude and silence."

"Oh come on, a padded room is star treatment. No one would bother you ever again, you'd have a lot of time to just think and babble about the stars," he joked.

The rest of their walk, they laughed and joked about various subjects. Mina was relieved Scott had let go of the subject and hadn't questioned her further. She certainly didn't want to tell him that she had come up with nothing.

At Mina's house, they said their goodbyes, and Scott started on his way home.

During his walk home, Scott looked again at the stars. Mina's words echoed through his head. He hated being nosy, but wondered if Mina was getting lost in the wrong kind of research. The wrong research hinders the life and mind whereas the right kind strengthens it. She had kept talking about the stars. What was so important about the stars being covered, he wondered.

Mina's strange attitude appeared, flickering off and on ever since...

His thoughts went back to a few days ago at his house, the day they researched missing cases. The pile of ash and a missing, unidentified girl. After that night, she started acting strange. Earlier today, she became defensive. Only the supernatural would be so important to her.

Scott sighed.

Mina truly did waste more of her energies than put them to good use. She was brilliant but her priorities were mixed.

Finally arriving at his house, he went upstairs and laid in his bed, contemplating what to do next.

***

In her house, Mina snuck past her parents in the living room, creeping quietly up the stairs.

Taking off her light jacket, she sat, once again in front of the computer. Turning it back on, she briefly thought about how concerned Scott looked. She was just fine though. She didn't understand the big deal they were making.

Entering in her password, she decided to try her search in a different manner. She had to figure out the differences and steps in fire burns and how it might be possible to burn fully without leaving remains. Pulling up information via one of the search engines, she learned that there were four main types of burns. She read the information from the site:

First-degree burns were the lightest, resulting in redness. They did not stretch beyond the first layer of skin, the epidermis. These types rarely left scars and typically healed quickly, possibly in less than a week.

The second degree penetrates deeper going through the epidermis, into the second layer, called the dermis. These take longer to heal, usually leaving scars.

Third degree burn destroys nerve endings as the skin becomes charred and leathery. It is not painful for this same reason, though the tissue damage extends to the third layer of skin, called the subcutaneous tissue.

The fourth degree burn was the worst one listed on the health site. When a burn is in the fourth degree, it involves muscle, bone, tendon and/or ligament. It may cause death or amputation.

She shivered uneasily with the information.

"No, but that's just not good enough," she said aloud.

She kept searching.

In other listings, one site named a fifth type of burn. This fifth degree burn topic was otherwise known as spontaneous combustion. And this was just what she was looking for. An excited glimmer of hope surged through her.

"Exactly," she said.

Rarely had she heard others talk about spontaneous combustion. As she read the information, it seemed, for the most part, to be a frowned upon theory by experts. In spontaneous combustion cases, the entire body allegedly caught fire, without the help of an external source. All parts of the body, skeleton as well, were turned to complete ash. But in some cases, bodily remnants were found within the ash.

Mina read on.

Along with the definition was a news story. Allegedly, a 16-inch pile of ash was found on the floor of a home where a missing persons case was filed. There was no external fire source around.

Mina eagerly read on, her eyes quickly skimming the pages.

An elderly man had been missing for a few days. When family members grew worried that he did not return their calls, they went to his home but he was nowhere around. Even the pipe he regularly smoked his tobacco in sat in its usual location on the living room table. In the basement, a pile of ash was found, exactly below the old man's favorite chair in the living room. Authorities are still unsure over what happened.

"Wow," Mina said.

She sat back in her chair.

What if all the cases she had read so far could be scientifically explained through spontaneous combustion? Then there would be no proof of deaths from a supernatural source. That would kill her case.

But it could very well go the other way. Spontaneous combustion could be an excuse for the supernatural, to try to keep people from the truth. Almost like a conspiracy of sorts.

She leaned forward again, reading several other listed cases of hypothesized stories on spontaneous combustion.

People didn't want to believe in either spontaneous combustion or a supernatural existence. They didn't want the fear of truth. No one wanted to know what the clouds hid each day.

She wanted to know.

CHAPTER 4:
LOSING SLEEP

The next morning at the library, Mina tried to force herself awake. The quietness of the surrounding rooms made it very difficult. She had found a book on burns and spontaneous combustion but that could not even keep her alert.

Last night, she stayed up much later than she anticipated researching her topic. Her search seemed endless so far. She reached for her coffee mug.

The work atmosphere was calm today, too calm for her. Typically, she enjoyed the solitude and lonely warmth of the library. But today, she wished there was more noise to keep her from falling into a drone of sleep. Luckily, her boss wasn't working today, or else she would be upset at Mina's tiredness. Though there was not much to worry about in a library, Ms. Diotese worried about everything. She wanted her employees to be sharp at all times, 'for security measures.' Mina had worked there for three years and didn't exactly see any threats.

"Ughh," she sighed.

She set down her book and stretched her arms above her head.

Observing the library she had seen so many times, she thought of the dull brown color, which composed the walls and desks. Three large wooden desks along with wooden chairs for group reading were directly in front of her, next to brown shelves containing a listing of every book in the library. This Dewey Decimal System seemed outdated since the rise of computers, but many libraries kept this reference method anyway. To the far left of the library was the kids' section, made up of small round tables and a wide variety of children's books.

Gray colors made up the remaining bookcases for adults, with narrow space in between. Curtains shaded windows near the walls to the right and left of the library, also in this dull gray color. The library colors were so boring, so calming; Mina was surprised she had never fallen asleep on the job before.

Cushions of chairs lined with a dim shade of brown were usually placed next to a window or in a grouping in the right corner, opposite the kid's section. She considered this the adult section, where reading could be done with less noise than sitting in the middle or to the left.

Perhaps if she moved around, that would keep her awake. She shook her head from side to side, rubbing her eyes with her left hand. Sitting quietly at the desk made sleep that much more inviting.

Mina stood from the desk, walking around it, stopping just in front. She looked around. There were very few people in the library today. An old, chubby man with gray hair and a solemn face, a regular named Mr. Riddle sat near a window along one of the walls. He sat on one of the brown cushioned chairs, browsing through a newspaper. Since he lost his wife a few years ago, the library had become his hangout.

In the center of the library, Mrs. Barnes, a middle-aged woman, sat at one of the desks. She was always deeply engrossed in a romance novel. These two figures were more like expected landmarks. It was early yet; though. After school let out, the library would be busy with young kids doing homework and reports, or just hanging out.

Still standing in front of the desk, Mina shook her arms a little bit, just enough to wake herself and to avoid interrupting the readers. She yawned and then looked at her watch. It registered 11 AM.

She didn't really like working mornings. This week she was filling in for a few days for her boss' vacation. Usually, she liked her job. It was easy work and she was able to research whatever she wanted.

Figuring she had stretched enough, Mina reclaimed her seat at the desk. She had only been there an hour so far.

Mina picked up her book.

She was usually revived while she read, absorbing every word. Today, it was like a sedative.

"That will teach you not to stay up past three when you have to work the next morning," she grunted to herself.

The next hour passed even more slowly. The coffee's effect seemed to be wearing off. Mina caught herself drifting off to sleep. She kept pulling herself out of it with a jerk, realizing the loss of control. Finally, after pulling so much, she just let go, allowing herself to drift off into a light sleep at the desk.

"Boo!" someone shouted.

Mina jumped in reaction, opening her eyes and blinking quickly in search of the noise. Her hands clasped the desk in front of her and her eyes darted forward.

Jesse stood in front of her, laughing his sarcastic ass off.

"What the fuck are you sleeping on the job for?" he asked.

She calmed herself, shook her head and took a deep breath.

"At least I have a job," Mina replied calmly, her hand on her chest checking her heartbeat.

"You scared the shit out of me," she whispered.

Jesse leaned forward, looking behind the desk.

"Really, let's see it," Jesse laughed.

Mina punched his arm.

"Ow, all I did was wake you up," Jesse reasoned, rubbing his arm.

"Yeah, then stand there and laugh," Mina said, still in a groggy state of shock, "What time is it?"

"Noon," he responded, still rubbing his arm, "Why were you sleeping? That's not like you."

"I'm just a little tired," she yawned suspiciously.

"Late night?" he asked, noticing the minor dark circles under her eyes.

"Yeah," she responded without giving details, "What are you doing here? I never see you in here. You're always on the computer at home."

"I come in once a week before you start work. You know, personal research," he said.

"I see," she said.

"You're never here this early," he commented.

"Boss is on vacation," she reminded him, since she had told the group weeks ago.

"Oh yeah. I remember now. You coming over later?" he asked.

"Yeah, I'll meet you guys," she yawned, "I am done at 3, when Brandy comes in."

"Ok, I've got some work to do," he said.

Without another word he moved away.

Mina watched him walk away. She didn't even know Jesse did normal research anymore. He must have been hiding it from all of them. Perhaps he just wanted everyone to believe that all he cared about were his sexual subjects.

"Huh," she said.

She felt awake now that her brain had a little rest. Her eyes drifted to her paper.

Security measures, she repeated the words in her head that her boss etched into her brain. Some need for security, she thought. What we should fear most is what we don't know or see daily.

Mina reached in front of her for the book she had set down before her nap. This book contained a subject we don't know much about, though it definitely intrigues us. She read on...

But her mind couldn't concentrate on the words. Instead, her thoughts wandered, seeking action.

All of the cases she recently read about were marked with similar stories to the ones she had researched the night before. There were no fire sources nearby, a pile of ashes was found on the ground, and all persons were missing.

"I don't think it is spontaneous combustion," she said aloud.

"What?"

Mina jumped in reaction and looked up. An unfamiliar elderly woman's voice rang out in a screeching tone directly in front of the desk. Startled by the closeness and loudness of the voice, Mina blinked harshly. She had not noticed the small, elderly woman who stood before her, a book in her hands, ready for checkout.

"Um, nothing," Mina finally answered after pausing to catch her breath.

The woman made no effort to speak. Mina continued her apology.

"I'm sorry, I didn't see you there, I was so engrossed in this book," she said, "You weren't waiting long were you?"

She looked at the woman's small, wrinkly old face.

"Hmph," the elderly woman grunted, "I want this book."

She handed the book to Mina, ignoring the question. Natural acerbity dashed across her old face. Mina couldn't help but notice an appearance of lifelong bitterness and social isolation.

Mina hurriedly stamped the book.

"There you go, thanks, have a good day," Mina said.

She rushed the words together, watching the woman's wrinkled face for an expression. The cold look upon her face did not change, nor did she even look at Mina.

"Hmph."

The lady replied with a mutter, as if cave man language was her main type. Grabbing her book and walking quickly, though with a slight limp, Mina watched her, wondering about her story.

Jesse had seen the entire incident. Two large, old gray bookshelves hid him from her sight, though the cracks in between the shelves allowed him space to nose into Mina's life. He hadn't initially come there to spy. He wanted to do some research and test some of his secret theories. It wasn't until he noticed her book on spontaneous combustion that he became intrigued. Mina's recent behavioral changes meant that this subject was important to her. He wondered what she was so caught up in that she seemed to be losing sleep.

From his position behind the shelves, he saw Mina pick up the book again. It seemed like an addiction to her, that book.

After waiting so long, Jesse figured he must have a short attention span, because he decided to take action again. He wondered if he could sneak up on her and cause another scare.

Creeping slowly around the bookcases, Jesse ducked down as he walked quietly, though swiftly to the librarian desk. He was proud of his swiftness and noticed that she hadn't looked up even once. Finally, he arrived at the desk and with one quick jump, he simultaneously shouted, "Ooga, Ooga, booga."

Mina jumped so fast this time that she fell backwards off of her chair, thumping to the ground. Jesse instantly moved to help her but she quickly clamored to her feet, and immediately charged at him. Pushing him backwards, impulsively, he fell onto the ground this time, landing on his butt.

"Ow!" Jesse shrieked, stunned at her action.

"What did you do that for?" he asked.

"I am not in the mood for your stupid games!" she yelled.

She sounded as if they were dating.

Jesse looked at her as if she were a stranger. Mina noticed the change in his eyes and looked away. Slowly he stood from the ground.

"I just wondered what you were so interested in that you were compromising your job," Jesse admitted.

The seriousness in his voice took her aback. But she masked her surprise.

"Well guess what, it is nobody's business but my own. You know I really wish you guys would mind your own fucking business," she said.

Jesse swallowed hard.

"Who else is wondering?" he asked.

"Don't act stupid, I know Scott put you up to this," Mina accused.

"I haven't been around Scott lately, not since yesterday afternoon," Jesse said.

"Well then why was Scott asking me about my research last night?" she asked.

"Maybe he noticed how weird you've been acting the past couple of days too. We're just looking out for you," he said.

It was strange for Mina to hear anything even slightly compassionate from Jesse's mouth. His words were foreign to her and she was sad she was unable to accept the concern. But she had to do what she had to do.

Quietly, with restraint of emotion, she said, "I don't need anyone looking out for me."

Mina walked away towards the restroom. Jesse looked after her. It had only been a few days and already he could see the changes. Whatever her topic was, it was ultimately important to her. All four of them knew the dangers of becoming obsessed with a project, but Mina didn't seem to care anymore of their discussions on precautions. They had made a pact not to allow each other slip into another dimension of reality- that is, one in which they created on their own. It was terribly easy to slip into another world, mentally, with obsessive research. They had all seen the effects of obsession, through one of their own friends of the past. It was something they were too logical to think about now, though it was definitely not a forgotten consequence.

In the bathroom, Mina splashed cold water on her face. Looking up from the sink, she noticed dark circles glimmering under her eyes.

"Huh," she laughed, "You miss one night of sleep and everyone thinks you are fucked up."

She shook her head.

They were all dramatically overreacting. So what, she found a topic that interested her and wanted to find quick proof. That didn't mean she'd become obsessed.

Turning off the sink, she reached for a paper towel. Mindlessly, she stared off, wiping her hands while deep in thought.

Four years ago. He was only seventeen. He just could not handle his intelligence as the rest of us could.

Do not think about that, she scolded herself.

That is why they are so overprotective of me. The circumstances are the same. But they don't know what I'm researching.

Mina sighed.

Her sigh brought her out of her daydream as she realized she was still rubbing her already dry hands with the paper towel. She quickly threw it away as if it were a toxic substance. She looked down at her hands. They were red from the constant rubbing.

Opening the bathroom door slowly, she was cautious to make sure Jesse wasn't hiding somewhere to scare her again. He was a pain in the ass sometimes.

Walking swiftly, she took her position at the desk once again. Jesse was nowhere in sight. He must have left. Mina was rarely physically aggressive, so she was sure he had gotten a surprise after he knocked her off of her seat.

Mina decided it would be best if she read something else. She found a music magazine. She loved music, perhaps more than the others, just like her interest in the supernatural. Music usually saved her from any subject she focused on too much. Music was a real, beautiful and true part of the world.

Reading through the magazine, she saw that her favorite band was coming, adding some excitement to her mind. She was not sure if she was convincing herself to be happy about it, or if she truly was. In the back of her brain, her research was calling to her, beckoning her, trying to control her thought processes. She didn't want it to do that. It could become a problem, an obsession.

Just like him…

Mina read the entire magazine, from front to back. Setting the magazine down, she looked around the nearly empty library. Unfortunately, she just wasted her time reading. The only part of the magazine she could remember was that her favorite band was coming to town. During her reading, she must have unintentionally zoned out, thinking of her other subject.

Lifting her left wrist, Mina looked at her watch.

It registered 1:15 PM.

Might as well go back to reading the book I have a real interest in, she decided. Reluctantly, she picked up the book on spontaneous combustion. Looking around the library, she decided she was safe from spies. Jesse was long gone.

She read for the next few hours. Time passed with rare interruptions. But soon enough, the after-school crowd was slowly burrowing into the library, making Mina more alert to their needs than when the library could have passed for a ghost town.

Brandy came to relieve Mina a few minutes after 3.

"Sorry I'm late," the bubbly teenager chirped, "I had to stay after class."

"As long as you weren't kissing any boys," Mina joked.

Mina was only smiling half a smile though, making her joke near ineffective. Her mind was lost on her research.

"I wasn't," Brandy giggled.

She looked at Mina and her laughter faded, "You look like you're sick."

Remembering her dark circles, Mina blushed.

"I'm just tired. Not used to the morning shift," she claimed.

"Yeah, mornings stink," Brandy said, "But Ms. Diotese will be back next week and everything will be okay then."

"Yeah," Mina replied, "Well hey, I'm going get out of here- gotta meet the boys. Have a good night, looks like it's going to be busy for you. Call me if you need anything."

She forced a smile that she knew wasn't genuine.

"All right. I think I can handle it though," Brandy giggled.

"Ok, bye," Mina said, still clinging to her half-assed smile.

"Bye," Brandy said, waving as a group of boys walked up to the desk to talk to her.

Lucky girl, Mina thought. Brandy was a high school senior. She was likeable enough. Her intelligence was that of the average person, though she seemed to pretend to be less intelligent to boost her popularity. She was a pretty girl with blue eyes and sandy brown hair. Thankfully she was sensible enough to keep ideas of college in mind. Mostly, Brandy looked up to Mina, as Mina protected her like a younger sister.

Mina's house was on the way to Jesse's. She decided to go home and change clothes before going over.

Marching up the stairs to her room, she quickly fumbled through her closet for something to wear. Surprisingly, the November day was warmer than usual. She found a sleeveless black shirt and a pair of dark blue jeans. She didn't need a jacket but took one anyway.

Just as she was ready to leave, a thought struck her. Maybe she should search the computer for a few minutes before going over. She looked at the computer. It seemed to be beckoning her, trying to draw her in. Nah, she had been giving in too much lately. It was time to control her research before it actually did become an obsession.

But still it called to her.

"No," she said aloud.

She forced herself to walk out the door.

CHAPTER 5:
HELP… A BLESSING

Arriving near Jesse's house, Mina admired the two-story, light blue home. The paint job appeared to be visually perfect, with every window lined in a frame of white. Not a single crack of paint chipped away from the home. Every year, his parents had it repainted and applied all of the weathering necessities.

Must be nice to be rich, she thought.

Mina observed the area, making sure no one planned to jump out and scare her. She was tired of their pranks. She looked up. The light was on in Jesse's top story room.

Continuing watching as she approached, she saw Scott and his shadow dance past the window. She hurried towards the house. A strong stone path led to a recently painted white elaborate porch. On the porch, white wicker rocking chairs and matching furniture lined each side.

Mina opened the large glass door, knocking on the interior cherry wood. Though they knew she was coming, Jesse's mother was weird about people just walking into her home.

Jesse's mother greeted her. Her face was almost fake in appearance with skin so seemingly flawless that it seemed to be made out of wax. Her curly blond hair always hung in perfect rings. She smiled like a porcelain doll, as if she only smiled because she had been made that way. Her naturally cheery demeanor made Mina a little uncomfortable at times. Most of the time when his mother spoke, she moved her head to the right side and nodded.

"They're upstairs, I presume waiting for you," Jesse's mother smiled.

"Yeah, thanks," Mina replied.

She started past her and up the staircase.

Entering into Jesse's room without knocking, none of the boys looked up to acknowledge her. She edged inside slowly, feeling high discomfort permeate through her.

Finally Scott looked over at her.

"What's up Mina?"

Her eyes darted around, stricken with uncertainty.

"Not much," she replied.

She watched Jesse, wondering how he felt after the incident at the library. No one else said anything in greeting. However, that was not abnormal. But today she felt like it was. Mina looked around the room, trying to ignore the pictures of half-naked women that hung on each corner of the wall. Her heart seemed in sink inside of her soul, hiding there like an anchor in an intangible place. For some reason, she felt isolated today, alone.

She took a seat near his bed, lingering in her solitude. But minutes later, they all talked as if nothing out of the ordinary had happened at all. Even Jesse began talking to her as they discussed job searches. They even spoke of the news of the day. No one bothered Mina about her research and she was glad.

"My mom's making dinner around seven if you guys want to stay," Jesse offered.

This was one of his few kind gestures.

"Hell yeah," Scott answered.

Scott was always hungry.

"Sure," Ryan replied quietly.

"What's she making?" Mina asked.

"Meatloaf, mashed potatoes, bread, the usual stuff," Jesse said and then looked at Mina, "You staying?"

"Um, I don't think I will. I don't know yet," she replied.

"Free food," Scott said, nudging her jokingly.

"I'm tired though. I want to get to bed early tonight," Mina said.

"You looked pretty tired earlier," Jesse said, "and crabby."

Mina made a face.

"Sorry. I don't like mornings," she said.

"Understandable," Jesse replied.

The feeling of lonely isolation entered into her again.

"I think I better head out now actually," Mina said, looking at her watch.

"But you haven't really been here that long," Jesse said.

Scott eyed her.

51

"You don't want to hang out?" he asked.

"Tired," she replied, her eyelids feeling heavy.

"Well, before you go, I found this for you," Scott said.

He handed her some papers.

At the top of the paper, in bold letters, Mina read:

MISSING CASES: UNEXPLAINED

Without reading more of it, she looked up abruptly. She couldn't cover the shock or the anger that widened her eyes.

"What's this for?" she asked.

"Read on," Jesse urged.

She began reading it, realizing they were digging into her research. It was a case similar to the ones she was searching for. She didn't even finish reading it before she looked back up.

"Look guys. I want to do this on my own," she said.

It took every ounce of restraint to hold back her extreme annoyance with them. Scott put his arms up in surrender.

"I just came across it," Scott replied, "No big deal, it's still yours."

"Thanks," she said.

Without another word, she hurried out of the room.

Taking the stairs quickly, once she was outside, she ran back to her house. When she got to her room, she jumped onto her bed. As angry as she was, she couldn't help but read the rest of the story. As she did, she realized that this story was better than the others she had found.

In summary, three people- all in their late teenage years, two males and one female, in Gallup, New Mexico went to light fireworks in a dark area around the Fourth of July. The boys were recklessly trying to light a computer monitor on fire with fireworks. The monitor wouldn't light, as they continued to set off fireworks. The female hid behind the boy's truck. She didn't want to get hit with debris. Both of the young men disappeared out of nowhere. There was no reason. Piles of ashes existed near where the vehicle had been.

Mina set down the paper.

The female was still alive. A victim, a witness remained.

"This is perfect," Mina said aloud.

The case happened over three years ago in the next state over, New Mexico. Now, she just had to find the girl. Since those involved were of legal age at the time it happened, all names were listed. It was initially assumed that the two boys left the girl there to scare her, but the truck remained with the keys left in the ignition. The girl finally left after screaming their names and then reported it to police.

"Greta Marhan, Nicholas Golden and James Greco," Mina said the names aloud, "Greta's the only one left."

This case held every answer she needed. This single case was already the most important. It would tell whether or not she should go further with her research or just leave it alone.

If this were supernatural, no one would have believed the victim, except me. I will.

Mina hurried to the computer. Searching for the name, she quickly located the girl's home address. Next, she searched directions to the house. To her surprise, it was only an hour and a half away.

As she printed the directions, her insides bubbled with excited but fearful anticipation. She had no idea what to do but enjoyed the excitement that now kept her animated.

How do I approach this? I'm just a girl, I'm not anything important, she realized.

Whose family would let someone in to talk to someone she didn't even know?

"Shit," she said.

She stood and paced around the room. The girl's home was close enough for her to find though. And it was close enough for her to find soon. Tonight.

Mina looked at the clock. It was 5:30.

Would it be too late by the time she arrived? Tomorrow she had to work early again until three. Should she wait until then? The boys would wonder where she was. She had to do it now. No one would know if she went now.

Running down the stairs, Mina moved quickly out the door.

"Later!" she yelled to her parents.

They would assume she was meeting the others.

"Bye."

Her mother's voice called out from behind her.

During the drive, she had to read the directions constantly to make sure she didn't get lost. At this point, she did not know if her mission was pointless. But she was anxious to find out. She needed to know now, instead of wasting her time on computer research that wouldn't give her the real answers.

Halfway to her destination, she saw the lights of a gas station. Realizing she hadn't eaten yet, she stopped for a Pepsi, beef jerky and a bag of chips. She munched on them as she drove.

Her exhilaration began to waver as she drove the second half of the distance. She began to feel like she had in the library. She opened her windows and slapped her cheeks until, some time later; she pulled into the neighborhood where Greta Marhan resided. As she pulled up next to the house, she noticed it was a nice, large home, almost the size and beauty of Jesse's. The outdoor lights shone bright, lighting up the dark blue and white colored home. There were small lights surrounding the walkway and the windowsills, adding to the illumination. Even outside, Mina could tell that many lights were on, on the inside as well.

"Wonder what their electric bill is like," she muttered.

Mina looked at her watch, noting that it was just a little after seven.

"Is it rude to go up to someone's house at this time? Is it too late at night?" Mina asked.

The lights are bright within though.

She tapped her fingers against the door handle, trying to make the decision.

Might as well get it over with.

The house had a welcoming look about it, as though it was a loving house, emitting feelings of warmth.

Strange, she thought of this vibe.

Mina reached into her glove box, gently pulling out an old newspaper clipping. It had yellowed in its time of abandonment in her glove box. It weathered more than she wanted it to. Her eyes scanned the writing without reading the words she memorized before. This paper should be in her home, laminated with plastic to keep it safe.

Looking at the picture, at his face, she wondered if she should bring it in to talk about her loss.

Hurriedly she decided against it and reached over, placing it back in the glove box.

It was time for action.

Leaving her car, she locked the doors and looked around the neighborhood. Wind blew a dry heat upon her face and she blinked against the mobile sands. She hurried towards the porch; taking the steps so lightly it was as if she floated up them. As she approached the large, wooden door, she felt a deep inner nervousness creep in.

What the hell was she doing here? What was she going to say?

Still standing outside the home without moving a hand to knock, her stomach rumbled with nerves that dreadfully lurched turmoil inside of her.

Why the hell was she so nervous? She was an independent, capable woman.

Her stomach continued to lurch, her heart joining in with the frenzy. She swallowed hard. She stopped to take a breath to calm herself. Sweat dripped from her brow. Just as she thought herself under control, the wooden door before her swung inward, without her knocking.

Surprised, Mina flinched. Her heart fluttered into a faster game of jump rope, her stomach following suit.

In front of her stood a small woman with curly dark hair and hints of gray streaming through. Her gentle face and dimpled smile was fueled by an oddly loving glow.

"Don't be scared," the woman said in a mesmerizing, gentle tone, "How can I help you today?"

Mina opened her mouth to speak but couldn't find any words. A short sound came out of her, immediately embarrassing her enough to force her to get her bearings.

"I, I…how did you know I was out here?" Mina stammered.

The woman smiled warmly.

"The cameras sweetie. We have cameras. Would you like to come in? We can help you here," she continued.

The woman's hospitality surprised Mina, especially inviting in someone whom she did not know.

Where the hell had she ended up?

Mina looked at the top of her head, wondering if there was a halo there that she couldn't see.

"Come on in," the woman persisted, "It's getting chilly out there. Sure isn't as warm as it was earlier today."

Mina felt really cold all of a sudden. She was seriously stunned by the woman's behavior. Since she was unaccustomed to this, she immediately became suspicious. The woman spoke to her as if she were her own daughter. Mina thought of the story of the kids and the gingerbread house. Maybe she shouldn't go in.

Grow up, she scolded herself, *this lady isn't a witch who is going to try to eat you.*

Reluctantly, Mina followed the small woman into her home. Mina did not even know how to begin her line of questioning.

"Would you like some coffee or tea? We have both," she offered.

"No thanks," Mina responded, "I have Pepsi in the car."

"Oh," the woman said, smiling at Mina, "I'm Dorothy Marhan. And what is your name child?"

She turned back to face Mina directly.

"Um, I'm Mina Clyne. I just had a few questions for..." she began, trailing off.

The woman smiled patiently.

"Well, always remember that God is with you," the woman interrupted, "And you shall not fear the words you must speak."

Mina suddenly felt the urge to flee. Her insides were filled with nervous jittering. Her eyes darted away from the woman, seeing nothing around her before they came full circle to study this woman, this figure before her. A gold chain with a large cross lined her neck. Matching earrings of the same cross design framed each of her ears.

Mina paused, preparing to speak but the nervousness silenced her again. With all of her hidden anxieties, she sure would make an awful detective. She wracked her brain for answers to the behaviors she was now witnessing. Mina could not understand what was going on but it frightened her because it was so out of the ordinary. Nobody ever welcomed strangers into their homes like this. Why would they?

What if she was a robber? Didn't this woman care? Was this even a private residence?

Why had this lady welcomed her so easily?

Mina felt the frantic urge to solve this mystery. Her eyes darted around the room in search of answers. White bulbs of Christmas style lights shone upwards, wrapped around the railing of the staircase, leading to the next level. Small, stuffed angel dolls followed the line created by the lights, but hovered just above the glow. Gowns of different colors framed the bodies of the countless angel dolls, with differing hair colors and nationalities.

Along every wall, paintings of religious figures lined the room. Peering into the attached living room, Mina noticed that various nativity scenes lined shelves. On a chimney mantle, most of these pieces dwelled in recognition of a higher power's presence. Along the windowsills, white candlelight added to the religious glow and decor. She had noticed these decorations from outside, though only thought of them as simple decoration.

On the television off in the living room was a religious station. Mina caught part of the words from the channel, talking about the evils of sin.

"Sin is everywhere…in our music…carried around by our youth…orchestrated by the devilish tendencies of mankind…"

Mina tuned out those words. Her eyes continued to curiously scan the scene in search of answers.

Above one of the paintings by the staircase, a banner with black letters set on a white background spoke the words:

GOD'S HOUSE OF HOPE

The scene stunned Mina. In an instant, a realization overwhelmed her.

Without even noticing, she had walked into a house, whose décor was similar to church. This was a religious venue- not just a simple private residence.

Suddenly, Mina did not know what to do; her words had now frozen within her throat. She looked back at the lady, Dorothy. A kind smile formed along the edges of the stranger's face.

"It's okay," the woman said.

She put her arms out and before she knew it, she was hugging Mina. Mina's eyes opened wide at the embrace, following the rest of the exasperating oddities of the night.

"You can look around first, and then we'll find out what we can help you with."

Mina realized that the warm woman mistook Mina's reactions-her confusion and surprise for some other outer source such as the shock of trauma. This woman did not realize Mina had not come there for comfort as many others probably had. This place was like a homeless shelter for the soul.

'God's House of Hope.'

The banner's words echoed through her brain until this saintly human woman pulled away from her, interrupting those thoughts.

"We help everyone who has love in their hearts," she began, answering Mina's silent questions, "I can tell that you have the love. From when I first saw you, you seemed to be in need of some sort of help or guidance. We will try to help you when you are ready. When you get used to being here, we will talk. Go ahead, have a seat in the living room," the woman offered.

Mina barely even hugged her own mother, let alone a stranger. She was in shock but quickly composed herself.

"I'm okay," she responded, "I'm just not from around here."

"Well, we welcome everyone, from anywhere," Dorothy smiled.

"Who's we?" she asked.

She hadn't seen anyone else in the house.

"My husband, Carl. He's asleep, and my daughter Greta is in her room. We help anyone who needs us," she said, smiling again.

"Can...can I talk to your daughter, Greta?" Mina asked.

Dorothy smiled politely.

"Well let me tell her you're here," she said.

The woman moved slowly up the brightened staircase, her feet invisible underneath a gown. She seemed to float rather than walk.

Mina looked around the house again. She wasn't a follower of religion and couldn't believe the work this family put into their faith.

But Mina scarcely had a chance to look around when a startlingly beautiful young woman descended the stairs behind Dorothy. Dressed in a flowing white dress, which accentuated her naturally blond hair, she appeared to be almost a real-life angel.

Mina's face showed her shock. Greta looked down from the staircase, picked up on her apprehension and smiled a caring smile. Her natural, bright blue eyes made her appear even more synthetic and untouchable than an angel.

When mother and daughter reached the bottom of the stairs, the girl stood directly in front of Mina. They were the same height and their eyes met. Mina unwittingly flinched. She was intimidated by the seeming pureness of the girl. Greta appeared perfect in every sense, making Mina feel impeccably flawed.

"Hello, I'm Greta. How are you Mina?"

The girl spoke softly and tilted her head to the side. Her voice carried a concern greater than anyone she had ever known.

"I'm okay," Mina replied.

The girl's face was like a doll- a porcelain doll with only slight movement. Besides concern, no emotion stirred on her face. The girl sensed something from Mina, but Mina couldn't be sure what signal she was sending off.

"Would you like to talk somewhere private?" Greta asked.

The soft words spilled out, as she cocked her head to the side in the same manner as Jesse's mom usually did.

"If you don't mind," Mina said quietly.

Her eyes dropped to the floor. Now the carpet caught her eye. The patterns in the carpeting were composed of angels as well. Visually, the home was crowded with this religious pattern.

Greta touched Mina's arm and then looked at her mother, seeming to ask permission.

"Mother, I'll help her out, ok?" Greta said.

"Absolutely, please do," her mother responded.

Still smiling, she gracefully waved her arm. Greta turned back to Mina.

"Please, come with me," she said.

Greta led Mina upstairs to her room.

59

"It will be more private here," Greta said, "Though God is everywhere to help."

Mina's lack of religion made her feel awkward and blasphemous as she entered the room. These kind people expected she needed help, and she was taking advantage of their gullible behavior.

Inside Greta's room, Mina first noticed that many porcelain dolls, mostly in angelic form, lined two bookshelves of the room. On another bookshelf, there were books. Mina could see that the titles were about various religious subjects. The room was much like Mina's, though in hers, the dolls were replaced with horror movies, books and a widely dispersed collection of mystical mythical figures.

Beside her, the light pink colored walls wore the decorations of angelic patterns. A few stuffed bears with halos sat at the top of her bed, staring with blank dotted eyes.

Mina looked up.

On the ceiling, a beautiful chandelier with intricately carved glass angels hovered above her dresser.

"What may I help you with?" Greta asked.

"Um…" Mina started.

Her eyes still traced the room. She wracked her brain for something to say. Greta smiled.

"It's okay. Have a minute to look around, have a seat if you like," Greta said.

Mina walked around the room, moving in closer to the girl's personal objects with unusual fascination.

On a wooden dresser, pictures of Greta, her mother and a man stood in the frame. There were various pictures of the three of them. Not one picture existed of Greta with friends or even a boyfriend.

Mina turned to look at her and words finally came to mind.

"Do you ever get lonely?" Mina asked.

The words came unexpectedly for both sides, impulsively for Mina. Greta still smiled.

"What do you mean?" she asked.

Greta's smile grew hesitant. She searched Mina's now emotionless face.

"Are you lonely?" she asked, wondering if it was Mina expressing her own feelings.

Surprised by the rebounded question, Mina thought for a moment.

"Well I don't know," she said.

She realized then that she didn't know after all. Greta seemed to pick up on this. She smiled, never answering the question herself.

"I can help you if you explain it to me," the girl said patiently.

Greta stood by a window, which was framed with white lace curtains. Her fingers traced the lace. Something secret was stirring inside of her now. Mina could tell. She took this as her opportunity.

"What happened three years ago?" Mina asked.

The words came quick and blunt. Simultaneously, Mina turned to face the young woman. Greta's smile remained intact, though had lost some of its gleam from their first introduction. However, she remained calm and patient.

"What brings this question?" Greta asked.

There was no emotion in the question. Mina moved closer. Her eyes pleaded with her words.

"I can't say because I don't know. Please just tell me," Mina whispered.

She moved to the window where the girl stood and faced her directly. She felt like a black cloud draping over a pure white one with the shadow of a storm. Greta smiled though before she answered.

"I am not ashamed or embarrassed of the past, but it is in the past. It is because of the past though that I am here like this today. If it hadn't happened, I wouldn't have found God. My family and I wouldn't be as close as we are now. Without the past, we wouldn't be able to help others, those others who need help in finding God. Those others like you," Greta replied.

Mina instantly paled at the conviction in Greta's statement.

"But..." Mina started.

"Shhh," Greta said, cutting her off.

She put one finger to her mouth before continuing, blinking like a beautiful statue.

"No one thinks they need God, but everyone needs hope. There is no hope in the past. Hope is brought with thoughts of the future," she whispered.

"But I don't..." Mina began again.

"Oh but you do. You just aren't ready yet. I will tell you of my past though, if you really must know. No one has ventured to ask me about that night since it happened. It's almost as if it didn't," she said.

Her eyelashes fluttered as if fingers had obnoxiously snapped in front of her face.

"I will only tell you because I think it might help you Mina," she said.

Mina opened her mouth to speak but decided against it. Instead, she watched Greta. Her eyes seemed to glaze over, trailing off into the dream of another place. Mina watched her catatonic stare.

A strange silence came between the two of them. Mina wondered of the aftermath of what happened to Greta. Usually, when one was traumatized, they fell into a shell, a depression. Greta had done the opposite and found great hope through religion.

The girl's eyes fluttered as she awakened from her trance. She walked slowly over to her large bed. Pure white satin sheets and pillows covered it. Sitting, she smiled and then waved for Mina to sit next to her. Mina complied. Greta studied her face.

"I can tell you what happened, though I am confident it will be hard for you to believe. Perhaps you won't believe it at all. No one else did," she said.

Mina caught residual resentment in her voice.

"I'm sure I'll believe," Mina said.

Her eyes spoke with the sincerity of her words.

The girl looked away, seemingly composing herself. Simultaneously, she pretended like she had gotten over the events of three years past.

CHAPTER 6:
AN OPEN PAST

Mina looked at her watch. 7:34 PM.

Greta spoke, her voice softening into a whisper.

"We must talk quietly. Mother will not agree with dark talk."

Mina nodded her head. Greta continued without stopping.

"There is so much light here that evil dissipates immediately. However, this rehash of my past will not help me, for I am well. It will only be serving your purpose. Perhaps it will help you find the light. That is why I do not hesitate to take on this good deed. I'll see this as a kind deed to you. You are not with a newspaper, intending to use this for dirty purposes, are you?" Greta inquired.

Her innocent eyes scanned Mina. Mina blinked.

"No, it's my own...personal research," she replied.

Greta nodded, seeming to believe her.

"When I finish, I request that you tell me about yourself Mina as an agreement for this discussion. Shall I begin?" she asked.

Mina nodded.

"When you're done, I'll tell you as much about me as I can," Mina agreed.

"Good," Greta said.

She smiled eloquently and then took a deep breath before she began.

"As a younger adult, I was immature to life. I dated many boys and enjoyed selfish events where I was a disgraceful sinner," Greta said, "I smoked cigarettes, stayed out later than curfew, partied and drank. All the time I disobeyed my parents, those who loved me the most."

Greta stopped suddenly, shuddering as if a wave of cold had suddenly struck her. Mina winced. She felt an odd awakening from those few words. She looked at Greta.

"You okay?" she asked.

"Yes," Greta said, a wide smile gracing her face, "Just remembering those awful sins that ruled my life."

Mina suddenly shivered. She was really glad Greta didn't know her own life, beliefs or thoughts.

Greta grimaced before beginning again.

"I had many friends, I was cool, but I was goalless and hopeless. I just wanted to live for the day, not caring if I died at any moment. I just wanted to have fun, without responsibility."

She paused again, her eyes seeming to drift into that other time.

"I met Nicholas Golden. He was the cutest boy around. Every girl wanted him, but I was the only one he wanted. We were inseparable. We experienced many first times together, even wanted to marry some day...in that rebellious sort of way," she paused as if a realization suddenly hit her.

Her tone changed, even becoming angry this time.

"But he was a sinner worse than I was. I realize that now. We thought we were in love, but it must have been young, foolish lust. For he is gone now," she paused again for a breath.

Mina knew that it truly did pain Greta, some aspect of it, but she hid it or didn't even realize her own feelings deep down.

Greta continued, her lip trembling with an awkward sort of docile hatred.

"We were always into some kind of mischief, always out for a thrill."

Regret whisked its way into her voice. Mina's curiosity grew.

"What happened that night?" Mina asked in a quiet, though persistent tone.

Greta looked at Mina, trying to read her face and then continued.

"It was a hot, July night. Nicky, his friend and I were on our way to the woods. His friend loved driving fast in his truck, crazily, without a care in the world. We could have flipped over many times on the rocky terrain he skidded through, but no one really cared. It was a big truck, dark blue. I was so scared of his driving that night; I even wore my seatbelt for the short distance he drove. Usually, I wouldn't have cared, but for some reason that day, I did."

She paused and furrowed her eyebrows as if trying to remember why she had been so scared.

Mina watched her in her own silent contemplation. Greta continued.

"Nicky was riding in the back of the truck as we hit the bumps. He and his friend thought it was fun. Boys I guess. I was worried he would fall out and get hurt, but he seemed to like getting thrown around like that," she said, frowning with worry.

Mina noticed the pet name, 'Nicky.' She interpreted this in that she really had cared about him.

Reluctantly, Greta continued.

"We had fireworks to light for the fourth of July. In the back of the truck was an old monitor from a computer, which had been thrown out in someone's trash. Of course the boys wanted to light it on fire for thrills. They would try to light anything on fire," Greta paused again.

Mina tried to read her face, but it was expressionless. No smile or frown lapped her features. Greta continued.

"For a while, I stood by the boys while they acted silly, lighting off various fireworks. Some of them were really pretty, shooting into the sky with different colors. Other ones moved fast on the ground, with small sparks following them. But after a while, the boys started getting crazy with them. I was scared they would set the trees on fire. Flames were shooting out in every direction of a small fire they created. The monitor would not light though. They kept kicking it, breaking it, throwing paper fireworks wrappers around it, trying desperately to build a flame out of it…" Greta stopped.

Her motionless face appeared as if she was in a trance.

Mina visualized the events as Greta spoke, wanting her to get to the part she desperately needed to know. Suspense and anticipation tensed her body, continuously building up within her. She allowed Greta her lengthened pause though, knowing she was lucky to get this far with information. Greta continued but with her eyes in another place, wearing that emotionless expression.

"I walked behind the truck, far away from the two. I didn't want a firework to accidentally explode and injure me. I decided to let the boys be boys, though I nervously smoked a cigarette on the other side. We were in an open area surrounded by trees, just along the outside border of the woods. Railroad tracks were to my right, as I just looked around the area. I'd never been there before, but I guess the boys used the same spot every year. It was a very dark night; I looked around in between watching them cause their fits of destruction," Greta paused.

Her face grimaced as if she was disgusted by their actions.

Quickly this time, she continued again, "Nicky came over to me, to see if I was ok. He asked me why I was hiding. I told him I didn't want to lose a body part over a firework. I was nice about it; they just thought I was scared. And I guess I was, sort of."

Greta stopped her story again. Her haunted eyes seemed to relive the fear of that night all over again. Mina watched her intently, understanding that the situation had been painfully buried so long ago.

Greta picked up her story again, "Then he went back to his friend to continue their destruction. I ignored them. Instead, I admired the stars in the sky. But as I looked around, I noticed that a lot of smoke and fog had built up. It was slowly surrounding us. It was so thick. It seemed to slowly rise from the ground. It started getting so thick; I could barely make out the guys. I tried to see them through the other side of the truck's window. I hadn't been around campfires or things of that sort very often, so I thought it was just natural, the smoke, the fog...."

Greta's voice instantly trailed off.

Mina gently touched her shoulder, accidentally surprising Greta into a jump. It was almost as if Mina had brought her back from another world. She looked at Mina then.

"Then they disappeared," she said.

The blunt ending surprised Mina, causing her to blink harshly. The two of them sat there in silence. Mina knew that they couldn't just disappear; Greta wasn't letting out the full story.

Mina pursed her lips together, contemplating.

"How exactly did they disappear?" Mina asked.

Greta's eyes peered into another time once again.

"They just left me," she said quietly, "But that's when I found God, because God could have taken me too. But He let me live because I was good. And that is why I have all that I have now. That is why I am still alive today."

Greta's voice perked up with these words, though she appeared to be in an even greater trance than when she told the story. Mina studied her.

"How did it really happen?" Mina persisted.

Greta sat there, silently. Her lip quivered. Mina wondered if she would continue. Greta didn't look at her. But she decided it was okay to continue.

"I told everyone they disappeared," Greta admitted, "They wouldn't have believed me. Even my own parents barely did."

"Maybe your parents really just knew that no one else was willing to accept the truth," Mina reasoned.

Greta looked at her and smiled.

"You have a kind heart," she said.

Greta's eyes moved back to her hands, which were now clasped together on her lap.

Angel, Mina thought of her pose.

She studied her and then spoke softly.

"So tell me the rest," Mina said.

Greta's eyelashes fluttered before her eyes lifted again.

"As I stood behind the truck, the smoke continued to build all around us. It was such a thick and tremendous fog. It thickened until I could barely see them. It seemed to encircle us and it happened so fast. I couldn't see him at all," she said, her lashes fluttering, her eyes drifting downward again, "My love," she whispered.

Then she stopped, hesitating for a moment. Her voice quivered when she began again.

"I yelled his name, I was scared and I just wanted to leave. I heard Nicky say, 'Let's get out of here.' I guess he was worried about all the smoke or fog, whatever it was, too," she said.

She stopped herself again, causing the anxious suspense to rise in Mina's chest. Now, Greta was the circus freak and Mina the selfish observer.

Greta's mouth started to tremble. But she regained herself as she spoke again.

"They were walking back to the truck, to me. I could hear their footsteps on the rough ground, coming towards me," she said, her voice grew shaky but continued, "Then, from nowhere, it swooped down. A fiery comet, with the shape, with the screeching sound of a loud demon, it shot right out of the smoke. It went directly for them, taking my boyfriend and his friend away. I didn't even have a chance to shout out. And just as fast, the monster disappeared too."

Her voice grew hysterical yet volume controlled. Mina empathized as best she could, feeling her pain through the words.

Greta continued on, "I stood there alone, screaming once they were gone. I fell to the ground and blacked out I guess," she whispered.

She wiped at the fresh tears that surfaced behind her eyes.

"I woke up hours later underneath the truck and yelled for them," an un-captured tear dripped slowly from her eye, "I looked for them everywhere. They were nowhere. They were gone. I had to take the truck and leave because I was still alive. The devil took them away, but he couldn't touch me, I was safe. I was afraid, but I was safe."

She looked at Mina with pleading eyes.

"But I've changed my ways, so that the devil doesn't take me like that. Not that way," she said.

The teardrops multiplied, now dripping nonstop from her eyes.

Mina sat in silence, taking in the trauma that surrounded her. The girl silently wept. Mina rubbed her shoulder. A question burned in Mina's mind. Before she could stop herself, she blurted it aloud.

"Do you miss him?" Mina asked.

Greta's shocked eyes scanned Mina's face. Greta looked away.

"He was a sinner," she replied.

Mina caught something else in her voice.

"But you loved him," Mina said.

"It doesn't matter. He went to Hell. He was taken by the devil. He was a sinner," she said.

Greta repeated herself as though she had been brainwashed, or had even brainwashed herself.

A knock startled both girls into a jump.

"Honey?"

The familiar voice of Greta's mother came through the door.

Greta quickly wiped the remaining tears from her eyes. She did not want her mother to know the tears had been for herself.

Mina caught a trace of shame, embarrassment from the girl. Greta explained.

"We're only allowed to cry for those who need help, not for our own self-pity," Greta explained, "But I think we're done here. I have to go to bed now; I'm worn from the day."

Mina blinked harshly at the way she was dismissed.

Greta opened the door, smiling her charming smile.

"Hello mother," she said, "Mina was just on her way out. You can show her if you want."

Dorothy's smile overwhelmed her with motherly concern.

"Yes, certainly," Dorothy responded.

Mina slowly walked to the door. There was so much more she wanted to know. She didn't want to leave yet.

At the door, Mina turned one last time to look at Greta. The girl was staring blankly at the floor. She suddenly looked so small, like a lost, frightened child who needed to find herself. Her trauma had been displaced into a façade. She really believed the devil would get her if she didn't change her ways and live by God's rules. She completely deprived herself of a normal life by helping others, rather than recovering herself.

Mina felt bad for her. She felt guilt for her own presence. It shook Mina's heart with a silent anchor. But she knew the girl needed to find herself on her own. Maybe this visit would help her.

"Thank you Greta," she said.

"Yes," Greta replied.

But she did not look up. Mina turned away and slowly followed the mother out of the room. As they continued to the stairs, Dorothy touched her shoulder.

"Did she help you well?" she asked.

Mina nodded.

"Um, yes, yes she did," Mina responded, "Very well."

"Good, good."

The woman shook her head as she spoke. At the door, she faced Mina and smiled wider.

"Goodbye and good luck Mina. Come back any time, my child."

She took Mina's hands, squeezing them affectionately with a vast expression of sincerity.

"Thank you," Mina smiled.

She hurriedly walked away to her car.

In her car, Mina cursed. She needed more. She had not gotten all that she needed. She looked at the clock; it was almost eight. She looked up again at the remarkably lit house. In the upstairs story, a silhouetted figure of a woman stood behind the glass of a window, partially covered by white lace curtains.

"Why is she watching?" Mina asked aloud, "She's really stuck there. She wants to come out into the world again. She's just too afraid."

Hurriedly, Mina put her car in drive and headed home. It would be over an hour before she got there.

As she drove the open road, her mind flashed back to their conversation. Was Greta even a reliable scientific source? She seemed so unreal, as if she was no longer a real person. She looked confused, lost, scared and still traumatized.

Mina tapped her fingers against the wheel.

Greta had said that her boyfriend and his friend were taken by a demon, by the devil. But the missing cases report read differently. In the report, there was a large pile of ashes on the ground, over four feet high. It was located right next to a computer monitor, which had failed to burn, along with other debris from apparent fireworks. The devil couldn't have taken them. They had definitely burned downward somehow.

But how? Was it a meteor, this devil she saw? Spontaneous combustion could be the answer, though only if an external force did not light them. But the ash pile seemed similar to this pattern of phenomenon. These questions were what Mina intended to get to the bottom of. She had to find out.

The ride home passed quicker than she expected. She barely remembered part of the drive since she was so deep in thought. And she felt so invigorated with her new knowledge that she didn't even think of falling asleep.

Pulling off the road in front of her parent's house, she turned off the ignition. Instead of running into her home, she stayed in the car. Her thoughts went back to Greta. Since Greta couldn't understand what happened to her, she used something familiar; she used religion to describe what she saw. The demon signified evil and her thoughts must have transposed, making it the devil's fault. That way, she couldn't mourn the loss of a boy she loved because he was a sinner. All Mina knew was the girl was covering up her true feelings for her religion.

Mina looked up at the night sky and spoke.

"Underneath those clouds, your true thoughts are lurking Greta. I hope some day you realize this."

She paused.

"They're just hidden, but they're still there. It is still here, that monster or demon. It is still here," she whispered.

Some part of her wished she could have shared these words with Greta.

Mina leaned her head back against the seat. She sat there still thinking. Her eyelids became heavy. Moments later she fell asleep at the comfort of relaxing on the headrest.

Four hours later, Mina awakened, cold, startled and disoriented. Initially, she didn't know where she was. She realized she had fallen asleep in her car when the coldness began to set into her limbs. Shivering, she reached for her keys from the ignition. Then she stumbled out the door, locking, and then shutting it. Walking very slowly, she rubbed her neck with her right hand. It had become really stiff in her nap in the car. Lifting her left wrist to view her watch, she realized how long she had been out.

"Holy shit," she mumbled.

She dragged herself up the stairs to the porch, remembering her dream. During her sleep, she had had a very strange dream. In it, she was running through the woods. Nothing else occurred. She had never seen these woods before, but she felt scared, like someone was chasing her, hunting her.

Before she knew it, she was already up the stairs and into her room.

"Too much research," she mumbled.

Still groggy from the nap, she laid on her bed without changing her clothes; quickly falling off into another deepened sleep.

***

By early morning, Mina was revived enough to awaken without her blaring alarm clock. Quickly she grabbed one of her small notebooks and a pen. She scribbled some notes of her last dream. This dream was very much like the one she had in the car. She started at the beginning of the woods, searching for something. Then, from nowhere, she started running. Soon, she was flying, escaping and feeling freedom. She wanted to interpret this dream later. But for now, she had to get ready for work.

Once she made it to the library, Mina took notes; reviewing the entire story Greta told. She had already discussed the events with herself, but knew her tiredness might have caused her to overlook something. Drawing large boxes on a piece of plain white paper, she sketched an outline of the events in the order they occurred, from Greta's perspective.

When she finished, Mina sat back from her outline, getting a full view of it. Stick figures were drawn to make up for the people involved. She had her own ideas, but needed more evidence to prove them. Now, she had to contemplate the causes of such a seemingly fictitious event.

If the devil were the cause, and was truly in existence, would it have honestly left a survivor? The devil, from what she had heard, had no pity and his wrath would extinguish more than just two boys in the woods. In addition, the whole surrounding area of wood should char to ash just from his presence. Of course, it could not be that phenomenon; the general idea of the devil is to allegedly cause death and pain. Mina didn't believe it was the devil.

Could it have been a meteor? Greta said it came from the sky, as meteors do. Perhaps it fell too quickly and was hot enough to cause the death of those two men, with ash the only remnants.

Mina sipped from her coffee mug, without moving her eyes from the paper in front of her. Just as she set the mug back down, a familiar voice spoke up next to her.

"Into your research?" Scott asked.

He stayed back, opting out of the surprise tactics he usually used.

Mina hurriedly covered the sheet with a book.

"What are you doin' here?" she asked.

"Just came to see how you were doing. I tried to call you last night but your mom said you were gone," Scott said.

His eyes were hopeful, inquiring. Mina smiled.

"Yeah, thanks for the research you guys did," she said.

But she offered nothing else. Scott frowned. Now, she rather wished that he could help her. He continued.

"I let Jesse look at it briefly, but I found it specifically for you. They don't really know what you're into, they just know it's important to you," he said.

Mina raised an eyebrow.

"And you do know?" she asked.

Scott smiled with a mischievous glint in his eye.

"Sort of. I can kinda guess how your mind is reeling," he said.

Mina grunted.

"That's how you found the case. But you don't necessarily know where I'm going with this," she said.

Scott smiled.

"It's definitely a supernatural search," he said.

He studied her for a reaction. She gave none. After a few more moments, she began studying him. She tapped her pen against her book and paper.

"You really want to know, don't you?" she asked.

"Sort of," he replied.

But he played it off as less urgent than he felt it was.

"I can help you," he said.

"Honestly, I can do this by myself," she replied.

She watched the disappointment surface on his face before continuing.

"But if you feel like you're up to it..."

She studied him for a reaction. He kept a stone face.

"I could probably use your assistance," she said.

His eyes lit up and she looked away.

"Well let me know and I can help out a little," he said, hiding his curiosity and joy.

Mina smiled half-heartedly and then looked back up.

"Everyone has a partner at some point I guess," she said.

She pondered the issue for a moment before beginning again.

"If you do help me, I do not want you to tell the others a thing about this. Is that a clear agreement?" she asked.

Scott frowned. He didn't agree. He believed in open, honest conversation. Mina also knew how tough it would be for him.

"You know I don't like to do that," he said, "but in order to protect your privacy I can keep my mouth shut."

He put his left hand in the air, the right over his heart swearing his secrecy. He was really too concerned about her recent behavior to say no.

"Well," she started, "Meet me back here for lunch, around noon with food. I'll fill you in. Sound good?"

"That works for me," Scott replied.

He kept his face expressionless despite the excitement he felt.

"What are you going to do now?" Mina asked.

"Just going to read for a little bit," he said, "I have to find a book for Ryan."

He looked back towards the numerous bookcases.

"Okay, see ya later," she said.

Scott nodded and walked away.

Mina sat there, collecting her thoughts.

Ok, only tell him some of it, not everything. Always keep one step ahead of him, she reminded herself.

Mina moved the book, exposing the doodle sheet again.

Let's see, where did I leave off, she asked herself. *Oh, that's right, the meteor that it couldn't be, or maybe could be. What else can explain it?*

Mina tapped her pencil lightly against her temple for a few seconds.

Could it be a small spark of intense heat from an illegally made firework? Nah. Maybe it was some sort of foreign substance, a terrorist idea. Nah, it would have been a more powerful explosion. Perhaps a biological agent of some sort? Nah, the girl wouldn't have survived. Whatever this was, it was a contained sort of destruction. It did not reach beyond the two young men who were lighting the fireworks. They were specific targets, singled out by whatever it was.

Lighting fireworks. The boys had been lighting fireworks.

What major harm does that do? People do it every year. They just happened to be hidden in the woods, near railroad tracks. Could it have been gas, oil or something derived from the ground? Some sort of substance had to spark. But if natural oils sparked, it would have spread, not singled out two men.

Mina stopped writing, instead looking at her list of other possibilities. None of the events were logically possible.

Another thought occurred to her again. Could she even trust Greta's recollection of events? Sure, she seemed like an honest girl, but she was horribly traumatized. The human brain can scramble events in a different way than they occurred. Perhaps Greta recalled the night differently than it happened.

Mina sighed out of frustration.

Now she had to quickly find another source to back up her research. Scott might not believe her at this point. He'll think she doesn't have enough proof. If he doesn't believe, he can back out.

Though she already knew he would not.

CHAPTER 7:
DAWN OF A DUO

After circulating through town with his errands, around noon, Scott found his way back to the library. Carrying a bag of Styrofoam boxes of food, he stopped just before entering the library.

Did he really want to become involved in her project? Anything dealing with the supernatural led to either a waste of time or high risks. He had never seen solid proof and hoped that she wouldn't get her hopes up too much.

Scott sighed.

Whatever happened, at least he'd be able to monitor, or rather look out for his best friend. Yeah, he decided, he had to become involved so that Mina wouldn't end up crazy like....

He stopped himself in thought, entering the library instead of dwelling on the past. Mina eyed him as he entered the door.

"It's about time, my belly's growling," she said.

"I'm on time," he claimed.

"I know, but my stomach thinks you're late," she joked.

Digging into the bag, Mina quickly found her sandwich and onion rings. Scott stood there, watching her bite into her food.

"When's the last time you ate?" he asked.

She continued to chew, swallowing her food.

"Seconds ago," she replied.

Scott shook his head in disapproval.

"Mina, Mina, Mina. You have to take care of yourself," he said.

She ignored his concern.

"Aren't you going to eat?" she asked, chewing again.

"Yeah, I was scared to put my hand in the bag," he joked.

"Here, have a seat," Mina said.

She pulled out a chair from behind the desk and pointed at it.

"I put it there for you," she continued, wiping her mouth with a napkin.

"Thanks," Scott replied.

Silently, they finished their lunch, each enamored by their own separate thoughts of dread and excitement over what was to come. Mina could not tell what was worse, the silent wait or actually getting to the subject.

When Scott finished eating, Mina held the silence longer.

As he sipped his drink, his mind pondered whether or not he should start the conversation. He was always the leader type, but didn't want to over step his boundaries.

Mina reached in the desk and pulled out her papers and sketching. She sat there silently, allowing Scott to look over the papers. Mina set the papers out in her own order on the desk, rearranging them, from left to right in order of her first research, up to the sketch of the night before.

"This paper," she said, pointing to the one on the farthest left, "is a case I found similar to that of the one we first encountered. You remember, the one with the log cabin, the casualties, the missing girl and the pile of ashes."

"Yeah, yeah, yeah, of course I remember that. So that's what sparked your interest?" he asked.

He knew it.

"Exactly," Mina said, "But when I looked on my own, I found this case," she said, pointing to another paper, then picking it up, "Two middle aged couples were at a picnic reunion at a park. Actually, here I'll let you read for yourself what happened."

She handed the paper to him.

Scott quickly scanned the paper, taking in the information up to the same pile of ashes. Quietly, he handed the paper back to her.

Mina scanned his face but he offered nothing.

"In both cases, there were no witnesses. The couple had gone to the restroom together, leaving the other couple there. They saw nothing," she started.

"I know, I read that," he teased.

"All right, all right," she said, "but just listen."

Her tone changed into a seemingly frustrated sound, though she was still in good humor.

"It took a lot of researching to find these small cases, a lot of hours of sleep were missed, with some results, though I believe we can figure it out..."

She paused before beginning again, "Now, back to where I was, the same pile of ashes was present, no bodies and two missing people whose vehicle was still there. Who would kidnap a middle aged couple without trying to collect ransom?"

"Maybe the kidnappers realized they weren't rich and just murdered them," Scott hypothesized.

"I doubt that, they would have at least tried. But, there's the pile of ashes. The fire was fully extinguished, though it was lit before the other couple ventured to the restroom. There were ashes close to the fire, though far enough from it that they weren't connected. The pile of ashes was a few feet deep, as with what occurs in spontaneous combustion," she started.

"Spontaneous combustion?" Scott asked, a frown filling his face, "That's been a tested and rejected theory for ages. Is that the research you've gotten yourself into?"

Slight disappointment sunk in. He assumed she was searching the supernatural.

"No," she said, "And from now on, no questions until I finish."

Scott zipped his fingers across his lips and then raised his hands in the air as a pledge of silence. Mina grunted.

"What I meant was that spontaneous combustion is the only semi-acceptable theory that the world will agree with, though it is even doubted. The manner in which the bodies were found would point to that theory, unless," she paused for suspense, "It really is some sort of a supernatural effect."

Mina looked at Scott, hoping he would believe the rest. Scott forced himself to keep quiet, though his mind was brewing questions and rebuttals.

She continued.

"In spontaneous combustion, there is no external source. No fire is present when the body inflames itself, but in these cases, there was fire present at least somewhere in the surrounding area. There is, however, no evidence that the flames caught the person. If they had, the person would not have burned completely to ash, before at least partially being put out somehow, if that were the case," she paused again.

Mina studied the profile of Scott's face. Scott kept his eyes averted to the desk as she spoke, taking in every word she said.

Mina paused, lifting her drink to take a sip. Her endlessly rattling nerves grew visible down to the tips of her shaky fingers. She was confident behind it all though. She knew there was something to find.

"So, I must thank you for the paper you found the other day..." she started again.

"You're welcome," he said; glad to use his voice again, though briefly.

Mina's voice ran over him as she continued explaining.

"With the case you found, there was a survivor this time, a witness," she said and then paused, "whom I visited last night."

"What?" Scott asked.

Stunned shock lit his face with the disbelief that she had gone to a total stranger's house, alone.

Mina smiled.

She knew he was worried just by the look of surprise on his face.

"Relax, it's ok. Everything went well."

But Scott was angry and he couldn't hide it.

"Mina, I love you like a sister, but you can't do stuff like that. I really wish you would have told me before you went to a stranger's house. I could have gone with you. You could have gotten hurt," he continued.

"Ok dad," she joked, "But really it was ok. You read the case that you gave to me that day right?"

"Yeah," he said, frowning, "But I wish..."

Mina cut him off, "Besides all that. The girl who survived, woman I should say, became super religious after the trauma she went through. She told me her story because she felt that she had moved past that time and that God was by her side now. She wanted to help me. Though I don't really think she got past it at all. But that's another story altogether."

79

Scott picked up on a note of sadness in Mina's voice and looked up. A matching frown, framed with that spoken sadness swept over her face.

But she continued again with a new, solemn expression, "Here are the events as she described them to me," Mina said, pointing to the last paper, which sat on the desk directly in front of Scott.

Mina put her doodled paper directly in the middle of both of them. Instead of having him read it, she wanted to show him the picture of events so he could understand it better.

"Nice doodles," Scott remarked.

Mina ignored him, continuing on.

For the next ten minutes, Mina described the events to him in nearly the exact manner that Greta had explained them to her. When she was finished, she looked at him intently, wondering of his response.

Scott sat there, staring at the paper without words.

Internally, he pondered the issue. It seemed too ludicrous, the devil coming out of the sky, burning two young men to death, to ashes. But then again, it was a supernatural subject, which leaves the question, is this story real?

"Well?" Mina finally asked.

Scott smiled, holding back a laugh at her impatience, though he didn't want to offend her or her research by letting it out.

"Well, how do you know what the girl said is the truth, particularly if she was traumatized?" Scott asked.

Mina knew he would wonder.

"Because this girl isn't the type to lie or exaggerate. I am a very good judge of character and she was very pure, wholesome. But that's not all," she continued, "These events, they aren't explainable at all. Nothing could selectively sear an individual, turning it to ash. Fire is wild, not specific. Any fire would consume more than just two men. The woods, the truck, the girl all would have burned and it would have kept growing at an uncontrollable rate."

"That's true, and yes these cases are strange- but the devil?" he smirked, "I don't..."

Mina quickly interrupted, "I don't think it was the devil either. I was just telling you what Greta thought it was. But I, I definitely don't think it was the devil."

"Well what do you think it was?" Scott asked, watching her intently.

"I don't fully know," Mina said, frowning.

Reaching into the desk, Mina pulled out one last sheet of paper.

"This is a list of my idea of possibilities, though they're quite debatable," she said, skimming her eyes across the sheet, "of natural explanations, there is spontaneous combustion, as I mentioned, though there usually is no external source present and in each case, fire was near. Another possibility, a terror attack, somehow a gas or something of any sort mixed into imported fireworks. Some new type of military gas that sears on impact, but fireworks were not involved in each incident. Now, some supernatural ideas, the devil…"

"Whooaaa…no devil," he said.

Scott smacked his forehead in disdain. Mina gave him a dirty look, though he turned away too fast to catch it.

"Supernatural ideas," Mina repeated herself, continuing through his stunts, "if it were the devil, it would not have left survivors. Not to mention the devil does not exist or else God would come down and extinguish fires at the same time."

Scott nodded his head in agreement.

Mina continued again, "A meteor would have left some sort of evidence or remains. Don't you think?" she sprang the question upon him, then changed it, "What do you think it is?"

"I," Scott paused as he thought about it, "I don't know," he paused even longer, "I think they are definitely strange situations, even if not fully supernatural. It seems like an interesting enough topic."

But Mina picked up on the tone of his voice.

"You don't sound very enthused," she said.

She scanned his face for a reaction.

"I just don't want it to be a waste of time," he said truthfully, "What if we never find anything?"

"We will," she said, "It just takes the scientific method."

Scott's eyebrows rose.

"Still there are no guarantees with this subject- it might be like chasing a ghost. A thin, transparent image that can never be held," Scott said.

"Look how much information I've acquired in less than a week so far," Mina said, attempting to sound convincing.

"Yeah, that's just information- the easy part. If this truly is the supernatural, how do you expect to ever see it without facing the consequences?" Scott reasoned.

Startled by the sudden thought, she said, "That's not going to happen. It will not go that far."

"Mina," Scott began.

"I know," she said, looking away.

A strange silence strangled the gap in between and around them. Scott knew that Mina was strong; he just cared for her and didn't want her to get hurt. Granted, they all lived for the strengthening of their own minds, but there were other subjects to discover that were just as fulfilling.

"If we figure this out, we will have made the biggest discovery in the world," Mina offered, attempting to convince him it was not a pointless venture.

"But..." Scott started.

"It will be the beginning of a legend, now an unknown story, until we discover the truth of it," Mina continued.

"But..." Scott began again.

"I know you're worried. It won't be like that though. Disappointment may come, but at least I'll know I tried," Mina justified her interest.

"As long as you know ahead of time, that you may find nothing and can deal with it, I'll help you," Scott said, "but, I do not want you to find some sort of depression. Promise me now, that you will not get yourself involved to an obsessive degree. We've seen the consequences, you know that as well as I do."

Mina contemplated his request and his emotional features. Seriousness stared back at her.

"I have no intention of becoming obsessed with this case," she said.

"A promise," Scott said.

"Damn it Scott, I'll promise that I won't be obsessed with this case for the rest of my life. For now though, it is good to have a small bit of that quality. It makes you work harder," she reasoned.

"Ok, but not to a dangerous degree. Promise that this case is not worth your life or anyone else's," Scott said.

"I agree," she said.

"Say I promise," Scott requested.

Scott knew Mina too well and understood that she would find a way to get out of anything.

"Ok, I...," she paused to tease Scott, "promise."

She scrunched up her face as if she had just eaten a lemon against her will.

"That's better," he smiled, "Where do we start?"

"Well, I stay here, reading possibilities, working my own brain until I'm done with work. You go home and search for cases. Sound good?" she asked.

Scott felt weird about being told what to do, but said, "Sure, it's so strange taking orders, especially from someone as bull-headed and unrestricted as you."

"I knew you'd feel that way. You," she paused, "can always back out if you don't want to take orders from a woman."

Scott smiled.

"Nah, I'm in too deep now. My curiosity's got the best of me. But..." he paused, "We could always be partners instead. I could just be 40% invested and you can be 60."

Mina tapped her pen against her temple.

"Let me think about it," she said, "Prove yourself to me, and we'll see."

Scott turned to her, pretending to look upset. Mina rolled her eyes.

"Fine. Partners, 65 and 35%?" she asked.

"Fine," he said.

But he still had that mopey look on his face.

"Now get out of here. I have to work," she laughed.

Scott turned towards the door.

"Stubborn men," she muttered.

A middle-aged man looked up at her comment. Mina's face flushed.

"Not you," she softly replied, "Sorry."

She picked up her book on spontaneous combustion in an attempt to cover her reddening face. To her relief, the man went out the door. Mina took a deep breath.

Meteors, Mina thought to herself.

Terrorism, her thought process continued.

The devil, a haunted lonely ghost, spontaneous combustion, gas, defective fireworks- what the hell was it? How does it work so well, so directed?

Looking up from the desk, no one was in sight. She gathered up her papers in the order of which they occurred. Her hands moved quickly through the first couple of pages, until she came to the sketch again.

A demon of the night, she thought, her eyes focusing on the last picture box of her sketch. Roaring through flames, a demon that breathes fire. Like a dragon. Perhaps a relative of the dragon. How far-fetched did that sound? A dragon was a fairy tale, a myth, or was it?

Mina's mind wandered more.

This case certainly was a brainteaser, especially for the early parts of it. One cannot just simply read information to solve a case. They would need more footwork in the future.

***

As Scott walked back to his house, he thought about the case.

Though it was seemingly interesting, he found it borderline impossible. It was going to be extremely difficult to prove something so intangible, particularly to a public, which is generally unwilling to believe. Movies and books were great sources of the supernatural, but no one wanted to believe they were a true concern in the real world.

Scott imagined trying to convince the world of the existence of supreme or supernatural beings.

I can see it now, Scott chuckled to himself. The world has too much to worry about already with normal everyday problems.

"Ah," Scott sighed.

But there were people who have suffered loss from this monster or meteor or whatever it was.

At least it will help them out, I suppose, he thought, trying to give himself a reason to stay involved besides helping Mina.

Scott's mind wandered over possibilities until he reached his home. As soon as he made it to his room, he jotted down a few thoughts that occurred as he walked. Immediately after, he logged on to his computer, searching for something either very important, or something entirely impossible.

CHAPTER 8:
A SECRET SHARED

After work, Mina expected to meet with Scott at his house to see what he found out. As soon as Brandy came in, she rushed out the door.

When she stepped out into the sunny day, she shielded her eyes and blinked harshly. To her surprise, outside sitting on the sidewalk with his back to the library, was Scott. He did not turn around as she walked out, and she assumed he was deep in thought. Sneaking up behind him quietly, she wondered if he had been overtaken by the same deep thought as she recently experienced.

"Hey!" she said.

Scott jumped as though he was caught alone and spooked by the devil on a darkened night. Mina laughed.

"Whoa, isn't it usually me who jumps?" she asked, smiling.

Now she was curious as to what thoughts separated him from the world. Scott brushed off his scare.

"I found another case," he responded.

"Ok, fill me in," Mina said.

Quickly she sat down next to him.

"Right here? Maybe we should…" Scott began.

Before finishing his sentence, he noticed Jesse and Ryan walking up to the library.

"Shit," Mina mumbled under her breath.

Four would be overcrowded. Unfortunately, it was a secret they had to keep together.

"Just remember, it's between you and me," Mina quickly mumbled.

Scott nodded. They watched them approach.

"What's up guys?" Jesse asked.

"Nothing," Scott said.

But his voice sounded suspicious. Ryan examined the pair sitting on the sidewalk.

"You guys look pale. Vampiric even," Ryan observed.

"I'm fine," Scott and Mina replied in unison.

"Okay," Ryan responded.

He was unconvinced but he looked away from them rather than pursuing it. Scott was beginning to get that strange look in his eyes Mina had lately. Jesse piped in.

"I've been calling you all day Scott," he said.

He too noticed a strange separation.

"Oh, sorry man. I've been running around all day. How is the book Ryan?" Scott asked.

"Exactly what I wanted. Thanks," Ryan replied.

But he kept his eyes averted. Of course, that wasn't exactly unusual. Ryan hated making eye contact at any time unless he was angry.

A strange silence grappled between them for a few minutes until Jesse broke into the quietness.

"So, what are we doing tonight guys?" he asked.

"Um, what does everyone want to do?" Mina asked.

Truly, she hoped that she and Scott could get away to work on their new project.

Scott studied them; his troubled blue eyes scanning his friends' faces.

"What kinds of projects are you guys into?" Scott asked.

"Nothing much- still meteors," Ryan replied.

"I've found an interest in those missing cases we were working on before," Jesse piped in.

Scott and Mina reacted, their facial expressions of shock giving them away.

"What, how, what kind of cases?" Scott asked.

Once his words jumbled together, Jesse immediately noticed his nervousness.

"Oh, any kind," he replied nonchalantly, "It is fascinating how easily people disappear."

"Did you find anything of interest?" Mina asked calmly.

She knew he could be bluffing and simply nebbing into their business.

"Oh, you know, the usual stuff," Jesse answered.

Mina didn't believe him.

"Huh," she said.

She got up and dusted off the back of her jeans.

"Well I'm going to go home and change my clothes. Where are we meeting tonight?" she asked.

"It's your turn," Ryan said quietly.

"Ok, well give me a few minutes before you come over," she said.

She turned to walk away.

"We were going to go in here for a little bit," Jesse replied, pointing to the library.

She turned back to look at them.

"Be my guest. I've been in there all day," she said, "Brandy's there now."

Mina smiled as she watched Jesse's face curl into a grin.

"I know," Jesse said, "That's why we came down now."

He grinned widely. He liked flirting with Brandy. Ryan rolled his eyes.

"Good luck," Mina laughed.

Scott got up, slowly following behind Mina.

"You're not coming with us?" Ryan asked.

"Nah, I'll see you guys in a little bit," he yelled behind him.

Watching Mina and Scott walk away, Jesse was the first to talk.

"Strange," he said, "It's like they're both in some sort of strange warp or something."

"Yeah," Ryan responded, "Something definitely is crawling in their brains that wasn't there before."

Jesse shrugged and then opened the door to the library.

"Hello Brandy, here I come," he said.

Ryan shook his head, rolling his eyes again, as he followed Jesse into the library.

***

Mina and Scott looked over their shoulders before talking.

"What's the case?" Mina whispered.

"You don't have to whisper, they're in the library far away," Scott said.

He whispered too but with irritation in his voice. Mina picked up on it.

"What's your problem today?" Mina asked.

"I hate keeping secrets," he mumbled, "I'm no good at lying either."

"Look Scott, can you imagine how crowded this would be if we involved them?" Mina asked.

"I know, I know, I just hate hiding stuff, that's all. They're our friends too," Scott reasoned.

Mina rolled her eyes.

"Ok, what's the case?" Mina asked again.

Scott mumbled a noise of disgust to himself and then remained silent. Mina looked at him with quiet impatience. The two continued walking in silence. Scott wasn't talking. With every step, suspense was building in Mina. She felt curiosity bubbling through the blood in every vein.

Scott still remained quiet.

They were coming closer to her house when, finally, Scott began.

"In this case," he began.

He noticed the tenseness dissipating from Mina's walking stance through his peripheral vision, "It was a car incident of sorts."

He paused. Mina grimaced.

"Missing people in a..." Mina began.

"I didn't look through missing cases this time," Scott interrupted her, "I couldn't find anything similar in the missing cases, so I tried something else."

"That was pretty smart," she said.

Scott continued talking with a serious tone, not even acknowledging her compliment.

"There was an accident report, a strange one at that. All I know was that they think the car must have caught fire. There were ashes inside, half the car was gone, but..." Scott stopped.

"Gone? But what?" Mina pushed.

"But there were witnesses this time too," Scott said.

"Are they still alive?" Mina asked.

"Yes, some of them are. Though sane, I'm not so sure," he said, "It seems that a group was traveling in separate cars, one following the other when it happened."

"Where did this happen?" Mina asked.

"In Gerlach, Nevada, just one state away," Scott replied.

"How far away is that?" Mina asked, "Driving distance?"

"I'd say about 17 hours, maybe less depending on speed," Scott replied.

But Scott was wary about traveling so far to talk to witnesses about an uncertain case.

"Here's the report," he said.

He pulled a paper from his notebook and handed it to Mina. She anxiously read it.

She skimmed through the names, to get to the most important parts. Four young adults were traveling for summer vacation, one car following the other. Two men in the first car, one man and woman in the second car. One car just wrecked, must have caught flames, the bodies disappeared perhaps burned alive, first half of car turned to ash. Eyewitness accounts were unstable, drivers wrecked after first car. Source of accident and fire: unknown.

"Huh," Mina said, "So when do you want to go?"

"I don't," he replied.

"Why not?" Mina asked.

Her disappointment bordered on anger.

"I don't think it's worth it," he responded.

"What?" she asked, pulling him to face her, "After what I told you happened when I spoke with Greta, you don't want to find out more?"

"It will take up at least three days to drive there and back. How can either of us get that long off of work?" Scott reasoned.

"I work tomorrow, then I have two days off. If we don't make it back in two days, then I'll call in sick. The boss will be back by then," Mina reasoned.

"And me?" Scott asked.

"You never take time off, I'm sure you can for once. You don't get to be young and adventurous forever," she responded.

"Who's to say we'll even find these people?" Scott asked.

"You can find anyone on the Internet. I'm not worried about that," Mina said.

Scott shrugged.

"How do we know they will want to talk to us? We're nobodies who have just taken an interest in a certain subject," Scott said.

Truly, he didn't want to go at all. Any reason would do.

"That is exactly why they'll want to talk to us- just like with Greta- because we are nobodies. They'll want to talk, because we'll listen," Mina said.

She studied him, watching for his response. When he didn't say anything, she felt the bitterness brewing a hurricane in her heart.

"You just want an excuse not to go," she said.

Her words were stained with disdain. Scott averted his eyes.

"Maybe I do," Scott replied.

She couldn't hide her anger.

"Why are you wussing out already?" she asked.

Scott's face reddened, blending in with his hair color.

"I'm not. I just have a feeling we should leave this case alone," he said.

"No chance in hell. I'll go alone," she continued.

Stopping outside her house, she considered running into her room and locking the door. But she wasn't a child and knew that wasn't what she should do.

A look of disgust brewed over Scott's face.

"When do you want to leave?" he asked.

"Tomorrow, immediately after I am done with work," she said.

She wore the serious face of a challenger.

"I'll work early so that I can get off a few days," Scott said.

He hated giving in to anything, but knew she would go alone. He cared enough about her that he did not want her to have to face that danger alone. But Scott wished he had never found the case now. Initially, he had contemplated whether or not to even tell her about it.

Scott started walking away towards his own home.

"Hey, where are you going?" Mina yelled.

He turned slightly to make quick eye contact.

"I have to get something from home. I'll be back in a little bit," he said.

Scott continued walking away. Mina watched him. She hated being the way she had been lately but this was important to her. She sighed, hoping to flush away the discomfort that settled over her life.

Unexpectedly, Scott stopped in the middle of the road. He looked around quickly on all sides and then turned towards her.

"We better think up something really quickly!" he yelled.

"About?" Mina asked.

"The guys and our vacation!" he said.

He turned back around again, walking away.

"Call me!" she yelled.

Quickly, she ran to her room. She hurriedly hid Scott's paper under a few books near her computer. Then she jumped on the bed. Lying on her back, she stared at the ceiling as she relaxed. Within the next few minutes, her phone rang.

"Well, what have you thought up?" Scott asked.

"Me?" she shrieked.

"Yeah, you want to go so badly," he replied.

"True," she said, "um…um…"

"Are you telling me you haven't come up with anything yet?" he asked.

"My aunt is sick and we are going to go see her, at my mom's request," Mina said.

"Where does she live?" Scott asked, wanting details.

"I really do have an aunt who lives here in Arizona. That's pretty close, we'll say we're just staying a few days to help her around the house," Mina continued with the story.

"And why can't they go?" Scott asked, making sure he had all the details.

"Small house, lots of people, not enough room. You're only coming because I don't want to travel alone. Parents can't get off work. I'll tell my parents I'm staying with a friend and for them to tell anyone who calls just that I'll be back in a couple days. No one should call though," she finished.

"Your aunt's name?" Scott asked.

"You've never met her before but her name is Marly- same last name as me," she added.

"Never married?" he asked.

"Divorced with three kids," she answered.

"Is that all then?" he asked.

"It seems that way. She just has an early winter flu," Mina added in.

"Got ya, ok. See you in a little bit," he said.

He hung up the phone. Mina hung up the phone without a goodbye. She resumed her relaxed position on the bed until she heard heavy footsteps on the stairs. It sounded like two people.

Jesse opened the door, peeking inside her room. Ryan was behind him. Mina looked at him with a funny expression.

"What?" she asked.

She felt odd at the expression on Jesse's face.

"You're daydreaming about Scott, aren't you?" he joked.

Mina scoffed.

"Shut up, can't you give that story up?" she asked.

The constant assumption annoyed her.

"Admit it and we'll stop," Jesse said.

"What do you mean we?" Ryan said, pushing Jesse the rest of the way through the cracked open door.

"Punk," Jesse said.

Ryan moved past him into her room.

"You look tired," Ryan said to Mina.

"Yeah, it's these damn morning shifts," she claimed, sitting up on the bed, "My body's just not used to it."

"Yeah," Ryan agreed.

"They'll be over with soon though," she mumbled.

"Where's Scott?" Jesse piped in.

"He stopped at his house to get something," Mina replied.

She wasn't exactly sure what it was. If he wanted her to know he would have told her.

Jesse moved to Mina's computer, taking a seat. He logged on without asking, though they were good enough friends that she was not bothered by it.

"No porn," she teased.

She wasn't against it; she just didn't want a virus or for someone to trace it to her computer, especially since it wasn't her search.

"I'm not," Jesse mumbled quietly.

Jesse searched the Internet while Mina and Ryan talked. Mina asked about meteors, taking interest in what he had to say about the subject. She didn't tell him how it had to do with her own research.

In the midst of their conversation, heavy footsteps emerged from downstairs. Seconds later, Scott came into the room carrying a handful of papers slightly disorganized as if he had rushed them from somewhere.

"What's all this?" Mina asked.

She hoped it had nothing to do with their case.

"Just some projects for us all to work on," he answered.

He gazed at her with a cool, confident expression as if to say 'don't worry.'

"What about?" Ryan's curiosity streamed out.

"Well, you guys said you were interested in missing cases, so I thought we'd work on a few," he said, nonchalantly.

Mina looked at him with apprehension. He had given her the 'don't worry' look, but his words were becoming something else.

"These are all cases of fire deaths," Scott began, looking especially at Mina, as he handed them out to all three of them.

"We should figure out how many of these truly happened how they did, that is, if the cause listed is correct, how long it took for the victims to burn to death, what happened in the end, etc., etc.," he continued.

Jesse and Ryan quickly began looking over the papers as Mina stared at Scott. He mouthed the words 'relax' to her as she lowered her eyes to the paper.

The story on her paper was about a couple on their second honeymoon, who were caught in a hotel fire. The cause was a dropped cigarette in a different room. The rest of the people in the small hotel escaped, besides the couple. DNA results from the remains of the bodies identified the victims.

Remains, Mina thought to herself.

There weren't remains in any of her cases. Maybe Scott was onto something. If he gave the others cases like this, they would all be involved, but wouldn't know everything. She really had to give him credit.

Ryan looked up from his copy.

"These aren't exactly missing cases," he said.

"In a way, they are," Scott shrugged his shoulders, "These few people did not make it out alive in these cases, but there were other survivors. Why didn't they survive? It leaves many questions we can ask and debate about. I just thought it would be fun to do before we started trying to solve missing cases, where there isn't much evidence involved."

"Sounds good to me," Jesse replied.

"Sounds fun," Mina encouraged.

Scott looked at her with relief that she understood his plan.

"All right, lets give it a shot," Ryan said.

Ryan and Jesse seemed happy that they were included in something. Each one read their stories in silence. Scott and Mina read theirs as well, just in case there was something in the elements of a natural fire that might explain a supernatural existence.

The four began their discussion of debate on subjects of less importance than Mina and Scott's. But Jesse and Ryan felt important in their new inclusion into the group.

CHAPTER 9:
TRAVEL AND THE EXPENSE

Mina threw her bag into the back seat of Scott's car.

"I'm so glad they believed it," Mina said.

The shining red 2007 Dodge Neon was spotless on the interior to match the cleanliness of the outside. Within the car, the floors had recently been vacuumed, the windows were spotless, the back seat free of debris- unlike Mina's car. Mina's own car appeared as though she lived in it- clothes were scattered throughout, food wrappers strewn about, the dashboard was full of dust and the floors even went months without seeing a vacuum let alone the daylight, since it was so covered with her messes. Silently, she admired his organizational skills as she thought of her own dirty car.

"Yeah, thanks to me," Scott prided himself.

"I agree, what made you come up with that idea so quickly?" Mina wondered.

"Well," he thought about it for a moment, "It was guilt. I felt bad that we couldn't tell them so of course I involved them. Though not fully."

"They even lightened up enough to think we really are going to see my sickly aunt. Perfect," she said.

But now she felt her own slight guilt at the secrecy.

After they finished loading the car, they were on their way to Nevada. The Internet offered directions to the survivors' homes. Besides the addresses, they had maps and listings of asylums in case the two were enlisted. Anything they could think of, they had planned for the trip.

Before leaving, Scott told his parents and job place he just needed to get away for a few days for a vacation. He didn't want to lie so he told them nothing important. Jesse still thought something romantic was going on between Mina and Scott, though it obviously was not.

With Scott driving down Interstate 40 West for the first hour, they talked about music, movies, everything but the mission they were chasing. It had been a long time since they just had friendly conversation. Usually, their conversations were about research, whether from the group or individually. But there would be plenty of time to discuss research topics later.

For the next hour, each one took to their own silence as, together, they listened to compact discs with intervals of switching to the radio. Admiring the scenery, separately, they each felt a quiet peacefulness in the drive. Last summer, they had not taken their usual trip anywhere- not even during spring break. Usually, the four of them took off together somewhere to expand their minds with experiences from being in nature's natural world.

Within the next hour, and though it was early, Mina decided to curl up against the window to take a nap. She worked the morning shift again and though she had gotten to bed early the night before, she wanted to be well rested for her half of the drive. They had taken his car since it was a newer model.

As Mina slept, Scott listened to the music while lingering in deep thought. Even if they didn't find what they wanted here, at least he was able to see all that he was seeing now. He had gotten out of that town for now and just enjoyed the new scenery of the surrounding area. It was only strange because he had not seen anything outside of his own town in at least a year. He was still young, though he seemed to have forgotten his love of travel until now.

Scott especially liked the highway's wide-open spaces and a greater ability to see what was coming from afar. He spent the rest of the time enjoying this spacious scenery.

Hours later, when it was Mina's turn to drive, Scott was glad that the time had finally come. The passivity of the drive had caused much tiredness in him. His stomach growled as he pulled into a diner. He knew Mina would be more than glad to have some food. It was late at night though early in the morning.

They had an early breakfast and before long, they were back in the car. During their breakfast, Scott had explained which highways they would merge onto. He asked her if she would rather find a hotel for the night, since she still appeared tired but Mina was in a hurry. She wanted to find out information, sooner as opposed to later.

This time, Scott curled up against the window. He had been looking forward to this nap for a long time. Thankfully, it was dark out. Within minutes, maybe even seconds, Scott was in a deep sleep. Even the coffee he had could do nothing to keep him awake.

Mina silently drove on in the night. She loved the night. But during her sleep, she had the same dream she was having lately. Running through the woods.

Weird, she thought, shaking her head.

She must have been sleeping deeply because, as far as she could recall, Scott hadn't stopped the whole drive. If he did, he sure as hell hadn't bothered to wake her up.

Mina turned up the radio.

She needed some sort of distraction to keep her awake. Doing the same thing in the same position was quite tiring. Concentration was a necessity now.

Within the next few hours, Mina looked at the clock. It was now 5:30 AM. She had only been driving for over four hours and already was feeling the exhaustion. Thankfully her mind was strong. At this point, though, Mina thought the hotel idea would have been a good thing.

As she continued driving, Mina spotted what looked like fire on the other side of the highway. The closer she came to the image, the more she could make out what it was. It seemed to be a mirage to her, a hallucination of fire, like a man searching for water in the sand paper heat of the desert.

Squinting her eyes to try to see clearer, she could tell that a car had caught fire from the front end. The fire was small, as if it had just begun.

Mina quickly slowed, pushing the brakes down slowly, though suddenly. Driving at 80 miles per hour, she quickly went to near 40.

Scott was abruptly roused from his sleep.

"What are…" he started.

Mina quickly spun the car through a dirt and gravel divider, crossing to the opposite direction. Moving slowly through the gravel, she made sure another car wasn't coming. Making a left, she pulled Scott's car off to the right side of the road.

Stopping at what she considered a safe distance from the car, she pulled the emergency flashers to make sure the car could be seen in those dusky hours between night and the coming day. Looking ahead, they could see that the car, a light blue vehicle, was partially engulfed in flames.

Mina quickly pulled her cell phone to call the police. She spotted a middle-aged woman off the side of the road, close to the vehicle. The woman was on a cell phone herself. Mina tried her phone, but the call kept fading and flashing out of range.

"Shit!"

Scott stared at the enflamed car with concern.

"She's standing too close to her car," he said, suddenly realizing the possibility of explosion.

Mina flung open the driver's side door, standing halfway, though trying to use the door as a shield.

"Ma'am!" she shouted, "You should move away from that car!"

Without speaking, the woman, still clutching the cell phone to her ear, ran towards Mina and Scott. Scott slowly opened the door, shielding himself with it just as Mina had.

As the woman approached, they could tell she was speaking with emergency workers on the phone. She finally hung up as she reached the two.

"My...my...my car," was all the woman could say.

"What happened?" Mina asked.

"I pulled off the side of the road, to look for something I dropped..." the lady started.

Her eyes averted.

"Ok, really, I had thrown a cigarette out the window, and I thought it came back in from the wind. I wanted to make sure it hadn't. When I started my car back up, it caught fire," the lady spoke quickly, leaving herself out of breath.

Just then, a wind blew up from the surrounding areas. It was a sudden wind, pushing forth the fire of the vehicle, making the flames appear higher. Smoke seemed to rise in almost perfect form of a tornado cloud as Mina watched it. The woman continued to speak, but she didn't hear her. Mina watched the funnel above the car. The tornado funnel appeared threatening, as though at any time, it could come out and disintegrate them.

The woman, noticing Mina's lack of interest and attention, continued with her story, though turned to talk directly to Scott. Scott in turn, watched Mina's expression. He noticed that the wind had picked up and that the smoke was funneling in a strange direction. He knew she would think it was supernatural, though it was simply a fire on a windy early morning. There was probably something wrong with the car engine. He'd seen this happen to cars before, though Mina would make something out of nothing. He was sure of it.

Suddenly the smoke of the fire began to take small form, though still formless it circled like an eddy of leaves in the wind around the blaze. The grayish cover of smoke seemed to curl up and grow strength at every gust of the wind and the ever-growing fire. The wind suddenly whipped with strength and a near feeling of dry heat around the three figures.

Scott's opinion suddenly began to change.

As he turned to look at the building fire, the smoke seemed to be taking form. The beginnings of a demonic form almost. The smoke circled in constant movement as a genie who was finally set free from a lamp. A fog seemed to overlap the area, making it more and more difficult to see the car.

Just as the form in the fog built to greater thickness, the sound of the blaring alarms of a fire truck crept up quickly. They could hear the sirens in the distance, coming closer. The fog seemed to continue to rise around the smoke with the prevalence of a film on the lining of the top of a pool.

"Scott," Mina said.

But she didn't look his way.

She was unsure if he was seeing this, though he had been watching the entire time. Quickly, she glanced at him to make sure he was watching. Satisfied, she continued to watch the developing form.

The woman, annoyed at being ignored, turned around to see what the two were staring at.

Just as she turned, the fire trucks came up over the hill behind them, shining through the fog and smoke design. The woman turned quickly back, partially blinded by the lights and looked to the ground as she waved her arms.

Firefighters quickly jumped from the truck, beginning to cool the blaze with a yellow hose. A screaming noise emitted from the small fire, as though a life form was being extinguished.

The fire was quickly contained as a police officer pulled close to Scott's car. Getting out of his vehicle, he studied the three figures for signs of suspicion.

"Hello," the officer said in a booming voice.

"Hi," the woman answered shyly.

The officer took turns staring from Mina to Scott.

"You mind telling me what happened here? This your car?" the officer asked, looking at the woman who stood directly in front of him.

"Ye...yes," she stuttered.

The woman repeated the story she tried to tell Scott and Mina, along with her name, telephone number and address. Mina and Scott stood there quietly, baffled at what only they had just seen, or at least only begun to see.

"And who are these people?" the officer asked.

He looked over the two young people, whose faces had reached an unhealthy pale shade.

"They," the woman started.

She looked at the two, pausing, noticing the changed color of their faces. She couldn't tell if those two people were on drugs or what from the way they stared at her car. The woman continued her pause, looking at the two, whose expression appeared similar to a mindless zombie in a horror story.

"These people were kind enough to stop. Must have seen my car," the woman replied, realizing their good gestures, even if they were weirdos, "Haven't said much since they stopped."

"Hello," the officer spoke directly to Mina, "You driving?"

Mina looked down. She had been clutching the door so hard; it left red-purple imprints into her palms and fingertips.

"Yeah," she answered, still in shock, "His car," she said, nodding to Scott.

Scott suddenly snapped from his frozen state as well. The officer studied him.

"We're not from around here," he quickly said, trying to give an excuse for his expression, "We've never seen a car on fire like that."

"Where are you from?" the officer interrogated.

"Oh, Joseph City, Arizona," Scott said.

"I know where that's at. Welcome to our town. Why are you driving so early?" the officer asked, looking at his watch.

"We left during the day yesterday. We were just looking for a hotel when I saw the car on fire. We figured we would try to help," Mina said.

The officer's face softened a bit. It seemed to sink in to him that he was only investigating a car fire.

"There's a hotel about ten miles down the road, if you're looking for one. You two look tired, either that or like you've just seen a ghost. Fires happen all the time," he chuckled, "It's just a good thing it was caught early," he continued, pointing off to the side of the road at the over hanging trees by the guardrail. "Dry season like this. Could very well have caused a forest fire," he said, shaking his head.

He turned his attention back to the lady.

"Ma'am," he continued, "I'll take you to your house."

"Thank you," the three said in unison.

The officer tilted his hat to Mina and Scott.

"You folks have a nice day," he said.

The officer and the woman climbed into the police car, as Scott and Mina slowly moved back into their seats. Neither of them said anything, as they waited for the cop car to pull out. They didn't know what to say, plus they wanted to pull back on the other side of the highway.

Finally, they were able to pull across the highway divider. Since it was so early in the morning, there weren't many cars traveling the road, making the transition easier to follow through with.

Silence lingered and floated about the car as the fog of the fire had around the ignited vehicle. Both Mina and Scott mentally traveled paths of justifications and possibilities of what they had seen. Each one silently questioned what it was. Initially, in his mind, Scott was in denial that he had seen anything at all, though he knew it was hopeless to pretend that he had not. Instead, he was trying to find a scientific explanation for the funneling form, similar to a tornado.

Mina, on the other hand, continued to find the supernatural explanation and possibility of how exactly it happened. On the list of possibilities, she wondered, what conjured up this demon? Was it fire of any sort? Was it in every state, every city? Did there have to be any similar circumstances surrounding its appearance? These questions needed answered, Mina thought madly.

Mina looked at Scott.

His eyes were wide open. They seemed to be following the pavement the tires tread.

He's not getting to sleep now, she thought to herself.

She continued driving on until they passed the exit the officer mentioned.

"Would you have preferred to get a hotel?" Mina asked.

"Hell no," Scott said, looking out the window, "At least not in this strange town."

Mina knew him well enough to know what he meant. Not near that crazy monster. Eventually, after the two had enough time to think on the subject, they would discuss it.

Perhaps at lunchtime, about six or more hours from now, Mina thought to herself.

Adrenaline pumping, though somewhat filled with fear, Mina turned the radio up much louder than before. The drive continued on, each of them staring fiercely at the road ahead. At the same time, their true concentration was deeply within their brains.

CHAPTER 10:
PIECES QUITE PUZZLED

The fall sun trickled through the trees in small, though blinding rays that reached Mina's eyes. Squinting, wishing she had brought sunglasses, she struggled to see the road. Road was all she had seen for the past hours. Thankfully, they were almost at their destination town. She looked forward to the end of the drive.

Mina looked over at Scott.

He was curled up against the window in a deep sleep, just as she had been so many hours ago. Mina was surprised he could drift off, after clutching the door handle and staring at the road for so long after what they saw in the dark hours of the morning.

Ah, to switch places now, in an uninterrupted sleep, she thought to herself. Her eyes moved back to the road.

From within her stomach, a mild growling noise began. It had been nearly eight hours since they last ate. She was surprised she stayed focused enough to drive for so long. It was about time for lunch, she figured, as she continued to struggle with the blinding sun. Mina's eyes scanned passing signs in search of a restaurant. She didn't like fast food very much. After all the driving, she would rather sit somewhere than eat on the go anyway. Getting out of the car was all she looked forward to at that moment.

A sign, Rush's Restaurant, caught her eye. She turned off towards it.

"Scott," she began.

Scott didn't budge.

"Hey," she said, reaching over to shake him, "Scott wake up, time to eat."

Scott jumped violently at the shake, emitting a shriek of surprise and then flinched as the bright sun hit his newly opened eyes.

Mina jumped simultaneously.

"What the..." she began, though maintained control over the car.

Scott looked around, disoriented and adjusting to the light.

Mina pulled into the restaurant parking lot, quickly finding a place to park. She looked at Scott. His eyes were wide open, as though he had once again seen the thing that formed in those early hours. His skin was just as pale and clammy as it had been when they drove away from the scene.

"You alright?" Mina asked.

Surprisingly, she found humor in his actions.

"Yeah," Scott replied, moving his hand up to rub his forehead, "I was just in a deep sleep."

"Now that you're rested, let's get some food," she said.

The two made their way into the diner, ordered their food and then sat in silence. Neither could stand to bring up the events of that morning, particularly in a public place. It just didn't seem like a good idea to talk about monsters and demons in a town where they were strangers.

When they finished, as they climbed back into the car, Mina wondered how she ought to approach the subject. She knew Scott wouldn't bring it up.

"How far away are we?" he asked.

"Less than an hour," Mina replied.

"We should get a hotel," Scott said.

"We don't really need one," Mina reasoned.

Adrenaline pumped in her veins now and she felt ready to talk with the survivors. She was actually was excited about talking with them now.

"You might not think we need one," Scott began, "But I want to take a shower and relax a little bit afterwards."

"Fine, we'll get one afterwards," Mina replied.

"No," Scott objected, "We'll get one before we go, to leave our stuff and then we'll stay overnight."

"Ew, someone woke up on the wrong side of the car," Mina joked.

When he didn't respond, she studied his face.

"A little demanding aren't we?"

Scott looked out the window.

"I don't want to be in a car for another day in a row. It will be the best for both of us," he replied.

He curled up against the window again.

"Well, what about this morning?" Mina began.

"What about it?" Scott asked, seeming evasive.

"What did we see?" she pushed.

"Smoke," he replied and then closed his eyes.

Mina looked at him incredulously. He knew it was more than smoke.

In his own mind, Scott was really stunned about what he had seen. He hoped with enough sleep, he could drown the memory and fog the image.

Nearly 45 minutes later, Mina pulled the car into a motel. But she did not awaken Scott. Slamming the car door to enter the motel, he awakened on his own with a jolt.

The motel doors were large and made of wide glass. Fingerprints were visible on the glass, as though they had not been cleaned for the day. Pulling the door open, she walked to the clerk, a small, chubby man with dark hair. His squinted, round features gave him the appearance of a troll. He barely looked at her as he spoke; and when he did use words, they came out in a hushed monotone.

After registering her information and paying, Mina walked back to the car with the key to the room. Scott had his head against the side of the window, though obviously awake. Mina started the engine again, pulling into a parking space directly in front of their room, number 166.

After pulling the car over to the door, the two unloaded their things, carrying them through the glass doors into the lobby, and up the stairs that led to the room. Inside, Scott quickly found a change of clothes, moving to the bathroom to take a shower without saying a word.

Mina debated leaving him, but considered it too rude. Instead, she pulled out a special notebook to document everything that happened.

Mina inscribed the accounts of the car fire as they had witnessed it. Her strong memory allowed her to visualize it precisely as it happened. She scribbled pictures of the rising fog until she heard the water stop in the shower. Finishing up her new accounts, she quickly tucked the notebook back into her bag.

Scott emerged from the bathroom with dripping wet hair and lounging, casual clothes wrapped around his body. He looked at Mina with suspicion. She wore one of her strange expressions on her face.

"What?" he asked.

"I was considering leaving you, you know," she admitted.

"I would have hunted you down," he joked.

"You wouldn't know where to look," she teased back.

"Of course I would, I have double copies of everything," he said.

"You ass," she said.

"Partners right?" he finished.

"I suppose," she agreed.

But she wanted to know more about the case than he did at all times.

"Sound a little more enthusiastic than that," Scott said.

"So what did we see this morning?" Mina asked.

Scott's eyes moved to the floor. He remained silent for a few moments, and then responded, "What do you think we saw?"

"I think we saw what we were looking for," she replied, "Don't you?"

"I don't know," he said quietly, "Maybe we saw what our own minds wanted to see, since we're on this subject. We could have imagined that."

Denial shaped his words, enraging Mina.

"Oh no," Mina boldly said, standing in unison, "Don't try pulling that bullshit. That's why no one ever finds anything out. Everyone thinks it's their imagination. It's not, we both saw it."

"For how long? How long did we see it Mina, a few minutes, a few seconds? How can we be so sure? We've been reading those cases so much, perhaps it's like making shapes out of clouds. The clouds are there, but the elephant you might visualize is not. An elephant in the sky?" he said incredulously, but with good argument, "No, an elephant cannot be in the sky, just as a demon did not rise in the shape of the fog."

"A demon?" Mina asked, "Is that what you saw?"

Scott's eyes blinked nervously. He realized his error and swallowed hard. Besides the missing case she investigated, there was

107

no other way she would know what he saw, unless he told her. But even if it wasn't his imagination, he felt this research was dangerous and they should not be risking it.

"I saw the demon too," Mina paused, "But you didn't really want me to know what you saw, did you?"

Scott remained silent as Mina continued on, "You're scared Scott, you're scared just like the majority of the rest of the world. You don't want to know if this creature exists."

"I wouldn't have taken the case if I didn't want to know," Scott said, looking up from the floor, "I just don't know what we saw, if we saw it, that's all."

"Ok, well, I think it's a clue. I know I saw it. So you can just remain in denial as we solve this case," she said sarcastically.

Scott said nothing. He didn't know what to think. No wonder their friend had gone crazy. Killing himself over a mission of research. Only a teenager at that time too.

Scott shook his head and sat down on one of the beds. Reaching into his bag, he pulled out two socks, placing one on each foot, his shoes following afterwards.

Mina stared at Scott, annoyed by his state of mind. Any other person would be happy at such a clue, though frightened, but not Scott. Scott would be in denial about it until it burned one of his friends' heads off. Then, he would want to study it even more before coming to a conclusion. That was one of the reasons she wanted him to help her, but she hadn't expected it to become such an annoyance.

Looking away from him, she plopped her body loudly onto the bed. Now, her adrenaline resurgence was all she had to keep herself awake.

"Aren't you going to take a shower?" Scott asked.

She knew him. He was trying to break the ice that had frozen between them.

He waited until she calmed down to say anything. He didn't want ripped apart by a vulture before experiencing his own death.

"No," she said, with a pouty voice.

She crossed her arms over her chest.

"Peeyouu," he joked.

Mina turned her head towards the wall and window away from him to smile. Admittedly, she was a stubborn girl, who did not like issues to dissolve easily. She wanted a resolution to the argument, even if there were angry words said. But she knew that Scott hated to fight, unless, of course it was necessary.

"Someone must be smiling," Scott teased.

He knew her so well.

"Shut up," she replied, using her angry tone of voice.

Scott started singing a song of his own creation, "I once knew a girl who was stubborn, she stayed so crabby, time and again," he sang out, rhyming more verses.

"Shut up," Mina said again, laughing loudly this time.

Grabbing a towel and change of clothes, she hurried into the bathroom to get away from the silliness. Mina slammed the door shut from the inside as Scott yelled from the room.

"Ha ha," he said, "that stubborn girl smiled, ha ha," he continued, until the sound of the shower drowned his voice from Mina's ears.

As she stepped into the shower, for the first time recently, she allowed her mind to relax rather than think of their research. Slowly rubbing the soap over her body, she just enjoyed the water and was glad she had shut her mind and thoughts off briefly.

Back in the larger part of the room, Scott was watching an old movie on the television. He was so engrossed in it that when she finished, he didn't look up as she entered the room. Her fresh clothes made her feel revived as her wet hair dripped slightly.

"Time to go," she said, interrupting Scott's concentration.

"There's only a little bit left of this show. It will be over in 20 minutes," he said.

"The TV will be here when we get back. Let's go. You can see this some other time," Mina persisted.

Since she did not watch much television, she could not fully understand how so many people became hooked.

"It's just 20 minutes," he pleaded.

"Well just stay here then, and I'll go," she said, grabbing her light jacket from a nearby chair.

Scott shut off the television, but wore a deep frown on his face.

Silently, they found their way to the car. Mina looked over the directions to the house. Scott stepped into the driver's side. Still, they did not talk to each other as he started up the car. Mina handed him the directions. After looking them over, he handed the paper back to her.

When they arrived at the listed house address, Mina observed that the house was poorly kept; unlike the last one she visited. Stepping out of the car, Scott followed Mina to a gray, weathered and cracked wooden gate. She carefully pushed it forward as she followed large, flat, broken stones up the path to the home. The dull gray color of the small house was faded and cracked as well.

"Looks like Ryan's," Mina joked.

Scott didn't laugh. Instead, he continued to silently walk behind her. This town and everything around it already freaked him out.

Approaching the porch, Mina slowly moved up the cracked cement steps. A doorbell with the sign 'broken' taped over it lingered next to the door. Opening the screen door, she knocked lightly.

Listening intently, Mina heard a television set. It sounded like an old western movie wrought with constant gunshots.

Mina knocked again, only harder this time. The television set volume lowered at her second knock. Mina heard a shuffling noise within. Her heart pounded quickly.

Mina reluctantly knocked one last time.

Scott began to speak when the door opened a small crack. A middle-aged woman's voice rang out.

"Can I help you?"

Her tone of voice was screechy and witch-like.

"Um, yes," Mina began, "We're here to see Robert Caset."

"Well are you old friends of his?" the woman asked.

"Well, no, we just wanted to talk to him," Mina said.

"Are you from his school?" she asked.

"Um," Mina began, and then thought about it, "Yes, we are from his school. It's about a reunion."

From behind her, she felt a slight pinch on the back of her arm. She jumped and then gritted her teeth.

"Sounds fun," the woman responded.

She opened the door widely.

"He prefers Bobby over Robert though, don't call him Robert," the mother warned, her cold facial expression unchanging.

The small woman ruffled her disheveled faded red hair. Her dark, brown eyes gave off a worried, motherly look.

"He's upstairs," she spoke again, "Where he always is."

She frowned, stepping back from the door and allowing them to enter.

Mina and Scott thanked her and then walked slowly up the stairs. Their hearts thumped with the uncertainty of what awaited at the top of those stairs. The woman hadn't told them which room either, but it became evident as they approached the second level. One room had a plain brown door with chipped paint- the other was decorated with posters of bands and TV stars clipped from magazines.

Mina knocked gently on the door. Inside the room, music blasted along with the sound of a television. Mina wondered how he could hear them both or which one he paid more attention to.

There was no response to the first knock. Mina knocked harder the second time, trying to reach over the muffled noise from within.

Finally, the door opened with one quick pull inwards, just enough to startle them with the suddenness.

A frazzled man with shoulder length, straight black hair stood there. His face was smooth despite some hair growth in the form of a small beard, which wrapped around his chin. His dark greenish brown eyes looked curiously at the two figures, without recognition. Mina was immediately attracted to his aura of loneliness and eyes of solitude.

The dark clothed man stood there ominously and without speech. Mina realized she was staring. Her face grew red and she forced herself to speak.

"Hello," Mina said.

Her lashes fluttered and she felt as if the breath had been knocked out of her.

"Hi," he said.

He had a confused look upon his face, as though he was searching his mental banks for some sort of recognition, where there was none.

"Who are you?" he continued.

"I'm Mina and this is Scott. Your mother let us in. We wanted to talk to you," she continued.

"About what?" he asked, a strange look gracing his face, "Am I supposed to know you from somewhere?"

"No," Scott said.

Mina cut in.

"No, but I did tell your mother we went to school together," she admitted.

For some reason, she felt like she could tell him her lie without major repercussions.

"Why did you...?" he started.

Scott interrupted him.

"We wanted to talk about what happened to your friends a few years ago in their car when you were going on vacation," Scott said.

The man uneasily ran his hand through his hair.

"Oh," he said.

He hesitated for a moment.

"Why that?" he asked, looking at Mina.

"We want to find it," she replied boldly.

"Are you with some sort of government agency or something?" he asked.

"Nope," Scott replied, "It's just her crazy idea of research."

Mina elbowed Scott just enough to quiet him.

The man ran his hands through his hair again and then shook his head.

"Come in."

The boy stepped backward into his room before continuing, "Though I don't know what to tell you. You'd think I was crazy. Although you are trying to find it so I guess that makes you crazy," he finished.

Inside the room, Mina immediately noticed that it was cluttered with posters, a desk, papers, a computer, television, vcr, dvd, a large stereo system and more less noticeable items. The walls were framed with posters of long haired men in heavy metal music bands along with a few posters of mostly nude women. A bookshelf was against the wall, holding endless novels.

Bobby cleared a few magazines and papers from his bed to give them a place to sit. After Mina and Scott sat, he cleared off a wooden chair and pulled it close to the bed. Sitting in the chair, he faced the two strangers.

"What makes you want to do this?" he asked, observing Mina's face.

His eyes were so intense on her. She looked at Scott, meeting his gaze before turning back to Bobby. But Mina was unsure how to respond. She did not want to offend him or make light of the subject in any way, since he lost friends. This man seemed nearly as intelligent and curious as they were, or at least observant and inquisitive.

"Well," Mina began, "A few friends of mine and I enjoy finding subjects of research to learn about to strengthen our minds."

Bobby nodded as if he understood.

"And one day, we came across missing cases. We've been doing this since we were much younger, but this time, something strange came up on one of our searches. It was a case, a missing case where a fire was involved. Two young people were burned to death in an accidental…" she paused, noticing that Bobby flinched as she said 'burned to death.'

Mina continued.

"Fire," she picked up where she left off, "There was another person there though. This person became a missing person. They combed the woods, searched the town, miles away, everything they could but found nothing. The only other strange clue in the case was a pile of ashes nearby the scene, a few feet high, unexplainable. Normally, people would overlook that aspect," she paused, "but I have a strong belief in the supernatural and decided to pursue it further. I found another case after that and I brought Scott into it and he found even more. He's a good friend of mine."

She nodded towards Scott but her eyes remained on Bobby. Everything about him seduced her as she sat there.

Bobby stared intently with interest beyond her words.

"So you've been hunting down the survivors?" he asked.

"Exactly," Mina replied, maintaining eye contact.

"Well, what if you were wrong and I had nothing to tell you?" he teased.

She blinked.

"Then at least we had a vacation from our normal lives," she said.

Bobby smiled, amused by her optimism. Leaning back in his chair, he studied both of them, as if memorizing their physical characteristics.

Scott felt odd, like a spectator at the beginning of a porn flick. Yuck. He knew that if he weren't there, their bodies would be tangled all over each other. He laughed to himself. They were both loners, perfect for each other.

"And you?" Bobby asked Scott, "Where is your interest?"

There was an obvious double meaning to his words. Scott was surprised someone had even talked to him.

"Ah, I guess I'm curious, and at the same time want to protect my friend from any danger. We all know the effects of obsession in research."

Mina looked down from the man, realizing the hidden mention of their former friend.

Bobby noticed the strangeness that had settled with his answered question, but chose to ignore it rather than pursue an explanation.

"That's very honorable," Bobby responded.

Mina looked back up.

"Let's get started," she interrupted.

The man looked at her, then looked at the wall, as if in deep thought.

"Where should I begin?" he asked.

"You could start from the beginning of that day to what you saw," Mina answered.

"The beginning of that day, lets see," he started, "I woke up late, had to rush to work. I was an hour late, still didn't have my stuff packed for the trip."

He winced, seeming to press to remember the early beginnings.

"Where were you going?" Mina interrupted.

"To our favorite camping spot. We go…" he stopped, "We went there every summer. Just the four of us. It used to be two, then it was three, we acquired a fourth that year. Lucky four," he mumbled, and then began again, "I was the only one that had to work that afternoon, only a few hours. Then I came home, finished packing and met them at Jared's house. Jared's one of the ones who died," he paused just as Greta had, seemingly in order to say, may he rest in peace, but without the words.

"We took two separate cars, my girlfriend at the time, the fourth addition, was going to leave the camp a day early to go back to work. We drove behind them most of the time. No offense or anything, but sometimes women drive way slower than men."

He stopped, looking for a reaction from Mina.

"Some," she agreed, with persuasion she was different.

He studied her for a moment, and then began again, "So we followed them. Usually, the three of us rode together, drank beer, smoked cigarettes on the way, but this time, I was a good boy for Erica. I went without the beer. There would be plenty of time to do that later anyway. I just smoked cigarettes."

Mina hadn't smelled smoke in his room at all.

"Do you smoke now?" she asked.

"No," he replied.

His eyes widened with a small glint of fear that attracted Mina to him even more. He began his story again.

"We drove about two hours on Interstate 40, the former Route 66. My girlfriend and I dodged the endless cigarette butts Jared and Frankie threw from the window. At that time, the season was so dry, there was actually a warning not to throw them out of windows or it could start fires. They didn't care. At the time, Erica was very girly, very picky. She didn't want any of the cigarettes flying into the car and starting a fire or anything like that. Most of the time, we had the windows up just to assuage her fears. Even outside, the heat made it possible to start a fire. But my friends, they didn't care, they just enjoyed their beers and smokes. I watched them weaving around in front of us, with a longing to be in that car with them like usual. But at the same time, I was glad I wasn't being so rude to my girlfriend or anyone else on the road."

He stopped and sighed before beginning again.

"Frankie called me from his cell phone. He was on the passenger side. Said he had to pee and we were going off the next rest stop. I could see them passing the lighter and whatever else back and forth in the car in front of us. It was getting dark out. Before we hit the rest stop, we started to pass through a fog. Sometimes the fog is only in a certain spot. Did you ever notice that?" he looked at Mina, "You could be driving and its clear, then suddenly, you pass through a short amount of fog."

Mina nodded.

"I know what you mean," she assured him.

"I mean, how does that really happen?" he asked.

He stopped and sat there quietly, seeming to be lost in thought.

"I don't even know," she said.

Really, she hoped he would get back to his story.

"But anyway," he began again, "Oh yes, we were passing the fog. The guys didn't slow down much, though visibility was bad. We figured we'd pass the patch of fog I guess. Erica, she was scared of rear-ending the two, so she slowed down, of course. Realizing she had to keep up though, she sped up again. The fog just seemed to get thicker though, rising from the ground almost. Frankie called me back on the cell phone. At the same time, we realized the drunken bastards missed the rest stop in the fog. He said he wanted to pull off the side of the road; he had to pee so badly. I could hear Jared in the background, 'pass me a cigarette dude,' he said. Just then, one last cigarette flew out their window; I'm guessing it was Frankie's. Then... it came," he stopped suddenly.

His eyes widened as if he had seen it again.

Mina watched him like he was a movie in a theater, waiting for him to end the suspense. Bobby put his hands in the air, moving them down to his lap in a swooping motion like a bird swiftly attacking its prey.

"It came out of nowhere. It was a large fireball, it seemed. Like a meteor had hit their car without knowing it would fall in the first place," he paused again, shaking his head.

His hands began to tremble.

Mina could see how the story affected him. But even now she wanted to know more.

"What was it? What exactly did it look like?" she asked gently.

For her, it was a struggle to speak so softly.

Bobby swallowed hard.

"The fire, the fire surrounded it, in the middle was a grayish brown image of...of...of...of," he stuttered, "Well it was a monster, a hu...human demon."

He quickly looked away, a slight flush sweeping across his cheeks. He didn't look up when he continued.

"But I could have imagined that. I've always been deeply engrossed in horror flicks," he said.

He blinked suddenly.

"Did your girlfriend see it too?" Mina asked.

"Yeah, I guess, but I don't really know. I don't have her brain or eyes," he replied.

"Then why don't you believe you saw it, if she claimed the exact image?" she asked.

"Because it was too surreal, too large, too frightening to be true, to be real," he said.

He shivered as if a cold air passed into the room, which did not affect Mina or Scott.

Mina stared at him. She couldn't understand how he could question what he saw, just as Scott had. That he couldn't believe he had seen it, even when another person had.

"What happened next?" Mina asked.

She clenched her teeth to hide her aggravation.

"It screamed, or the wind did, I don't know what it was. Then the entire car swerved in front, then...then...part of it vanished, as if it rode into hell. Maybe another universe. Only, it didn't ride upwards, it just fell to the ground. Somehow," he said.

His eyes widened incredulously, remembering that night. He paused as Scott and Mina watched him more intensely now.

"Ughh," he moaned, "Then the old girlfriend hit a guard rail on the side of the road, bumped her head. I don't know I might have been knocked out too. All I remember is getting out of the car and walking to...where the rest of the other car was. The car was still intact from the backseat on. Ashes composed the front end. I walked all around the tremendous pile of ash, which steadily, slowly blew away with the wind. I was kind of hoping my friends were hidden in the ashes. I dug for them."

He paused with another sigh. His eyes grew watery but no tear fell.

"What did you tell the cops?" Mina asked.

"Well," he laughed, despite the circumstances, "We told them that the car turned to ash, must have been a meteor or something. Of course they didn't believe us, blamed it on the bump to the head. Still, there were missing persons and there was some evidence of fire, though nothing to merit a claim of a fireball," he said.

He looked directly at Mina.

Mina nodded. Bobby shook his head.

"You know, seeing something like that happen to your friends can cause many problems in your life. Death happens, but not in that way. It was so unexpected, nearly drove me nuts trying to figure it out," he said.

He looked towards his books with a distant aura in his eyes. Mina broke into his thoughts.

"We want to find out what happened, find out what it was," Mina whispered.

Her eyes were in a daydream but they came back and focused on him.

"How did it affect your life, if you don't mind me asking," she asked.

"If you would have known me before," he chuckled, then paused as if reliving a high school football game, "I was very outgoing. You'd never find me at home. My girlfriend and I broke up after that. She didn't want me anymore. Wanted to forget what happened, I suppose. I never smoked another cigarette or lit another fire. I was nearly a pyromaniac before that incident. Once, I loved flames. I barely leave the house now," he said.

But he spoke without self-pity, just as an explanation of the man he'd become.

"Do you want to do those things again?" she asked.

She felt comfortable enough to grow more personal with him.

"I don't know," he paused, "I don't know where I would go. They were my best friends for about ten years. You can't just replace them so easily. I suppose I'm content as a loner now," he said.

He was confident but there was still a hidden sadness in his voice.

"What about Erica? Do you still talk to her at all?" Scott inquired.

"No, not at all. I guess she doesn't want to be reminded of that night. She later convinced herself it didn't happen," he said.

A look of sadness washed over him.

"Do you want to go with us to talk to her?" Scott offered.

He actually felt sorry for the man, especially if his story was true.

"I...don't know if I should," Bobby responded, "I don't think she would be too happy to see me now. You know, the reminder part."

Mina shook her head.

"I think you should accompany us anyway. This demon, or whatever it is, it is still out there, taking lives from anywhere. We need to find where it originated and hopefully, a way to stop it," Mina said.

Bobby sat there studying her and then leaned back in his chair again. He remained silent as he looked up at the ceiling. He was quiet for a long moment.

"I would love to stop this thing. Truthfully, I had just let go of it, trying to forget it happened. Now, I suppose I'm going to be caught once again in this miserable curiosity," he finished.

Mina and Scott were left silent with his words. They hadn't realized that they might send this man backwards. They looked at each other with worry.

Bobby said nothing more.

CHAPTER 11:
CLOSER TO THE MIDDLE

Mina and Scott made their way down the stairs and out the door before they spoke to one another. Scott began first, whispering so his voice could not be overheard.

"Do you believe it?" he asked.

"Of course, this story is very similar to the one Greta told me. The only difference is the manner it occurred. She was hiding behind a truck, not actually in a vehicle," Mina paused.

When they reached the car, Mina immediately grabbed her special notebook. Scott looked at her from the driver's side, but said nothing. At least one of them was keeping notes, he thought. Scott put the key in the ignition. Before he could start the car, Mina looked up at him.

"Wait," she said, "Let me finish this before we drive," she continued, going back to writing in her journal.

Scott dropped his hand to his lap.

He studied the neighborhood while Mina quickly scribbled away in her book. Some of the houses nearby were just as poorly kept as the one they had just been in. Those houses seemed to be on the right hand side of the street as well. On the left side, the houses were in much better shape, though not exactly richly designed.

Mina interrupted his observations.

"I want to do this before we talk to the girl, just so nothing becomes blurred or intermingled," she said.

She waved her hand in a circular gesture as she spoke, "Besides," she continued, "he's coming with us."

Scott leaned forward and looked at her.

"What was the last part?" Scott asked, baffled by her.

Mina looked up, "Come on," she began, "Couldn't you see it in his eyes? He wants to go. He wants to get out of that house and find out what it is that made him suffer so long."

She studied him.

"You didn't see that?" she asked.

"I'm sorry," Scott said sarcastically, "But I'm a guy and I try not to stare deeply into another guy's eyes. Though you definitely were."

His voice trailed off teasingly. Mina's eyes grew wide.

"What?" she asked.

Scott smirked.

"You know what. And I know you. You were very attracted to him. I almost wasn't in the room," he said.

Mina laughed, "You're nuts. You're not supposed to notice that stuff," she said.

Suddenly she was embarrassed that it was so obvious. Scott took the opportunity to tease her further.

"Yeah I was pretty sickened by the sexual tension between you two. I almost thought to get up and excuse myself," he teased more, enhancing her embarrassment.

She laughed even harder, knowing it was true. Suddenly there was a tap on the window. Mina jumped quickly but turned her head. She was just inches from Bobby's face. A pane of glass was all that separated them. Her heart thudded with wild anticipation.

Quickly rolling her window down, her face reddened more. She hoped he hadn't heard Scott teasing her.

"Hey," she said softly.

"Hey," he replied his face reddening too, "I guess if you guys are going to sit and tempt me, I might as well come along. I just hope Erica isn't pissed off that I'm coming too."

Mina shrugged.

"You probably won't have to see her after today," she said.

Suddenly she realized this might bring them together again.

Oops, she thought.

Bobby got in the backseat. Scott started up the car. Mina had gotten her main points etched in her notebook, but not all that she intended to record. She had enough of a start and was sure she would remember the rest. But she quickly put it away, not knowing how Bobby would react to part of his life being documented.

"Turn this way," he said from the backseat, "It's a shortcut."

Scott followed his instruction, knowing that Bobby had probably been there many times before.

Within a few minutes and turns, they pulled into a gravel driveway that led to a small, though beautiful white house with an extremely large yard. When they reached the front of the house and the end of the drive, Scott parked.

"I think I'll just wait in the car until she comes to the door," Bobby said, "Her parents didn't like me very much. They'll slam the door if they see me."

"Okay," Mina agreed.

Scott and her stepped out of the car.

On the front porch, Mina immediately noticed the fall decorations framing the windows.

Scott rang the doorbell as Mina looked around.

The door opened quickly and a tall, thin older man answered it. He looked like an old farmer who opted for a button down shirt rather than overalls. Behind him stood a woman near his age with curious gray eyes.

"Can I help you?" the man asked.

"Yes, I'm looking for Erica Waters," Scott said as politely as he could.

The man eyed him.

"Whom may I ask are you?" he asked.

"A friend, an old friend from school," he stuttered.

Mina almost chuckled at his bad lie but kept her face composed. She thought of pinching him back but figured he had it bad enough.

The parents peered past them at the car parked in the driveway. Concerned, Scott and Mina turned to look at the car as well. It appeared empty. Bobby must have ducked down when he saw the parents.

"She doesn't live here anymore," the father answered.

The man still studied Scott with great suspicion.

"What's this all about?" he continued.

"Um, well, we wanted to plan our, our reunion," Scott stuttered.

Mina was terribly amused by Scott's discomfort and inability to properly lie. The father grunted.

"We never did that when I was a boy, went door to door. We sent out letters," he said.

Mina stepped forward and smiled brightly at the man.

"We felt it would be more personal if we visited our fellow classmates individually. Everyone doesn't always decide to come to the reunion and we want to assure them that they are definitely welcome," she said, sounding sincere about it, "Other classes haven't had a very good turn-out. We want ours to be great."

Scott was suddenly envious of how easily she could tell a story.

"Kids," the man finally grumbled, "Well, Nancy," he said to his wife, "Grab some paper and a pen so we can give her the address."

The woman ran back into the house. The stern man questioned them more.

"Did you know our little Erica very well?" he asked.

Mina smiled in an endearing way.

"Sort of, everyone pretty much knew one another, we just didn't really hang out outside of school," Mina answered coolly, before Scott had a chance to try.

"Oh."

The man seemed to lighten up towards Mina.

Nancy brought out a piece of paper with her daughter's address scribbled on it.

"Here you go," she said with tight, rich facial expressions, "I'm happy to meet you, and who are you again? My husband seems to forget manners," she said, moving her small frame in front of him.

"I'm Melissa and this is Shawn," Mina replied before Scott could.

"I'm Nancy and this is Bob," Nancy gracefully replied as she shook Mina's hand, "I hope she'll join you at the reunion. She really needs to make new friends."

Mina smiled wide.

"We hope she'll come too," Mina said as she turned to walk away, "Thank you very much for your time and enjoy your evening."

They started down the porch, catching one last glimpse of her mother's smiling face, mixed with the stern scorn of the father. Scott and Mina hurriedly walked back to the car.

They climbed in and Scott didn't hesitate to start the engine. As he was backing out, Mina noticed the figure of the old man in the window, staring down on them.

"Stay down," she warned Bobby.

Scott backed fully out of the driveway and headed away. Mina reached back and handed the piece of paper to Bobby.

"She doesn't live at home anymore. Where is this place?" she asked.

"Not far from here. About ten, fifteen minutes. Just keep straight," he said, "Did they say if she lived with anyone?"

"No," Mina replied bluntly.

Shortly after, they pulled in front of a small apartment building in relatively good condition. On the short trip there, Bobby explained how her father hadn't liked him and the strict, snobby nature of her family, particularly the mother.

Finding the exact apartment, the three of them stood outside the main door to her unit, knocking. The first few knocks were ignored.

On the third knock, a full figured woman answered the door. The woman had blond hair, close to her mother's color, but with strawberry red streaming through it. She wore large black sweatpants and a white t-shirt with an apron tied around her waist. Her apron was covered in what appeared to be flour and cake batter. Similarly, some of the flour was smeared in splotches over her face, with powdery fragments lingering in her hair. Her eyes were wide with wonder at the strangers at her door.

"May I help you?" she asked, clearing her throat.

Mina was confused; this girl was not what she had pictured. She was too surprised to speak, allowing Scott to take charge again. But before Scott could say anything, Bobby gently moved in between the two.

"Holy shit," the woman said at first glance, "What, what are you doing here?"

She started to back up.

Bobby hesitated for a moment with his eyes open wide. Apparently, he too was surprised by her appearance, but didn't let it stop his words.

"We have to talk," he said.

"Ah... about what?" she asked.

A look of lost love cascaded through her eyes. But there was something else there, something like embarrassment.

"About what happened that night, about what we saw," he said.

She shook her head back and forth.

"I don't know, my doctor said..." she began.

"Forget your doctor. Look what we've become," he said.

She blinked harshly and then eyed up Scott and Mina. She hesitated for a moment.

"Come in," she said.

The three of them walked into her home, entering through an immaculately clean living room. The sweet scent of homemade cookies and cakes lingered throughout the apartment, growing stronger and ever so inviting, the farther into her realm they walked.

The four were silent. Erica tried her best to be hospitable; though it was obvious she didn't have company very often. Allowing them to take their seats in the living room, she brought out some of the cookies she just baked.

Scott looked around the room.

The carpeting and walls were a light gray color. A couch and loveseat were lined up perfectly to the shape of an L. Where he sat on the couch, directly in front of him was a television set, while the loveseat was to his right. Mina and Bobby sat on the couch with him, while Erica offered out cookies.

Scott felt antsy and stood from the couch. At the farthest left corner of the room he noticed a few pictures in frames on a table. Moving slowly towards them, he bent over to catch a better glimpse. Contained within the frame was the older couple they had just seen, along with a girl. She was a very thin but attractive girl, with long blonde hair and strawberry streaks running through it.

"Wow," Scott said, before realizing he had.

"What?" Erica asked from behind him.

Scott's face flushed.

"Just admiring your pictures," he said, trying to brush it off.

Embarrassed, he quickly moved back to the couch.

The girl did not say anything, though she had a growingly saddened look upon her face. She took her place on the loveseat, which her body all but devoured.

"Where should we start?" Mina asked.

"Where…where do you want to start?" Erica asked nervously.

She wrung her hands together, showing her uneasiness.

Scott decided he could be gentler on her, so he leaned forward and spoke up before Mina could.

"We just want to know what happened that night. What you saw," Scott began.

Erica took a deep breath. She wiped some of the cake batter from her face before she began. They sat there as she uneasily relayed nearly the exact same story as Bobby had. The only differences were her female perspectives and the lack of attachment she had to the men in the car in front. But right in the middle of her story, she began to cry. During her description of the fireball, she never mentioned that it appeared to be a demon.

When she was finished, she ran to the bathroom for tissues to blow her nose and wipe her eyes. When she returned, Mina felt it was her time to question.

"What did the fireball look like?" she asked.

Bobby sat there silently, waiting for her response.

Her now dry, though puffy eyes fluttered and blinked with nervousness.

"What do you mean? It looked like fire. It was a mixture of yellow…and red and…"

Her voice trailed off, as if she seemed to remember something she didn't want to.

"What was in the middle of it?" Bobby asked.

"I don't know, I blacked out after I hit my head," she said.

Bobby scoffed.

"We've fought about this Erica. Just tell them what it was," he pushed.

"Oh, I imagined it," she said.

"Erica," Bobby scolded, "I thought I imagined it too but I know I didn't."

"It looked like, but I could have imagined it," she stopped and then whispered, "Like a demon."

The words were very hard for her to say. Mina leaned forward and lowered her voice.

"Can you give us more details of the demon?" she asked, much gentler than usual.

Erica's eyes drifted into another time.

"It looked gray maybe brown with rippled skin, like a ghoul or something straight out of a horror movie. Only it was really mean, it opened its mouth and let out this terrible sound. Right after, these flames shot out. Just like a dragon. Such a small amount of flames and the whole front of the car was gone in seconds. Gone. We almost rode through it, but I swerved at the last minute. Or it could have done that to us too. I hit something. And then I must have blacked out. When I came to, the fog was dying down and ashes were all over the ground. The cops, the ambulance were there- they didn't believe our babble. They thought we were on drugs. Hell my own parents didn't believe me. But he believed it, he saw it too," she said, nodding towards Bobby.

Erica's voice babbled on in a whiny tone, as if she were finally relieved to get out the truth, "And then..." her voice trailed off.

She seemed like she didn't want to finish the last part.

"Then what?" Scott asked.

He noticed that her eyes were staring directly at Bobby. Bobby nervously looked away.

"Is this why you quit seeing each other?" Scott pried.

Silence fell over the room.

Finally, Erica began again, "My parents thought that I had gone crazy since I bumped my head. They never liked Bobby. They blamed him, saying he slipped me drugs. They made me tell him I didn't want to see him anymore because he was a crazy drug head. And we didn't really see a demon take his friends away. And that was the end, after that I did my best to get over it, but I never did," she admitted.

Bobby sat there, lingering in his own bubble of silence. He didn't know what to say. All that time, he assumed that it was at least some of her decision not to see him. Then, he couldn't understand how he had lost two friends and his love all in the same week. Suddenly Bobby looked up.

"You're depressed, aren't you?" he asked.

"Why, because I gained so much weight? Of course I'm depressed. I don't even know how to live anymore," she admitted.

The tears began to fall swiftly from her cheeks again. Bobby leaned forward.

"That thing messed up my life too. But these two are here to find out what happened that night," Bobby began, leaning even further forward in his seat, "They're going to figure out why that happened and why it took my friends. Then we should be settled enough to take control of our lives."

Erica looked up through her tears.

"What happened to you after, after...?" she asked.

Bobby sat back in the couch.

"I barely leave my house now," he said, "I'm afraid of everything outside. I can't be away from home for very long."

Mina and Scott sat in silence. Suddenly, Mina had a thought. It seemed like a long shot, but she figured it was worth a try. She had to find a common denominator between these events. This demon couldn't just be random. Something had to fuel it.

Mina leaned forward again, looking between Bobby and Erica.

"Can you think of anything major that was going on at the time you saw this demon, besides the warning against throwing cigarettes?" she asked.

"Do you mean in the world or community?" Bobby asked.

"Either, as close as possible to where you were when it attacked," she asked.

Each of them maintained the silence, as if forcing themselves to remember that time.

Bobby spoke first.

"It was summer time, very hot of course. We had that dry spell, not much rain. We had to monitor water use, couldn't wash our cars, that stuff. The winds were very, very dry," he remembered.

Erica's eyes lit up.

"Yeah, that's right. I remember that summer. Do you remember there was a fire that spun out of control, just a few hours away? A family went camping in the woods. They didn't put out their campfire and it started up a small forest fire," she said.

"Small forest fire?" Mina asked, unconvinced, "How small was this? Was anyone injured, property destroyed?"

"One man was killed," Erica remembered, "My parents didn't agree with me going camping in the first place, so they told me about the fire. They said one man was killed, the father who started the campfire. Somehow, the rest of the family got away. Some of the trees caught fire with the dry heat. The fire only lasted two days, compared to some of the others. Sometimes it takes weeks to clear up a big forest fire."

The gears of Mina's mind were turning. But she kept her thoughts to herself. She stood up from the couch, almost as if it were an automatic response. All eyes drifted to her. She looked at Erica and nodded her head.

"Thank you for your time," she said.

Scott followed her lead. He stood up, Bobby following suit. Left in suspense, Erica's eyes latched onto Mina.

"Do you think the weather had something to do with it?" she asked.

Mina shrugged.

"It could have been anything, but I don't know just yet. We'll figure it out," she said.

Mina turned away from the girl, walking out the door. Scott lingered for another moment in the apartment. He shook his head. Sometimes Mina came off as rude even when she didn't intend to be.

"Thanks again for your time," Scott said.

Erica looked at him with pleading eyes.

"How will I know if you find anything out?" she asked.

There was a definite need to know in her voice.

"We can take your number and give you a call," Scott said.

"Just let me get a pen," she said, waddling into the kitchen.

She returned with a phone number on a napkin.

"Please don't forget to call," she pleaded.

"I won't," Scott agreed, "One more question," Scott asked, "Where did the forest fire occur that you were talking about?"

"In Goldfield, Nevada," she responded, "I'll never forget the paranoid things my parents instilled in me."

Her eyes grew wide for a moment and she turned to Bobby.

"You know," she said, "None of this ever would have happened in our lives if it weren't for that, those things…they made me vulnerable," she said, her voice trailing off.

"I know what you mean," he said.

He looked away, staring off into that night all over again.

"We're both young yet, we can start over elsewhere," he said.

He turned quickly, following towards the door behind Scott. As he reached the door, she said one last thing.

"You know, you can stop by any time you want," she said, "as friends."

"I would, I really would. But I can't afford for your parents to get in the way," he said then finished with a whisper, "Again."

He continued out the door.

As he shut it, Erica realized that she couldn't blame him for feeling that way after all he went through then. She shouldn't have given him up so easily.

"Ah," she sighed.

Her thoughts wandered. She couldn't hide anymore.

Erica looked at the tray of cookies. Gently picking up the tray, she walked into the kitchen. She turned the oven off, in the middle of baking a cake. With the other hand, she went directly to the garbage can, dumping all of the cookies away. Next, she took the half-baked cake out of the oven, dumping it into the trash as well. Going through her cupboards, she put every cake and cookie mix she had in a brown box for donation.

"This isn't me," she said, "but I'll find her," she announced with new determination.

CHAPTER 12:
AS IT FALLS

Parked outside Bobby's house, Mina's mind traveled with possibilities. She almost forgot how attracted she was to him. The three of them sat in the car for a few more minutes before he spoke.

"I would like to know as well, what you come up with if you don't mind," he said.

Mina turned around, looking into his eyes. They were the darkest, most beautiful shade of hazel brown green she had ever seen. His intelligence, his vulnerability and the seemingly gentle aspects of his personality tempered his former bad guy image.

"Sure," she said.

She handed him a piece of paper, along with her pen. He scribbled his name, phone number and address on the paper.

"Where are you going from here?" he asked.

"We're staying in a hotel tonight. Long drive back home tomorrow," she said.

"How far away?" he asked.

Bobby saw admirable strength, intelligence and beauty in her.

Mina's voice softened, "Very far away, a whole state. Arizona," she said.

She regretted having met him so far away.

"Oh," he said.

He felt partly crushed by the thought of never seeing her again.

"Here's my number, if you get a chance," he said, handing it specifically to her.

"I'll try," she said.

She feigned coldness, trying to keep a professional distance.

"Thanks," he said.

He got out of the car. Bobby rushed quickly up the stairs to his house, as if it were a sin to be away for so long. Mina watched him ascend.

"Let's go," she said.

Scott put the car in drive.

***

Back at the hotel, Mina immediately jumped onto her bed, pulling out her notebook again. Scribbling for nearly an hour, she was uninterrupted by Scott as he watched television. She knew they needed to talk about the witnesses, but wanted to get her thoughts in order first. Besides, they had the whole car ride home to discuss their theories.

When Mina finally finished, she was exhausted. Her mind was swimming. Fighting fatigue and exhilaration from the case, she finally gave in and decided that she needed to take a nap. Looking at the clock, it was already three in the afternoon. They had estimated leaving at four o'clock in the morning, after they were well rested. Scott, feeling just as exhausted, shut off the television to get some sleep as well.

After nearly five hours of sleep, Mina's body awakened her. As she opened her eyes, the darkness of the room let her know she had slept through the remaining daylight hours. Rolling over, she looked at the clock. It was 7:47 PM. Scott was still in bed, though seemed to be tossing and turning.

Mina stood. Still slightly groggy, she decided to take a quick walk. Walking always invigorated and relaxed her mind.

Scott, awakening at her movement, asked what she was doing. Mina assured him she was just going for a walk. He was concerned she would be kidnapped, but she joked that she was just too mean for that. Finally, she left as he drifted off again.

Mina walked through the outer glass doors, into the coming night. The air was warm, with the smallest hint of mist on it. It was dry compared to the way the weather had been lately in their town. As she walked along the edges of the hotel, she muted out the voices she easily heard from within the rooms. Some were filled with people drinking and partying, others with arguers. Nonetheless, she did not want to hear any of it.

She rounded the building to the front where the worker sat at the desk, smoking a cigarette and reading over the day's newspapers. As she began walking past the glass windows to the entrance, she

132

heard her name. At first she wasn't sure and thought she'd imagined the sound until it repeated again.

"Mina!"

It wasn't Scott's voice and she didn't know anyone else from the area.

Turning around quickly, Bobby stood there; at the door of a car she had seen near his home. She remembered it, because most of it was black, with a spray-painted white hood.

"What are you doing here?" Mina asked.

"I just," he paused, "wanted to talk."

Shyness crept over his face.

"How did you know where we were?" she asked.

"There aren't many hotels around here," he laughed.

"I didn't see any headlights. How long ago did you get here?" she asked.

"Just a couple of minutes. I sat in the car, wondering if it was stupid of me to be here," he said.

Her eyelashes fluttered but her words came out cold.

"Huh," she said, "Do you have more news to tell?"

"No, none at all," he said.

His eyes lowered. Her voice changed again, warmly inviting this time.

"Well then, want to go for a walk?" she asked.

He quickly looked up, his eyes shining bright.

"Sure," he said.

They continued Mina's walk, rounding the hotel again. Initially, neither of them said anything. The sexual attraction was still there at a high and dangerous degree. But as intelligent beings, they could tell there was more to them than just the desire for physical stimulation.

"How did it feel? Seeing her today?" Mina asked.

Mina's curiosity of human emotions was never ending.

"Like I never expected," he said.

She looked at him but could read nothing.

"Specify," she demanded.

He didn't look at her before he began.

"Well, for a while I dreamt of this meeting, that there would still be something there. All this time I wanted to see her. But to my surprise, nowhere in her eyes tonight could I see what I wanted. I don't know if I changed or what, but it just wasn't there. Maybe it never was, maybe I just thought it would be harder than that to see her again. She was a coward. Or else it might have been more," he said.

"Hmmph," Mina said, "But at one point you thought it was love?"

He nodded but then shook his head.

"I don't know. We never said the words but I guess later, when you have no one else in your life, you have these thoughts that it was perfect before, like fooling yourself. An illusion," he finished.

"Interesting," she said.

He looked over at her.

"You," he began, fluttering his words, "Ever been in love?"

She pursed her lips together and did not say a word. The initial silence seemed penetrating of his mental interior.

"Nope," she said.

He looked her over with surprise.

"Never?" he asked.

"Nope," she repeated.

The silence grasped them again. The two continued walking. Tension seemed to overlap their time together. Close to the hotel were shallow woods. Beyond the woods were partially visible stores, all of which were closed, though streetlights illuminated their signs.

Suddenly, Mina grabbed Bobby's arm, shocking him into a jump. Her eyes grew wide with excitement.

"Let's go on an adventure!" she shrieked.

Bobby's eyes searched her face. Dread and fear began to brew inside of him.

"Where?" Bobby asked, confused.

She looked forward and then back at him, making direct eye contact.

"Into the woods," she said.

She watched a glimmer of fear take place in his eyes. He shook his head.

"I...I don't know," he said, blinking uncomfortably.

He had sworn off the woods ever since it happened.

"Come on," she said, "Let's find out what's down there."

"I can't..." he started.

But Mina wouldn't wait for excuses. She started running.

Her tall, lean figure moved quickly towards the edge of the woods. Hesitantly, Bobby ran after her. Mina jumped into the bushes and trees that rimmed the outside, the beginning of the shallow woods. Seconds later, she disappeared from sight.

"Mina?" he yelled.

She stuck her head out from the brush, only partially visible via a street lamp. She waved her hand at him.

"Come on, they're shallow woods," she said.

"I don't," he started.

"I'll protect you," she teased.

Bobby moved slowly to the woods' edge.

Darkness fell within the spot of woods in which he walked. Mina grabbed Bobby's hand as he approached, dragging him deeper into the blackness. Bobby looked around, heart pounding, at the appearance of the dead, old and haunted trees. After what he had seen, he feared everything. Now, even the trees could come alive and swallow him whole. His experience turned his thoughts backwards, allowing him to understand that the world was wrought with possibilities. Nothing would ever be impossible again. He feared a rain would come and turn him into ice; he feared the dirt would turn to quicksand and swallow him alive; he feared that fire would turn into a demon and singe him whole... It could all happen so quickly, so unexpectedly.

Mina dragged him further along. His head did somersaults as he tried his best to maintain his fear, to keep himself from running out and away, back to his car, to the safe shelter of his home. He had barely left his house, driven a car, gone camping or anything in the past years. He hadn't even thought much about it until he met Mina.

"God," he gasped.

Panic dashed through him, choking him. He had no air. His heart squeezed abnormally against his chest. He hadn't felt this much fear in so long. They continued walking forward and a branch nearly smacked him in the face. He imagined that the branch would suddenly

135

grow thorns that could capture and leave him forever tied to the trees. Sweat dripped from his body. He felt nauseous with fear. He began to shake; his skin grew clammy almost as though he was suffering from shock.

For the next few minutes, Mina, not noticing his state, pulled him even further into the dark woods. She felt no fear, only the curiosity of nocturnal life around her.

Abruptly, she stopped. The excitement still lived within her voice.

"By my estimate, we're approximately in the center of these woods," she said, looking around.

Her eyes adjusted to the darkness, though it was still difficult to see.

"Now," she said, "What are you afraid of?"

She finally looked at him, barely noticing his inner pain.

"Honestly," he said, his voice shaking, "All of it. Everything in the world that *can* happen. The dirt under my feet, the rain, the sky, the trees and wind and fire, all of the earth signs, all of them. If one can emerge, then they all can," he said.

Mina rudely scoffed, though she didn't really think before she did it. Suddenly she realized the true depth of his fear. He was scared so badly, but she didn't want him to be.

"So is life a game of witchcraft, or is it natural? Is it normal?" she asked.

"I don't know," he said.

His voice was still shaking, quivering like a lost child at the county fair. She looked him over again in the darkness.

"Is never leaving your house normal? Just because you saw something you didn't want to see?" she asked.

"No," he said.

"Don't you miss life?" she continued.

"I guess," he said.

His voice began to grow calmer with her words.

"Then it's time for you to look around and see again," she said.

The two stood in silence for the next ten or more minutes, just listening. The night was quiet, despite the sound of the crickets chirping and an occasional stray animal rustling through the brush.

Every time Bobby heard movement, his heart jumped full throttle in his chest. He held tightly to Mina's hand, silently begging the sweat to stop making it so easy for his hand to slip away. But every time Mina spoke, he felt calm overwhelm him again.

"When I was a child," Mina finally said, "My mother told me that if the crickets are chirping, then there is nothing to fear. When something scary is near, the crickets fall silent because they're scared too."

Bobby had always been strong, but realized fully that he had been isolated so long because of his fear of the world. Indeed, he enjoyed his time alone, but he had taken excess of that desire. Now in the darkness, he was able to quickly, mentally contemplate and flash through the past years. And it was the woman beside him who finally made him see.

Suddenly, Bobby pulled Mina close to him.

Their bodies aligned in the right areas, arousing even more the sexual tension, which had been building most of the day. Despite the dark, he quickly found her lips, kissing them with a passion he had nearly forgotten. Those years alone had built into a cyclone of desire for this one woman.

Mina returned his eagerness with a passion of her own. It had been a long time since she had this desire for someone. Fiercely kissing him back, it was as though a fire in itself burned static electricity between the two.

Mina's hands looped around the belt buckles of his pants, pulling his hips closer to hers. Slowly, she moved her hands to unlock the button on his pants, quickly unzipping them. Bobby countered by pulling off her light jacket. She helped struggle out of it, while their mouths remained locked in full movement.

He quickly unbuttoned her white shirt, pulling it free of her body. Struggling with her bra strap, she reached behind her back, placing her hand over his. Moving his fingers in the proper motion, together, they unhooked it. She moved her hands upward and underneath his shirt, feeling the defined muscles lingering there.

Enjoying her touch, he threw his shirt off, finding her mouth again. Pulling her close to his body, the feeling of her skin and breasts made him tinge with excitement. Her soft body was a contrast to the strong, independent person she showed herself to be. His arms quickly wrapped around her, joining his hands behind her back, his squeeze tightening until they were both nearly lost in each other's breath and bodies. He wanted to feel every inch of her surrounding him. Enjoying the feeling she hadn't had in so long, Mina couldn't help but moan with pleasure.

Bobby and Mina joined together like two animals in the wild, needing each other's bodies. Moaning loud enough to drown out any other noise, pangs of pleasure gouged and moved throughout their bodies, leaving her feet trembling with overwhelming enjoyment. Together, they moaned like two werewolves on the night of a full moon. Their howls were animalistic with desire until they faded into the silence of the night.

Together they laid in the dirt and grass. Bobby's arms held her tight. But Mina's mind wandered as it always did. Her thoughts continued on the rational side of the situation, rather than the feelings side. Though she did realize immediately, she had not used her brain in this situation. She had never before experienced a moment like this.

"Thank you," she whispered softly.

She turned and looked into his eyes through the slight light.

"It was my pleasure," he said.

He squeezed her into a hug. She quickly broke free and began searching for her clothing. Separately, in the dark they searched for the rest of their clothes. He found her shirt and she found his. Nearly knocking each other over in the darkness, they switched shirts with a giggle from both sides. When they finished dressing, they sat together against the tree they just marked.

"It's times like these where a cigarette would become necessary," Bobby said, remembering his life long ago.

A wind briskly moved through the trees at those words, though it quickly faded away.

"There are some parts of your old life, those ones that are detrimental to you, which you should not regain," she said.

Bobby wrapped his arms around Mina from the side.

"You are right," he said.

He looked up at the sky, past the trees. Suddenly, the darkness and surrounding woods did not seem so intimidating anymore. It was almost as if all of his fears had vanished as though they never really existed. The stars were beaming bright. The distant lights of commerce and the busy cities didn't shield him from seeing this beautiful part of the earth, which he had neglected enjoying.

"Mina," he began, "I really…feel something for you. Something I never felt before."

The coldness returned to Mina's voice.

"I believe it is your loneliness that persuades you to feel in such a way. I am no different from other women. You should not fool yourself like that," she said.

She understood what he meant though. It was almost as if they were meant to meet. Even she could feel the strength of the two of them together.

"No," he said, understanding her stance, "I know how I feel."

Mina stood. Reaching out her hand, she helped him up. He stared at her, searching her in the night but she looked away, keeping her eyes from him. Together, they quietly made their way out of the woods.

Back at his car, he wrapped his arms around her again. She could feel the connection, as strong as natural radio waves in the air.

"Can I stay with you tonight?" he asked.

Mina finally looked into his eyes again. The level of sincerity was strong and deep. She almost couldn't handle it.

"Scott's sleeping," she said.

"I'm sure he won't mind. Especially since I may never see you again," he said.

"I'll keep in touch," she promised, "I'll call and update you every couple days. Work on rebuilding your life," she said.

He backed away, watching her.

"I suppose I have to agree to this," he said, opening the door to his car, "Good night Mina, and thank you. You've helped me more than you could know."

He stepped into the driver's side, his eyes never leaving hers.

"Nice car," she said, "Drive often?" she teased.

He shook his head.

"I gave it to my mom after it happened. She never drove it much. It just kinda sat there. It feels good to drive again," he admitted with a smile.

"Good night," she said.

She walked towards the motel. Bobby sat in his car, watching her walk to the lobby door. Before she went into the door though, she paused and looked back at his car. He drove past, shouting out what he wanted to say.

"Mina, I love you!"

Her mouth dropped open in shock. She didn't say a word. He drove off. He did not expect her to respond, but her shock was just enough. He smiled as he drove. He really did love her already.

Mina remained dumbfounded by his comment. As a logically scientific person, she just simply did not believe in love as a quick accomplishment.

Quickly opening the door to her room, she found her way to her bed. On the floor, she groped for her bag, pulling the zipper down. Feeling, based on the material type in the darkness of the room, she found her nightclothes. Taking her shoes off, she quietly crept to the bathroom.

"What took so long?" Scott asked.

He was still in a partially deep sleep.

"I thought you were sleeping," she said.

"In between worrying," he answered, "I looked outside and you weren't around. Since you're a big girl, I didn't search. I knew you'd be mad if I did," he mumbled.

"Bobby came by. We went for a walk," she answered.

"Okay," he said, "Good, not alone, good night."

He drifted off to sleep again.

Mina quickly changed in the bathroom, noticing smudges of dirt on her clothes and body. Turning around in the mirror, she looked at the scratches on her back, which the tree and ground had left.

Mother Nature strikes again, she thought.

Though it was their actions, which provoked those wounds.

It was worth it, she thought, reminiscing.

Creeping back into bed, she expected sleep to come immediately but the case resurfaced in her mind. She wasted too much time tonight despite her enjoyment. Her case, the demon-monster, well she had to find out what it was. The case ran through her head as she lay there, staring, but not seeing the wall.

But somewhere between her thoughts and excitement, she fell into a deeply devouring sleep.

CHAPTER 13:
THE FLAMES

Scott's blaring alarm clock awakened Mina from a deep dream state. Opening her eyes slightly, the street lamp cascaded in small amounts through the partially open blinds of the hotel room window.

Turning away from the window and wall, she noticed that the clock registered 3:30 in the morning. Checkout was not for almost eight hours, but they would be leaving shortly. Looking up, she noticed that Scott wasn't in his bed, alerting her at first. Mina sat up abruptly.

The calming sound of the shower in the bathroom assured her that he had simply gotten more sleep and was out of bed early. She hit the snooze button on the alarm clock.

Lying back down, Mina reminisced the events of the night before. In her research and personal life, everything had gone well. Better than she expected. Soon, the hard part would come, discussing these events with Scott. He was so stubborn and hardheaded.

Not wanting to think of that now, Mina closed her eyes again. Allowing her thoughts to become blank, she envisioned a screen of gray in her mind. Relaxing the muscles in her face, she quickly nodded off into another sleep.

Whip! Smack!

A stinging sensation burned at the flesh on her side. Her brain quickly imagined flames and she jumped back, recoiling in fear. When she quickly jumped up, she saw Scott standing beside the bed with a towel in his hands. A wide grin stretched across his face as the light of the lamp caught his eyes.

"Asshole!" Mina shrieked.

She looked over at the clock. She had only been back asleep for about eight minutes. It was one of those sleeps where you drift off so suddenly and deeply that anything can scare you from the world of the awake.

Mina rolled back onto the bed face first. Moving her hand to her right side, she gently rubbed the spot he hit. As she pulled her shirt partially up, Scott noticed the scratches on her back. Sudden guilt sprang itself upon him.

"Oh shit," he began, "I didn't do that, did I?"

He leaned to get a closer look.

"What?" she asked.

Her voice was muffled from the pillows, though she suddenly realized what he had seen. At the same time she remembered the marks, Scott lifted the shirt slightly, just enough to reveal more scratches, deeper than the one he initially saw.

"Damn Mina, what happened to you?" he asked.

She quickly jumped up to hide the scratches.

"Nothing," she said.

She tried to ignore the horrified look on his face.

"Did you see that thing, that monster last night?" he asked.

"No," she laughed, "But I'm glad you recognize that it exists."

Scott stood there, a look of ignorance upon his face, as though he still didn't understand. Mina laughed.

Scott stood there, slowly trying to figure it out. Mina was bright, but very spontaneous at times. He was naturally concerned about her. But she was always so difficult about everything. He wondered if he should press the issue or just let it go.

"What?" she asked.

The smile upon her face only grew larger.

"Nothing," he replied.

Scott sat on his hotel bed, ignoring the issue since it did not seem to bother her. Reaching into his bag, he pulled out a pair of fresh socks, putting them on his feet, beginning with his left foot. He thought of how he had decided not to pursue his questioning. From research to her personal life, there was always a hidden part in everything involving Mina. But as long as no one hurt her, he wasn't going to press it. From the smile on her face, he could tell it hadn't been a bad situation, whatever it was.

Mina slowly moved herself from the bed. Quickly glancing at the clock, she realized she only had a short time for a shower. Without another word she ran to the bathroom with a fresh change of clothes.

After quickly showering, Mina stood for a minute in the mirror, looking at her scratches.

Mother Nature has marked me, she thought, giggling to herself. *But so has he.*

This second thought she did not intend to have. It seemed to have been conjured up from somewhere else, unwillingly for her.

First she scolded herself for allowing a thought of emotion towards someone and secondly for even acknowledging her heart. She wondered where the thought had come from in the first place. She did not allow her heart to make decisions as most girls did.

Mina quickly dressed, trying to blank Bobby out of her mind. By the time she entered into the main part of the room, Scott had already loaded their things into the car. Gathering up the rest of her stuff, she joined him outside.

They jumped into the car, heading home. Scott drove for a while with Mina looking over her notes before she engaged him in conversation.

"We have to find a similarity between this case and the woman I talked with alone," Mina said.

"I have a thought, as I'm sure you do," he said.

"Of the connection?" she asked.

She gently moved the hair away from her eyes, where it had been caught by the wind through her cracked window.

"Forest fire?" she asked, wanting him to be the descriptive one.

"Yup," he replied.

"But, what is your thought on that?" she asked, wanting to know more.

"I don't know," he said, seemingly frustrated.

Turning his head to the left, he seemed to search the countryside for answers as he drove.

"Yes you do. You're just embarrassed to say it," she pushed, "I won't think you're crazy. By now I'm probably thinking the same thing," she finished.

Scott didn't hesitate this time.

"Maybe it was sparked by the forest fire. Maybe that is the connection; maybe it wasn't a demon at all. Perhaps that is where the idea of spontaneous combustion came from. As you have said, with spontaneous combustion, the fire is not ignited by an external source. Maybe it isn't, but if a fire is close to the victim, perhaps there's a charge in the air that ignites it, almost like gasoline. In such a case, the fire would not start from another fire, but an alternate route, such as a charge in the air. Perhaps it's something scientific which has not yet been discovered," Scott said.

"Bullshit!" Mina shouted.

She looked at him incredulously now. She already knew he would continue to feel this way.

"We saw it, this demon. The others saw it and we know it is real," she said.

Scott shrugged.

"Maybe we didn't really see it. The brain favors speed over accuracy. Maybe the others just felt some sort of guilt and created the visual. For example, Greta may have felt bad about the reckless ways in which she lived. Erica may have felt guilty about going out with a man her parents did not approve of. Bobby may have felt bad that he couldn't be with his friends, like he was letting them down. All of them may have allowed their minds to think they saw something they did not see. A demon coming for them as a form of punishment for being bad- something linked to their individual guilt. Perhaps that's what happened with those three. They weren't exactly the most stable people," Scott said.

Mina scoffed.

"Define stable in this society," she demanded.

Anger pulsed through her now. Her nostrils seemed to flare with heat. Her body felt afire. Scott said nothing. She took his turn.

"Regardless of what it was, they each experienced a traumatic event. Similarly, they found their own way to deal with it. You know psychology obviously, but that can't explain why they all saw the same form, with the same description and they are all different people, strangers even," she said.

"Yes and just like I said- they weren't exactly the most stable people- not enough to take their word on it. Besides, tabloids are full of creatures; maybe they just used the same one as a form of coincidence. Like alien abductions," he repeated.

"There's nothing unstable about them. They're just scared, scared from what really did happen. Believe me, I know how scared they are," Mina argued.

"How do you know?" he asked.

Mina bit her lip, deciding to give in.

"Ok, when I ran into Bobby outside the hotel, I dragged him into the woods. I made him stand there in the darkness to let him know there was nothing to be afraid of."

Scott nodded, understanding now.

"You showed him the woods could be fun," he teased.

"Shut up," she said, "Why do you have to be so difficult? Why do you have to fight me on everything? Why can't you just believe what you see?"

Scott started mocking pornographic music. A laugh forced itself out of her.

"Just shut up," she said.

Another laugh brimmed at her edges.

"But are you sure that was a good idea? I mean you barely knew him," Scott said.

"I knew him enough from the look in his eyes," Mina said.

Scott debated within himself whether or not to bring up the past. Finally, he felt it would be best for her well being if he did.

"Mina, you know, Brandon had a look in his eyes too."

Mina's smile immediately turned into a frown. A grave silence fell over the car. Scott bit his lip and then continued.

"Brandon was just too intelligent. He became too obsessed with his own project. He became caught up in too much bullshit and his subject was quite similar to what you like to study the most. The supernatural, as you know," Scott spoke slowly, struggling with the words.

"Scott," Mina began, uneasily.

"You should never become personal with your cases, your research. God, he was so brainwashed," he continued, aggravation in his voice.

"Scott, please, I..." Mina objected.

"After all the years we made fun of it, he decided to study it. Oh, just for fun. That's what he said, right? Who studies Satanism, a fucking cult for fun? He even bought a black bible for research he said. Then what happened? They wanted him to kill his own friend.

For initiation. And it had to be a girl. But instead, he shot his fucking head off. A sacrifice to the god of doom," he said.

His hidden resentment over the ordeal surfaced, vulgarly eating at him as he drove.

"Scott, that's enough. I'm not susceptible like that," she replied.

She felt tears drifting up from the back of her eyes. Hurt avalanched through her chest as her mind flashed memories of that night. That awful night.

Scott continued.

"In your house. With all of us there. Right in front of us. That stupid girl he met, who told him she loved him. He fell for it too, especially when she told him to kill you for their god and they would forever be alive. All over what some stupid girl said and probably believed in her demented mind. Psychologically, it was just some dumb girl's jealousy over your friendship and it nearly got you killed. Instead, he became a sacrifice of his own," he said.

His voice rose in sarcasm with every word. Tears drifted from Mina's eyes as she remembered. But she pushed them back and then wiped them away, staring enviously at the dryness of the desert landscape.

"Just stop. I know all of this," she said, "And I know why you're worried, because we were so much alike. And I helped him with some the research on the occult. Yeah, I never saw it coming. The whole time I helped him, I just thought he was devoted to his research like me. He couldn't do it though, he couldn't hurt me, he was a good person and he was just lost. I saw a lot of the shit those people did to others, but I was in no way associated with it. In the end, Brandon was weak; he just wanted to be a super power. I already know that is impossible," she began to yell at him, "I'm sick of you acting like I need a guardian angel! That happened long ago and Brandon's gone now!"

She fought the fresh tears that wanted to be set free. Scott continued.

"I just don't want you to kill yourself or hurt someone else over something that doesn't even exist and isn't worth the effort," he said, "And you shouldn't believe what someone tells you just because you think they have honest eyes."

A solemn silence swam throughout the car. She thought of the putrid gray film he had just cast upon her life.

"So, I guess you took this case with me just to sabotage it. You really don't want me to find anything out," she said.

"No, that is not it. I just don't want you to get hurt, that's all," he said.

"I can handle myself," she claimed.

"Yeah, you already got injured," he said.

She looked at him with wide-open eyes. Anger brimmed in every corner of her body.

"Did I fucking complain?" she asked.

Scott said nothing in response. The two of them sat in silence again for a long while until Scott began to speak.

"I think we should go to that place and talk with the people who were at the campsite when the small forest fire caught. It's on the way back," Scott said.

He was trying to please her without apologizing.

"I would like to look up a couple of things on the Internet when I get back. Before we talk with anyone else," she said.

"That's fine," Scott mumbled.

He could tell by her tone that she did not want to talk to him anymore.

***

When they finally made it home, Mina was glad that the trip was over. Her hours of driving left her tired and worn. But instead of lying down as she really wanted to, she dragged herself to the computer.

Immediately after logging on, she searched the area in New Mexico where Greta lived. Checking newspapers, she quickly found that a forest fire had been near the town, around the same dates of the deaths of her boyfriend and his friend.

A newspaper headline read:

FOREST FIRE CAUSED BY NEGLIGENCE IN THE WOODS

"Unbelievable," she muttered.

She read the article and then sat back to think about it. Apparently, someone had started a fire, a group of kids, in that particular area of New Mexico, close to Gallup. They had been partying in the woods when their bonfire went out of control. One of the kids turned up missing; they figured the fire had taken him. The other three ran once they noticed the fire growing out of control. No one saw what happened to the fourth person, nor were the remains ever found.

Mina realized that she knew what happened.

This left one question.

There was no doubt that this monster, this demon could kill, but why were there survivors in some cases? Why weren't they all killed? The monster definitely had the ability to cremate an entire person, so why not all of them every time?

"Endless," Mina whispered.

The questions bubbled endlessly in her mind.

Searching the Internet again, she wondered where or how such a thing could originate. If she could find evidence of its origins...Perhaps if she began by checking the *way* in which the demon killed, by swift cremation, then there might be answers there.

Mina searched with the keyword 'cremation.' Reading the results on the screen, she found that the first crematory was formed in Washington, Pennsylvania. Dr. Francis Julius LeMoyne started it as a way to burn bodies when it was found that illnesses from dead, buried bodies were leaking into the soil and streams, causing others to become sick and die as well. The very first cremation took place in 1876, she discovered.

"Pennsylvania," she said, "Seems so far away. Though it might be a possibility of where the demon could have originated. Maybe they knew about the demon then when they created this first crematory. Perhaps its ability is how they got their idea."

She tapped a pen against her cheek.

"But the demon probably strikes every state."

She changed subjects, starting quickly onto a different search. Pulling up a list of large wildfires in history, she realized the first one ever was listed in October 1825 in New Brunswick and Maine. That was even before the first crematory was invented, she realized. Forest fires have been happening for centuries. As she read, she observed that this fire consumed 3 million acres of land.

"Wow."

That was all her energy could manage for her to say.

Most of the other fire cases were in areas close to her state. The majority of them seemed to occur in California, a state she hadn't even bothered to check before. Others were Idaho, Montana, Florida, Nevada, Colorado, and Wisconsin but the list went on endlessly. Forest fires were constantly occurring. That meant these cases with the demon were probably ongoing as well.

"Pennsylvania," she said aloud, "No extremely large forest fires in Pennsylvania. Closest state of historical fires in relation to Pennsylvania is New York. Pennsylvania has so many more trees than other states, though. Maybe it's the climate factor."

The idea hit her as she talked to herself, causing her to continue her search into a delirium. The more she searched the more her words were mumbled, though her thoughts were surprisingly still precise.

Searching the engine again, she pulled up a map of drought areas. She had done this sort of geographical research before; she just wanted to make sure her facts were correct.

She looked over the screen.

"Exactly," she said.

The cases of extreme forest fires were all in drought areas. The climate caused the dryness, which made forest fires harder to avoid. Arizona, her own home state, was one of them.

"What causes forest fires?" she asked aloud, searching again.

Her fingers keyed the search.

"The main cause is lightning? A natural attack?"

She sat back in her chair, asking herself again as if she didn't believe it.

"But lightning is natural."

She looked over the screen, seeking the second cause. She read the words aloud.

"The second cause is human error. Exactly," she said.

She looked away from the screen and thought about it.

"Human error," she repeated the words.

"Okay," she said, tapping her brain for more info.

She changed subjects despite her tiring mind.

"What was the name of the man who was killed in the last forest fire?"

She strained her brain to remember. But now that she thought about it, she had not asked Erica where the family was camping when the victim was killed. She had been too anxious to leave. She hadn't even attempted to find that detail.

"Damn," she said aloud.

She threw a pen at her desk. She screwed up. She shook her head in anger at herself but then quickly shrugged it off.

Though a third resource would make the case more, she did not feel it was terribly necessary. She had enough evidence accumulated. Now her mission was to prove it. Based on her favorite theory derived in science class, so far she had followed all the steps in proving her experiment.

Initially, she *observed* cases of supernatural phenomenon. The first case was with the group; the others came later, through her personal time.

Next, she sorted through a list of possibilities, forming the *hypothesis* on her own. Though still unsure, she had ideas close to what it could be.

Then, after to listening to survivors and linking the similarities by *gathering evidence*, she still had to consider places in which it was likely to occur again.

Now that this third step was mostly completed, tomorrow it would be time to carry out the final step. *Testing the theory.* The experiment she had put so much work into was to be tested in the final step of the process.

With these last thoughts in mind, Mina finally laid down to sleep.

Tomorrow, she would talk with Scott about their research. It was truly discouraging that his scientific/ psychological thoughts differed so greatly from her ideas. She was ever so familiar with the workings of science, but was always open to anything beyond the realm of it. Why couldn't others be that way?

Incredibly tired, Mina kept herself awake with these stirring thoughts. How could she convince such a stubborn, levelheaded man into believing in her?

"Damn it," she cursed aloud.

But it came out slurred more like a cartoonish word than an actual cussing.

Still, she felt too edgy to sleep. But the fatigue fought hard for the win. Finally, her mind still brimming with thoughts, she gave in to sleep. The brain shut her down to rest and prepare for the day to come.

CHAPTER 14:
PLOT OF EVIDENCE

Though it was 10:30 AM and she had gotten a good bit of sleep, Mina was annoyed by the obsessive ringing of her home telephone. She had set her alarm clock for noon, and it was quite important to her to receive the extra sleep.

The first ring she answered. This call was from Ryan, wondering how the trip had gone. She immediately mumbled that she would call him back later. The next call, she hadn't bothered to answer, though she knew it was Jesse or Scott. After that, the phone rang every ten minutes it seemed, until finally, she took it off the hook.

She flipped on her back again but had to be careful how she slept, given her scratches.

***

When noon arrived, the blaring trumpet of her alarm clock awakened Mina. Then, she knew it was truly her time to join the world. Reluctantly reaching onto her nightstand, she put the phone back on the hook. Not more than a minute later, it rang.

Still annoyed by the ringing sound, Mina answered it with resentment that echoed through the one word she crackled out.

On the other end, a male voice replied shyly with a simple 'hi.' The sound was familiar though it was not one of her close friends. Still half asleep, she couldn't hide her continuing annoyance.

"Who is this?" she asked.

Pause.

"It's me, Bobby. Remember?" he asked.

Mina was stunned he found her number. Sitting abruptly in her bed, her heart fluttered with the oddest of motions.

"How did you…?" she began.

"The same way you found me," he said, "Well, not the exact same way, but the same method. The computer."

He stumbled on with his words. Mina used her cold voice.

"Is there any reason you called? Research?" she asked.

Silence answered her. Then a voice, the seductive voice.

"I just wanted to see how you were. I, well, I..." his voice trailed off.

"You what?" Mina asked.

Suddenly she remembered what he had said at the motel before driving off. She gulped, hoping it wasn't a repeat of that.

"I want to come and see you where you are," he said, "I miss you already."

Mina sighed and then rolled her eyes.

"Bobby, I know how you feel, but right now, I have a lot of research to do. You see, this case is very important to me. It will open the eyes of average people, letting them know that these supernatural events, they do exist. So many of us are so blinded," she said.

"But Mina, I can help you with it. I need something to keep me busy. I need a change. I need a new life. I'm willing to come to you, to start out there with you," he said.

"Whoa. Look," Mina began, "I think you're a great guy from what I know of you and it seems really sweet, your words, but you can't consider me to be your main source of a new life. Yes, I helped you see what was missing, but that may be why you feel this way. Besides, where would you live or work out here?"

"I've already thought all of this through, believe it or not," he began, "And no, I do not plan on becoming some sort of attachment just because you helped me out. Over my years of isolation, I spent a lot of years reading and researching. I didn't even fully believe in love the way I do now...now that I met you," he said.

Silence fell between them. Mina's heart raced with desire, aching for him. Through the silence, an invisible, electrical wave seemed to pass through the phone, showing their mutually felt connection. He seemed able to read her thoughts through the phone.

"It isn't just the thought of having someone to be with. It is the way the air feels when I'm around you, the aura that ran between us and throughout. I know it is meant to be, or else I never would have taken the time to find you and call," he said.

The passion in his voice caused her aching heart to throb. She closed her eyes. Mina knew the feeling, the air and aura he explained.

She felt it too. It was nothing like anything she had ever seen or felt before. Desperately, she wanted him to come to her, but knew there was too much at stake. Her research needed finished and her methods would not be approved by anyone. They would try to stop her. She bit her lip and suppressed her heart. Her heart ached as she spoke the next words.

"I don't know what you mean. What you feel…" she began.

Her voice cracked as she spoke. The lie sounded as forced as it felt.

"Yes you do," he said, "I know you felt it too."

Silence greeted them again. She could tell that he was annoyed by her denial. She looked at the clock; realizing time was escaping her fast.

"Ok, well, how about I just call you and tell you what I've come up with in a few days," she said, rushing off the phone, "It may be more than a couple of days. I have to finish this and I'm sure you can understand how important it is to me."

"I'm sure it is, but I don't want you to get…" he began.

Mina interrupted, "hurt," she said mockingly, "Look, I will call you but I have so much to do."

"Mina, this, this demon…I've seen it. You don't know what you're dealing with," he persisted, "I should help you. I can be out there in just a day or two. Besides, that thing took my friends away. I have a score to settle."

"Look, I have seen it and I am not scared of it. Also, this case is mine. You gave up on it years ago. This is mine to figure out and damn it, I will do it!" she shouted.

She slammed down the phone without even realizing why she was yelling or why she had reacted so quickly. The mild fire in her heart burst into a storm of hot, aching flames.

"Ugghhh," she sighed.

She buried her face in her hands but her body was too stunned to weep.

Nearly immediately after hanging up the phone, it began ringing again. Lying back on her bed, she pulled the sheets over her head, trying to ignore it.

Within the next few minutes the ringing stopped. Slowly, she took the sheets away from her head, looking at the phone in its relieving silence.

"Good," she muttered, "No use getting anyone else involved or hurt."

But secretly, deep down within the flames in her heart, she felt a sad lonely heart ache. She did want him to come. Had he really given up so easily?

Just as she moved towards her desk and computer, the phone rang again. She answered it, hesitantly though hopeful. The voice wasn't the one she wanted to hear.

"What's going on sleepyhead? Thought you'd be outside, enjoying the day."

Scott's voice sounded far too cheerful on the other end. Slightly disappointed, though also relieved, Mina responded.

"Nah, I just got out of bed, after all that driving shit yesterday."

"Well, what have you come up with? Anything good?" he asked.

"Yeah, actually, I have a few theories we should discuss soon," she started, "When and where would you like to meet?"

"We can meet here, when you get out of bed and everything," he said.

"Alright, be there in about a half an hour," she said.

"Good," he finished, hanging up the phone.

Mina quickly got ready.

The phone did not ring anymore in the entire time it took her to get ready. But she kept looking at it and waiting for him to call.

***

Now at Scott's, Mina showed him the maps she printed the night before of likely forest fire areas, drought areas and the list of extreme forest fires. On the forest fire map, little red dots showed the states, which had a major forest fire. Orange dots showed the zones of medium sized forest fires while yellow dots showed the smallest forms. The cases they had where the demon appeared were all in the red areas, the grandest scale of a fire.

156

Mina pulled out another map, while Scott absorbed the information from the first one. She pointed to her new paper. Scott's eyes followed her fingers.

"This is a map of risk areas and places with drought," she said, "A forest fire is most likely to occur in any one of these areas."

"Whoa," Scott whistled, "Most of them are pretty close to where we live."

Mina looked up then, nodding.

"Exactly. This is why it has either happened or will happen here some day. It is now also a threat, not just a case," she said.

Scott nodded, seeing and feeling the imminence in her eyes. She continued.

"But I'm sure no one here noticed it either. Probably because no one wants to believe in it. Or no one could see it because it was masked by a natural force, fire," she began, "But, we should be able to find more cases now that we've narrowed down areas where it has occurred or where it will strike."

When she stopped, Scott smiled at her.

"Good job," he said.

Mina scoffed though.

"Yeah, but we're far from finished," she said, "It's time to search even more. Like now."

Together, they went to Scott's computer to begin yet another search.

After an hour of aimless searching, they found speculative cases in each state marked in red. Listing the dates of such cases, they checked to see if a forest fire had happened in the exact month and year for each time period. In every case it had.

Scott sat back in his computer chair. Dazed and dumbfounded, he rubbed the slight stubble on his chin.

"Well, what next?" he asked, looking over at Mina.

"Well, now we search the ones in orange," she said.

She tapped his shoulder, motioning for him to move so that she could sit in front. Scott reluctantly moved, switching to her former chair.

Within the next hour, they found fewer living victims. But the cases were still there. Instead of stopping there, Mina continued forward, searching the states coded in yellow.

This time when she was finished, Mina leaned back in the chair.

"Well, we've confirmed these fires occurred in places where the deaths happened, though not always in the precise location of the fire. The age group was always different. It does not discriminate in any way when it wants human blood."

Scott shrugged and rubbed his eyes.

"We still don't know what it is, if anything," he said.

Mina bit her lip, controlling her frustration with him.

"Scott we saw it, they saw it. It's a demon. A demon that attacks..."

She stopped suddenly. A thought popped into her head. There was another idea she had to check. She thought of it before, but had somehow forgotten in all the research.

"Night or day?" she asked.

"What?"

She shook her head and began typing into the computer again.

"Because most cases were the same, we need to find out when this demon monster attacks, day, night or both," she said.

"Good thought," Scott said.

She really did impress him sometimes, though he was still unsure if it was a demon they were chasing or a natural, undiscovered phenomenon in the science of nature. His eyes lit up and a smile swept across his face.

"We definitely want to find out if it's a vampire demon or just a regular demon," he joked.

She flashed him a dirty look. He put his hands up in surrender.

"Just seeing if you're paying attention," he said.

She flashed him a fake smile and turned back to the computer. Searching again, Mina sporadically checked the deaths.

"Night time," she said.

She tapped a pen against her cheek.

"You didn't check them all," Scott said.

"We don't have to. It only attacks at night," she assured him.

"So it must be scared of the day time, like in all the horror movies. Those vampire demons- better watch out for them. I wonder if some of them suck blood out of their victims too," Scott joked.

"Real funny," Mina commented, "But we have to find out why it only attacks at night."

Scott shrugged.

"Who knows? I think that's irrelevant," Scott said, "So where do you want to go from here? Should we visit the person Erica mentioned?"

"I forgot to ask where that was," she said.

Scott smiled.

"Have no fear, because I caught it and I did ask," he said.

Mina's eyes opened wide with surprise, "You did?"

"Yup," he answered, "And I already checked it out. The family's actual home is less than half the distance of the place we just came from."

Mina thought about it for a moment.

"I don't really want to go on another trip," she said.

Scott raised an eyebrow and looked at her suspiciously.

"As involved as you are in this case and you don't want to find out more?" he asked.

"I just," she hesitated, "Don't really want to go."

Scott shrugged his shoulders.

"Ok then. I guess we lose some possibly crucial data," he said.

She eyed him.

"Well, that doesn't mean you can't go," she said.

His eyes widened.

"Alone?" he asked.

"Yeah, I did it before. Are you frightened?" she asked.

She was intentionally appealing to the image of toughness men sometimes carry.

"No," he said defensively, "I just would…probably get lonely in a strange town not knowing anyone."

"Aww," she said, feigning pity.

"Shut up, I'll go, but just because I feel that it is important to the case, particularly since the man who started the fire died in this one. I'll just have to take more time off of work," he grunted.

A frown swept across his face, causing Mina to feel a twinge of guilt. She swept the guilt away for now.

"When are you leaving?" she asked.

"Well, I'll probably only get one more day off of work, so I suppose I should leave today," he said.

Feeling guilty about her deception, she asked, "Are you sure you should go today, you have been driving a lot. I don't want anything to happen to you. I'd never forgive myself."

"I can handle it. Besides, I'd rather go today than lose another day's worth of work," he claimed.

She studied him.

"Ok, but call me if anything happens. I'll be around researching," she said.

"Just find the exact address and I'll be off," he said.

On the Internet, Mina printed a map for Scott to his destination, along with reverse directions.

"It should only take five hours to get there," he said.

Mina scanned the directions.

"It says seven to eight on the paper," she observed.

Scott grinned mischievously.

"Like I said, it should only take five hours," he repeated.

Mina frowned, partially ashamed of herself though unwilling to admit it.

"Well, be careful," she added, "Are you staying in a hotel or will you be driving straight back?"

"I don't know yet," he said, "Work starts early after tomorrow, but I might just take another day."

He frowned now and studied her face.

"This case, I hope it's worth it to you," he said.

"It is," she smiled, "I only hope it eventually means as much to you."

"We'll see," he said, "Well, I have to pack some shit."

Mina helped him pack. She was sad that she could not join him, though it was her choice after all. Helping him carry his things to the car, she stood on the sidewalk and watched him drive away. Looking at her watch, she noticed that it was three in the afternoon. He would arrive by eight o' clock or later. Mina guessed that Scott would get a hotel room and that he would be back the next day around four or five. That was plenty of time for her.

Slowly, she walked to her home through the dry, heated air of the day. Dread and guilt bit at one side of her but the fierce evil of determination was a great conqueror.

At home again, Mina went to the answering machine. She was surprised Bobby had not left any messages. Maybe he realized he wasn't in love with her as much as he assumed he was. Jesse and Ryan each left messages, which she ignored. She hadn't even bothered to turn her cell phone back on in the past several days.

In her room, Mina searched for necessary supplies. She always had a good supply of matches to light her candles. She owned a single lighter for the same purpose. Mina knew how to start a fire; she had been camping so many times. Her tomboy ways were always prevalent in her personality.

Mina's mind drifted to the previous trips, when the four of them had gone camping. The others were always impressed with how well she started a fire. Her memories went back to the time she had let Jesse try to start a fire. Thinking he was just as smart and tough and that he could build one without ever doing it before, he learned quickly that he was not in touch with nature living. In his life, he was accustomed to throwing a log into a fireplace where the fire was already started. That same night, he struggled so much with keeping the fire going. He had definitely given them all a laugh with his sheltered, pretty boy ways.

Mina smiled.

She had some great memories. They had some really great times camping. Her favorite thing besides starting the fire was roasting marshmallows and hot dogs. Never, in their camping experiences, had they seen anything out of the ordinary. She always put the fire out when they were done with it. Mina was well aware of the risks of forest fires.

She just never thought she would be plotting to start one.

Mina sat on the edge of her bed with a large box of matches in her right hand.

"Ughh," she sighed, looking down at the box.

She had to think this through. All her life, she loved nature, from bugs, to fish- every living creature. She never wanted to hurt any of them. This was going to be an extreme pain when it was all over.

What she was about to do could cost human lives as well, including her own. She was also breaking the law. Even if no one was injured, she could still face penalties of imprisonment. If anyone was killed, she would have to live with that guilt on her conscience forever.

"Ughh," she sighed again.

When she first thought up the idea, she didn't realize it would be so hard to finalize her decision. She knew her own death might be certain, and that didn't matter so much since it was a risk she chose to take. It was the part of hurting others, which pressed on her mind. Scott was far away and Jesse and Ryan wouldn't be anywhere near the fire. The same went with her family. No one would be near the woods she intended to set ablaze.

Mina looked at her watch. It now registered four pm.

She had to wait until at least seven, when the night began to fall. She could go sooner, but didn't want to be seen.

Firewood, she thought.

She needed firewood. The winters weren't so cold here, so she didn't know how difficult it would be to find firewood. Many people liked to light their fireplaces just for fun, the romantic aspects of it, she supposed.

Then a name came to mind.

Jesse.

Jesse's family was one of those strange romantic types who carried wood right in their backyard. She knew they kept a small stack right next to their shed. Initially, she thought she would gather natural wood that covered the ground, but this would be easier. And since the logs were larger, they would burn longer. Also, she had lighter fluid from their last camping trip to keep the fire going.

She just had to give herself a little more time and think this through. She had to make sure this was something she really wanted to do.

She had to make sure this was something she could do.

***

162

Hours later, all packed and now in her car, Mina drove slowly down Jesse's street. Pulling past his home, she parked in the hidden, woodsy road near the driveway of a neighbor a few houses down. The lights were dark at their house and no cars were near. That signified to her that they weren't home.

Mina's watch read six o' clock.

Though it was still daylight, Jesse's family would be enjoying dinner on the entire other side of his house. Conveniently, he would be directly opposite from where she would be stealing the wood.

She contemplated the morality of what she was about to do to her friends, to strangers. Then, as she always did, she thrust those thoughts out of her mind, sticking solely to her scientific side. She grabbed an old, used gym bag out of her back seat. Before she could think twice, she quickly ran through the yards in between her car and Jesse's house. Honestly, she didn't want to steal too much wood from them, thinking it rude in the first place, despite the fact that they could truly afford more.

Looking up at Jesse's house, she observed that most of the lights were out, except for in Jesse's room. He always left it on. A small stream of light, obviously coming from the dining room, shone through the window nearest her. Mina looked beyond the house and at the neighbors' homes. All of them seemed still. No one was there to bear witness of her deception.

Quickly finding the shed, she struggled against the stubborn blue tarp that shielded the wood from the elements. One final tug and the right side of the tarp flew up quickly, whipping with the wind but making only slight noise. Quickly, Mina unzipped her gym bag and then threw it to the ground.

She quickly fitted the smaller sized, nearly perfectly cut logs into the bag until she could barely zip it. She had gotten at least twelve logs into the duffel bag. Pulling the tarp back down, though loosely, her long tall figure quickly jogged through the yard to her car. Dumping the bag of logs into her trunk, she grabbed the second empty gym bag from her backseat. In the same manner, Mina coursed through the path to the pile she had taken from before.

"Just a few more," she whispered.

At the pile, she threw her bag down in the same location she had loaded before. Swooping down to lift the tarp, she reached out to grab another log, when she heard a voice from above.

"Hello?"

Looking up from her spot, Jesse's figure rimmed the window. Guilt spread itself upon her face like that of a spoiled child who hurt his mother's feelings. Worry spread its wings around her. He had seen her standing there, though nothing else she hoped. She squinted her eyes to see better. He had a glass in his hand; probably filled with milk. He always drank milk with dinner.

"Hi," Mina said.

The guilt continued to spread across her face, though she knew he wasn't observant enough to pick up on it.

"What are you doing?" Jesse asked.

He snorted with obnoxious humor. Mina slowly stood back up.

"Just coming over to see you," Mina lied.

Jesse scoffed.

"You didn't call me back earlier," he said.

He looked behind him before turning back.

"Do you want to eat dinner?"

Mina's stomach growled at the mention. She realized she hadn't eaten at all.

"What are you having?" she asked.

"Lasagna," he answered, "And other stuff."

He burped before continuing.

"Well? Want some?" he asked, lifting up his milk for a drink.

She contemplated for a moment. The anxiety of discovery, the nagging pressure of time and the guilt of her mission could not stop her overbearing stomach. Besides, it would look really bad if she declined.

"Sure," she said.

"Door's unlocked," he said, "You know where we are."

He belched again and then walked away from the window without suspicion.

Mina paused for a moment, watching the window and letting out a deep breath of relief. But then she realized something- Jesse didn't think she was doing anything wrong because he trusted her. The overbearing nagging of conscience came at her again. As usual, she shoved it away.

Still watching the house, she wanted to make sure Jesse's face didn't resurface. Finally assured, she quickly lifted the tarp, filling the second bag. This time, she only took ten more, struggling with fitting them in. She must have picked bigger ones this time.

Rearranging the logs so that they looked undisturbed, she quickly tied the tarp back down and ran to her car. Opening the trunk, she tossed the bag in, hurriedly jumping in the driver's side. Quickly, she backed onto the road, pulling her car directly in front of Jesse's house. He wouldn't notice her car had just appeared. Jesse's intelligence was limited to brain and memory, not his eyes- he was truly as observant as a lemming.

Walking through Jesse's front door, she immediately found her way to the dining room. Jesse and his parents were enjoying their dinner, but still offered a richly gracious greeting with partially full mouths. His mother didn't even give her a dirty look for just walking in. Before she sat down, his mom was already ready to feed her.

"Have some lasagna," she offered in her seemingly fake voice, "There's mashed potatoes, garlic bread..."

Her eyes traced Mina's face before continuing, making her paranoid.

"Are you ok honey? You don't look like you feel well. You're awfully pale in pallor," she continued.

Mina smiled half-heartedly.

"I'm fine Mrs. Webber. I just have to use the restroom if you don't mind," she said.

Quickly she left the room, closing herself in the bathroom. Looking in the mirror, she could see her clammy skin and the sweat that moistened her face. She looked down at her hands, which wore small amounts of dirt from the firewood.

"Shit," she said.

Mina scrubbed her hands with soap and water, trying to clean them as best as she could. Then, she rinsed her face of the sweat in order to look more presentable. Checking her clothes, she was thankful she hadn't gotten much dirt on them either, besides a few wood shavings from the logs.

Finally, she returned to the dining room.

"Oh you look so much better now," Jesse's mom remarked.

"I just didn't eat yet today. I think I forgot to. I'm starving," Mina smiled.

"Oh dear," Jesse's mom said, "Here, I dished you out some lasagna and potatoes."

"Thank you," she said.

"You're welcome honey," she replied.

Jesse's mother was very big on manners. Mina was very thankful for the feast. She quickly scarfed down most of what was on her plate. They were all used to the way she ate, though still baffled by her.

"Here's some more garlic bread," Jesse's mom offered.

With a mouth full of food, Jesse spoke to Mina.

"What were you doing out there? Behind the house? You get weirder and weirder every single day," he said.

His mother gave him a disapproving look.

"Jesse don't talk with your mouth full," she scolded.

He ignored her, chewing heartily, his eyes searching Mina and awaiting her response.

Mina swallowed her food and took a sip of water.

"I wanted to play a joke on you," Mina quickly exaggerated, "But I forgot you were having dinner."

Jesse smiled while chewing more food. He took a sip of milk.

"What kind of joke?" he asked.

"I'm not telling," Mina said, "I might use it on you some other time. Besides, you and Scott get me all the time."

Jesse took a huge bite of his garlic bread before beginning again. He pointed at her with the remainder of his bread.

"Fine, but I bet you won't get me good. Not like we get you," he said, "Where is Scott anyway? I've been calling him all day too," he mumbled through his food.

His mother shot him another disapproving look. Jesse ignored this one as well.

"He's not feeling very good," Mina lied.

"What did you do to him?" he joked, chewing faster, "Did you guys go away and fall in love?"

He chuckled obnoxiously

"No, don't be stupid," Mina said.

Jesse's parents were used to their squabbles.

When they finished eating, Mina thanked his mother and helped her clear the table.

"What are you doing now?" Jesse asked.

"I haven't been feeling too good either. I think I'll go home and go to bed," she said.

She looked at her watch. It was nearly seven.

"Geez," Jesse said, "I don't see any of you for a couple days and already you don't want to hang out," he joked.

But there was hidden seriousness in his voice.

"No, Jesse," she started, "It's not you at all, I just think I'm coming down with something."

But guilt erupted, stopping her there. She couldn't think of many more lies. She looked up at him, her eyes shining with regret.

"It's better to hang out tomorrow when I'm better rested."

At least she hoped she would still be around tomorrow. At this point, she almost talked herself out of doing it.

Almost.

"Ok," Jesse smiled.

She sensed his disappointment.

"Get some sleep," he said, "But both of you better be better tomorrow."

"We will," she said.

She turned to leave but couldn't complete her escape. Halting, she turned back slowly and studied Jesse's face.

"Thank you Jesse," she said.

Moving towards him again, she wrapped her arms around him in a huge hug.

"What the hell is this?" Jesse asked, "What a way to say goodbye. I think I kind of like it."

Goodbye, she thought to herself, continuing the embrace. She had just wanted to say thank you. But maybe it truly was goodbye.

Finally freeing herself from the hug, she turned and walked out the door in silence. Jesse watched her leave with confusion filling him.

As she got into her car, she looked back up at Jesse's house.

"Hopefully," she began aloud and to herself, "This won't be the last time I see this town, this house and these people."

Pausing for a just few more minutes and observing the neighborhood, she finally started the car and slowly drove away.

CHAPTER 15:
LIGHT AND EMPTINESS

Mina continued her drive slowly out of the neighborhood. It was now 7:08 pm.

Her thoughts pulsed on what she was about to do. Maybe she was a little crazy just like Brandon had become. Yes, he killed himself- he had actually committed suicide. But wasn't that, in a way, what she was about to do?

"Can't back out now," she sighed.

It was all in the name of a good cause. She continued to try to justify it in her head.

Mina looked at the packed bag on the seat beside her. She had matches, lighter fluid and a digital camera. Her biggest concern was that if she did die for her cause, how would anyone see the footage? She couldn't have asked anyone to tag along. None of them would have helped her, but they all would have tried to stop her. She couldn't have that. The she realized something. Brandon would have helped her...

Mina shook the thought away.

She drove slowly. Her destination was not far away, though she had much to think of in a short time. The thoughts continued to haunt her mind.

Finally, at 7:23, she reached her destination.

As she got out of the car, she studied the thick woods that framed every corner of the area. It was their main camping space. They had been playing in these woods since they were kids and now, all of those memories could become ash.

To the left of the woods was barren land of archaeological importance. During the summer months, archaeologists worked near daily uncovering remains. Thankfully, now was not a popular time for camping or working there.

Standing next to her car, Mina nearly cried at the thought of all of those memories burning. But she was older now and she could deal with it. Right?

They're not so important now.

She told herself this in order to prevent the teardrops.

Slowly, almost dreadfully, regretfully, she opened the door to the passenger side of her vehicle. Grabbing her bag off the seat, she shut the door and then unlocked the trunk, retrieving the two bags of wood. Marching forward, she followed the path she knew so well. The darkness did not bother her. Surprisingly, she felt no fear. All she felt was the dread of the future she intended to create.

Inside the wooded pathway, her world grew darker with each step. Colorful images- memories haunted her at every turn. There, just a few feet ahead of her was the large tree Scott would hide behind when he wanted to scare her. Sometimes Jesse would steal Scott's place behind the tree. They took turns, thinking their joke was so great. Even though she knew where they hid, they still succeeded in surprising her most of the time.

She sighed and pushed the memories away. She asked for blankness of mind as she stared around the dark scene.

Twenty minutes into her walk, she stopped. By her estimate, she was now nearly a mile into the woods. She was not yet far enough to prevent it from consuming the town.

Mina continued walking, with two bags slung over her shoulder, the other one dangling in her clutched right hand. The load grew heavier with each step.

Ten minutes later, she stopped again.

She was almost to the point of their favorite set-up, where the four of them loved to camp out at. But she just couldn't bear to start the fire there.

***

Scott looked at the clock on his console above the compact disc player in his car.

It registered 7:50 PM.

"Huh," he said loudly to himself, "About ten more miles to go. I told Mina it would only take five hours."

Scott looked at his speedometer. Currently, it registered 75 miles per hour. That was much slower than what he had been doing.

170

He only stopped once for a restroom break and to grab a pop and chips. Then he had to make up for that by driving faster.

"Only a few more minutes," he reassured himself.

Adrenaline and excitement kept him from fatigue.

***

Finally, Mina found a place to set up.

Branching off from the path she had taken was a small clearing, just big enough to fit a tent. Small bushes and trees hung over this spot, making it an easy catch. Mina threw down the bags of firewood. Reaching into her other bag, she pulled out her flashlight, zipped it up again and threw it onto a level spot of ground so that it wouldn't roll.

Kneeling down, she unzipped the bag of firewood. She found a relatively dry spot of ground. Rocks, she needed rocks. Mina searched for large rocks. Finding some, which were not quite large enough, though workable, she dug and picked them out of the ground, holding the flashlight under her armpit. Carrying them to her chosen spot, she laid the rocks to form a circular pattern. Needing just a few more, she searched the ground again, resulting in the same pattern of movement.

After her circle was complete, she dug into the unzipped bag, carefully removing the logs, one at a time. The first three she laid flat against the outline of the rocks, only in a triangular pattern. The next two, she stood straight into the air, leaning them against each other to form a triangle. She did the same with two more across the two, which leaned together. Digging into her other bag, she pulled out some newspapers. Crinkling them into a ball, she moved one of the logs out to fit the newspapers in the center, needing the paper for initial ignition of the flame.

"Good enough for now," she said.

Picking up her bag of wood and newspapers, Mina searched for another location to build a pile.

***

Scott rang the door bell of what appeared to be a nice home, though neglected in the same lack of time and care in which Ryan's home had become.

His nerves began to replace the excitement he felt on the drive. Before, they had spoken with younger people. What if this woman was unwilling to talk?

The door opened quickly inward as though she was expecting company. A middle-aged woman, with a medium build and straight brown hair stood in the door. Her face was streaked with worry lines and she appeared as if she was afraid to laugh.

"Can I help you?" she asked.

A glass screen door separated them. A friendly, though unmistakably stern tone reigned in her voice.

"Yes, Mrs. Adams?" he asked.

"That's me, but if you're selling, I'm not buying," she replied.

"No," Scott said, "No selling, no scams, I just, would like to talk with you about something if you have the time."

"About what?" she asked, her eyes darting around uneasily, "Do I even know you?"

"I've come from a relatively far place," Scott began, "My friend and I, well, we're trying to solve a case, a mystery that has caused many deaths and trauma to more people than we even know about."

The woman's face changed, darkening around the corners.

"This is about Mike, isn't it?" she asked.

"Your husband, yes," Scott said.

She studied him, searching for a clue to his motivations.

"Why is this your interest? You look like you just came out of high school. You aren't with a paper or some tabloid or something, are you?" she asked.

"No, not at all," he said hurriedly, "Mainly, I'm helping a friend. It was her idea."

"Why? What interest do you have in this?" the woman inquired, "Why my husband?"

Scott's pale pallor felt the flush.

"Well, because, we're almost sure we know what happened and it's not what they wrote in the paper," he said.

He studied her face. She gasped. A far away look appeared in her eyes, as though she saw something different but ever so close. Now, Scott knew that she had seen it. His test worked.

Regaining herself, she studied him over.

She said, "I don't think you know what you're talking about."

Simultaneously, she stepped backwards, slowly beginning to shut the door in front of her.

Scott became frantic.

"Wait!" he yelled, "Don't you want to know what happened?"

"I know what happened," she replied, "My husband died in a fire."

She continued her slow pursuit of shutting him out.

"But what was in the fire? What did you see?" he asked.

His voice was growing even more desperate now.

The woman stopped. Through a small crack between the door and the frame, she looked out at him in silence.

"How do I know that's what you're here about?" she asked.

"I wouldn't know that much," Scott gasped, "If I didn't know even more. Please. We just need to solve this."

After pausing a few more moments, just searching his face for honesty, she said, "The kids are asleep, don't be loud."

She opened the door, pushing the glass screen door outward towards him. Scott grabbed the door, following her into the home. Inside, the home appeared much nicer than the exterior. It had a womanly, motherly touch of matching curtains, rugs and sofas in a light shade of blue. Pleasantly framed pictures of flowers hung in various corners of the room.

The woman eyed him suspiciously before sitting on the couch. Scott took a place on a wicker chair diagonal from her.

"Well?" she asked.

Scott leaned forward.

"Can you tell me what happened that night? What you really saw? It would help us solve the case," Scott said.

The woman sighed and looked him over. Apparently deciding he looked safe enough, she continued.

"Sure, I can tell you. As long as this doesn't become some sort of story in a wacky paper. They'll think I'm crazy and take my kids away from me if you do. I can't have that. They're all the strength I've got now," she said.

Seriousness graced her face. Scott shook his head.

"I wouldn't do anything like that," he said.

Although, he was quite unsure about Mina's plans for proving the existence of the creature. Suddenly he had a thought that opened his eyes.

Knowing Mina, she might still go to extremes to achieve results.

***

Mina found another location just a few feet away from the last pile of wood. With the same method, she quickly built another stack with the firewood and papers.

One more, she thought to herself.

That was all that she had enough wood for. The first two piles had taken 7 logs each. The last pile would be slightly larger.

Searching for an opportune location, a spot that would ensure the greatest chance of a large blaze, she found another place where dry leaves hung low from trees and bushes or plants framed the area. Building her last pile, she stood back, envying her job, before returning to the location of the first woodpile.

Reaching into her final bag, Mina pulled out the lighter fluid, matches, her lighter and the camera. Putting the matches and lighter in her pocket and setting down the lighter fluid, she stood with the camera in hand. A flashlight in her other hand, she shone the light so that it pointed directly at the location of the first woodpile. Though the camera had a light on it, she wanted the best picture possible. Turning the camera on, she began to speak her narration without showing her face.

"Forgive me for the damage I am about to cause, but it is all for good reason. I believe there is a demon that exists and emerges only in places where fire, forest fire burns the grounds of Mother Nature. This recording is to let society know that this creature exists so that many people can quit living in misery from traumatic events that occurred in their lives..."

She paused briefly in her narration before beginning again.

"I began this project no more than two weeks ago. I have talked with survivors as well as researched. All of my papers and documents are in the top drawer of my computer desk, along with a notebook dedicated specifically to this case..."

She paused again and then put the camera up to her face.

"My name is Mina Clyne. I am not much of a talker, so I'm going to begin now and you can watch," she finished.

Simultaneously, she moved the camera back to her woodpiles, slowly sinking to the ground with the camera level with her face. She reached for the lighter fluid. Grabbing the lighter fluid bottle, she squirted it in a circular motion over the pile, making sure the wood and newspapers were sufficiently wet, but not doused too much.

Then she reached into her pocket for the lighter.

***

After some natural trepidation, the woman began to tell her story to Scott. She took a deep breath, just as all the others had before they began.

"We went camping, as always. We always drove an RV. It was much more comfortable for the kids, plus they were so young. We didn't want to risk wild animals at night," she began.

Scott listened patiently, absorbing her words, though he felt like something wasn't right somewhere else. He pushed those thoughts away, letting them linger in the back of his mind.

"We always had a fire to roast marshmallows, hot dogs, we even cooked burgers with a rack over the fire. It tasted better that way," she continued.

A small smile crept over her face. The distant look in her eyes came back again.

"What happened that day with the fire?" Scott asked.

She shook her head back and forth.

"I kept arguing with him. Our usual fire spot, well someone had taken away the stones we built there. They were always there, every year except that one. He decided it was time for a change. He wanted to build the fire closer to the woods so that it wasn't near the camper. It would also be easier to scare the kids during story time too. We built a fire early in the day to cook with but he put it out, since there was still a lot of daylight left," she continued.

Her mind ran off in thought as she remembered that day.

"I told him it was too close to the woods," she said, her eyes seemed to glaze over, "Too close to the woods," she repeated.

She stopped. The woman sat quietly, building up the strength to continue. Scott wanted to know. He waited for her to speak.

"That night, when it was dark, we had our marshmallows ready. We sat next to the fire, roasting them as dad told the kids stories," she stopped again, "The kids had to use the bathroom so I went to take them in. But before that, the wind started blowing hard. I told him to put the fire out. I kept telling him to put the fire out. It was time to go to bed. And it was our last night there," she said.

She paused again.

"When I was in the bathroom with the kids, I heard the wind beating against the camper. I hoped he put the fire out and would come in for the night. When the kids were done, I was tucking them into bed when I heard yelling. It was Mike yelling but it sounded like the wind it was howling and screeching so loud. I had no idea what he was yelling about," she said, pausing again, "I told the kids to stay put in bed."

She trembled in her seat, quivering from an unknown cold. Her voice began to shake.

"When I got to the window, I saw that the fire had spread. It had latched onto the trees. I told him it was too close to the woods. All day I told him that," she said, shaking her head before continuing, "Mike had taken off his shirt and was trying to put it out. But it spread so darn quickly; I was watching and I can't even describe how fast it went. It was a dry summer but I never expected that. No one ever does," she trailed off.

"What did you do next?" Scott asked.

"I ran out to try to help him, but..." she stopped.

"But what?" Scott asked.

The woman flinched as if she'd been slapped on the hand. Instantly she started crying. The tears dropped so quickly down her face. This was becoming a natural visual to him after seeing the traumatized survivors. Still, Scott felt guilt for his persistence. But he knew it was better for her to let out the truth. He was probably one of the first people to listen to her telling what really happened.

She wiped her eyes.

"I think about it every day, how close I was," she mumbled.

Stopping, her face reddened with the tears and pain of thoughts from that night.

"I was so close to saving him and yet so close to my own death. And those kids never would have survived on their own," she said.

It was obvious to Scott that she was rationalizing; she had blamed herself for not being able to save him.

"There was nothing you could do," Scott said, trying to comfort her, "What happened, exactly, after you saw the fire?"

"I made it out the camper door. Already three trees had caught fire by then. I started to yell for him to come on, it was moving too fast. But he kept trying to put it out. We had to get out of there. He turned around, but just as he did, out of the fire, something just came..." she said.

Now she was shaking hard, her body vibrating at the memory.

"What was it?" Scott asked.

Tears in her eyes, she looked up incredulously, "It was brown or gray, it...it looked like a...a...demon," she said, rushing the words out, "I, I, mean I never saw one before, except in pictures and movies but that is what it was...a...a...demon," she stuttered.

Great fear rose within her. Her stomach seemed to tighten into knots and her body began to quiver and shake.

Scott's curiosity was full blown. He leaned further forward.

"What did it do?" Scott asked, "How did it attack?"

"It just shot out of nowhere and took him with it. He was gone, he went down, and he just blew away. He was a person before, but now...now...he was part of the ground. I watched his face..."

The tears resurfaced, harder now, forcing tremors through her body.

"His face..." she said.

She quivered uncontrollably. Scott didn't know how to stabilize her. He feared she would have a seizure; the emotions were so intense for her.

"I'm sorry," he said.

Silence surrounded them. Tears and shakes spewed forth from her for a great while. But slowly she began to calm.

He wanted to comfort her, but suddenly he was concerned about Mina. Why wouldn't she come with him on her own case? Thoughts of her extremist ways finally dawned on him.

***

After digging out her lighter, Mina paused for a long while, contemplating whether or not to move forward. She didn't have to do this. The legal and moral ramifications ran through her. If she didn't die here, Scott would kill her for trying such a stunt. Sudden fear eclipsed her.

Perhaps I have lost touch with reality, she thought to herself.

Did she really want to go out this way? Was this really worth her own life?

Mina shut off the camera.

She kneeled on the ground next to a pile, contemplating her decision. Would she be able to go on, knowing she had given up an opportunity to see the supernatural in its true form? Would she wonder forever about this day with regret? Would she prefer to live than die for a cause? She was no martyr.

After a few minutes of debating, she made an agreement with herself. She was already there and she was already ready. She might as well do it. But if she didn't see anything within six minutes of all fires flaming, she would go home. She chose six, because allegedly that was the number of such evil beasts.

Turning the camera back on and with her flashlight following her, Mina lit the first fire. It ignited quickly, the flames reaching as tall as the wood within it, flicking even higher above its top. Silently she prided herself on her fire starting skills. Recording the flames to the camera, she moved on to the next pile. The quicker she moved the better.

178

***

After the shaking and the tears had died down, the woman began again with her story.

"I got back in the camper and drove off, leaving him there," she started, "The kids were screaming the whole entire time. I drove like a maniac down the hills. The whole time, they were screaming for their daddy and me and I couldn't comfort them, I was in too bad of a shock. I tried to think rationally despite the shock. I had the little ones. I had to maintain my sanity as well as theirs. For them…" she said.

Scott fidgeted in his seat, but still listened intently as she continued again.

"I went to the police station, told them the fire started and that my husband was missing," she said, "They quickly sent people out there. But I knew it was too late. I held my kids tightly in the station. Eventually, everyone assumed that the fire had gotten him. I was the only one who knew what really happened," her voice trembled, "I only told one person, my sister. She thought I was just in shock and that I imagined seeing things. I knew no one would believe me, so I never told another soul until now," she said.

She eyed him. Looking at Scott with a desperate mixture of sadness and confusion, she asked, "I'm not crazy, am I?"

Scott shook his head.

"No, you are not crazy at all. What you saw that night is real. And you're not the only one who has suffered from it. My friend and I are going to solve this, and a lot of people will be able to speak the truth," Scott assured her, seeing this as his way out, "I thank you very much for talking to me today," he said, moving closer to her, "I know it was hard for you."

He reached in his pocket for a piece of paper he had scribbled his name and phone number on before he got there, just in case she didn't want to talk.

The woman looked down at the paper. Scott continued.

"That is so you can call me. When we solve this, I can fill you in on what happens. Call in a couple days for an update. You

179

shouldn't have to suffer like this, never knowing, never camping again. We're going to try to stop this thing, whatever it may be, before it can hurt anyone else," Scott said.

"Thank you," she said.

She looked up at the younger man. Scott could see in her eyes that she needed someone to confide in for so long.

"I have to go," Scott said, looking at his watch, "It takes a long time for me to get home and there is a lot of research to finish. Please keep in touch."

The sincerity rose in his voice. Scott moved to the door quickly.

Looking at the paper again, observing his name, which she had not initially known, she said, "Scott."

He turned around quickly.

"Thank you," she said.

"You're welcome," he said.

He nodded. Without hesitation, he walked out the door.

In his car, Scott picked up his cell phone. It registered 'OUT OF RANGE' across the screen.

"Shit," he said.

Scott suddenly knew Mina was up to something. He had suspicions before but was in too much of a rush to question her. He had to find a payphone and fast.

***

Mina was starting up the third and final pile. The second one had been stubborn and wouldn't stay lit. She blamed the wind. It was that same wind that was already helping her first fire spread.

Kneeling next to the third fire, Mina's lighter wouldn't light.

"Shit," she said, "I can't be out of fluid, I barely use this," she continued aloud, realizing she had caught that on tape.

Shaking the lighter, she tried it once again. This time it lit.

All right, she thought, forcing the newspapers to accept her flame. This fire started even slower than the second one. She fiddled with it, camera in one hand, lighter in the other.

180

***

At a gas station, Scott put coin after coin into the phone. Calling Mina's cell phone, he hung up before voicemail came on. Like usual, her cell wasn't on. He quickly dialed her house. Her mother picked up the phone.

"Is Mina there?" he asked.

"Scott?" she asked, "No she's not home yet."

"How long has she been gone?" Scott asked.

"A couple hours at least," her mom answered.

Her voice was unconcerned. She was used to her daughter's sporadic disappearances.

"Do you know where she is?" he asked.

"She just said she was running out. She's probably with the rest of the boys," she said.

"Okay. Thanks," Scott said.

He quickly hung up.

There was no use alerting her mother, especially since he didn't even know what she was doing, if anything. His worries might not even be accurate.

Scott piled coin after coin in again. The phone rang. Ryan answered.

"Ryan," Scott began, "Have you seen Mina today?"

"No, not at all. She never even called me back. Is everything ok?" he asked.

Worry ran rampant in his voice.

"Yeah," Scott lied, "I'll call you later."

He hung up the phone before Ryan could question further.

One more call.

But he had to rush into the shop to get more change and then hurry back out. Quickly, he dialed the numbers.

"Jesse," Scott said.

Jesse laughed in his trademark way.

"What's up goober, you never called me back earlier," he said.

"Hey," Scott began, "Sorry, but have you seen Mina today?"

Jesse made kissing noises on the other end of the phone.

"Scott and Mina sitting in a..." he began.

Scott rolled his eyes.

"Jesse just answer me!" he hollered.

"Yeah, geez man. What's your problem?" Jesse asked.

Ignoring him, Scott continued, "When did you see her?"

"You know, she gets weirder and weirder all the time. She was standing in my back yard. I saw her through the window so I invited her up for dinner," he said.

A sudden realization dawned on Scott.

"Jesse, do you still have firewood in your backyard?"

"Yeah, duh, we have it all year round," he answered.

"Shit!" Scott screeched.

His heart raced with ravenous, nervous fear. The tension in his voice rose even higher.

"How long ago did she leave?" he asked.

"Maybe an hour ago, I guess. What's wrong?" Jesse asked.

"Just do me a favor," Scott began, "Drive around to our usual places and look for Mina's car. Go close to the woods. If you see her make sure you stay with her. Don't let her out of your sight," Scott said.

"What?" Jesse asked.

All obnoxiousness grew obsolete from his voice. Now, he was filled with curiosity.

"Just do it, it's very important. I'm far away and I'll tell you everything when I get back," he promised.

"Fine," Jesse said.

The disappointment in his voice rang thick. He didn't really want to do it. But he knew Scott had no other option.

Scott hung up the phone, running back to his car. He had to get back fast. Much faster than he wanted to.

***

Mina's third fire spun out of control with the first two. Trees quickly began to catch. She stood mesmerized by the way the flames flicked and licked upon each other, encircling one another, crowding each other in an orgy of enchanting lights.

182

Mina moved slowly away from the fires, closer to the path to the road. She set the camera down on the ground behind her, pointing it towards the fires. She crouched off to the side in front of the camera, kneeling there, watching the endless fury of the flames.

She looked back at the camera. If something happened to her, she wanted it to be seen.

CHAPTER 16:
LEFT IN THE DARK

With dread, Jesse grabbed his jacket, ready to search for Mina. He didn't know why he had been assigned to do it; he certainly didn't want to. He just knew that Scott had a tone of urgency in his voice.

What the hell were they getting themselves into? And why had Scott asked about firewood? Maybe Scott was becoming just as crazy as Mina.

Just as he was leaving, the phone rang.

"Damn it," Jesse said.

But he picked it up anyway. He was unable to mask his irritation.

"What?"

On the other end, Ryan's worried voice drifted into his ear. "Jesse?"

"Hey, I'm in a hurry," Jesse said.

"Did Scott call you about Mina?" Ryan asked.

"Yeah, I'm going to look for her car now," he said.

"What?" Ryan asked.

"I just have to go," Jesse said.

He hung up the phone immediately. Scott never really asked anyone to do him a favor, so it must be an important one. Without hesitation, Jesse ran to his car.

Before he made it there, a thought occurred to him. He quickly ran over to the pile of wood. Easily lifting the tarp, he could tell that someone had been in it. It also looked as though they had tried to fix it so that it would look normal. But they had forgotten to secure the tarp in the same way his family did.

"Why would Mina steal our firewood?" he asked.

Jesse decided she must be doing something she wanted to keep secret from all of them if she couldn't even ask for the wood.

Running back to his car, he thought of how Scott told him to check the woods. Why would she go camping by herself? She took a lot of wood, almost as though she intended to stay for a couple days. Alone? What fun would that be?

Driving toward the park he tried to figure out this mess. He thought of the cases Scott had given to him and Ryan. Then he thought of how they left for a couple days. In those cases, there were fires. Something in his brain clicked.

"Oh no," he muttered.

He really hoped she wasn't stupid enough to experiment with fire. Suddenly he began speeding. It would only take him a few more minutes to get to the park.

***

The six-minute countdown had just begun. Feeling the heat of the fire behind her, she slowly inched closer down the path towards the road. Each time, she had to change the place of the camera. With each movement, she peered behind her to see if the demon monster was in sight. All that she saw was the dreadful fire she had created, tearing into the beauty of nature.

Though she desperately wanted to see the creature, the fire itself held a certain beauty. But she couldn't bear staring at it for too long, knowing guiltily that she had started it.

Mina looked at her watch.

"Only five more minutes," she said.

She knew those minutes would quickly pass.

Mina set the camera down behind her again, as she turned to face the fire. Sweat dripped from her face and body as the flames, though a few feet away, pushed off its heat with deadly intensity.

Mina sat in silence, without moving. The fire wasn't moving so fast towards her, which she found to be a relief. Nervously looking at her watch, she realized another minute went by. Gripping her bag tightly, she prepared herself to move backwards again. Peering upward, beyond the trees, Mina noticed an immense smoke and fog building high above her. Thick walls of smoke prevented her from seeing the stars in the sky she so often admired.

Her heart started to race into a frenzy. The fog was a sign.

Another few minutes, she thought to herself, looking at her watch.

Mina continued to look around, trying to be fearless, storing this night in her mind.

The night was so beautiful. Despite the dreadful fire she had started, it still somehow seemed to light up the night, to almost scare away any monsters, rather than bring them out. But she needed to see this. Even if it scared her.

"Where are you?" she yelled incredulously, "I did this to see you!"

Silence filled the night besides the crackling sound of the fire devouring the wood. Crouching in the silence, watching, she wondered when it would come.

Mina looked at her watch again.

Over four minutes had passed now. Lifting the camera from the ground, she videotaped the fire, the smoke and the fog one last time. This evidence could be very incriminating if the demon did not appear. This would be her confession to the crime of arson.

Standing silently, staring blankly, what she had just done started to really sink in. Maybe she hadn't enough evidence to have taken this step. Perhaps the third case might have held a different theory. If it was true, she allowed impatience to rule her mind, rather than rational thought. And everything she did tonight was in vain.

Flames fed their appetite on the dry leaves of the Arizona trees. Mina watched it silently grow, the crackling sound the only noise that haunted her ears.

Looking at her watch, it had been a little more than the six minutes. Slowly, she gathered her bag, turning to walk away. Listening as she walked, the fire seemed to squeal as if it itself were suffering the pain of being burned alive. Turning back around, camera in hand, she expected the demon, the monster to arise.

But nothing brewed there. Disappointed, it was just the flames. The smoke made no furrowing movement, no shape emerged, nothing. Nothing was visible but the light of the flames and the darkness of the night.

Turning around again with her head down, she ran the path to her car. Though disappointed, she knew she had to report the flames, to try to stop them before it was too late, before all of the woods burned away.

***

As Jesse was driving towards the park, he was just in time to see that a fire was quickly consuming some of the trees in the distance.

"Holy shit," he said.

He was still a far enough away but as he pulled closer to the woods, he saw Mina's car. It was where they always parked when they camped. Pulling behind it, he suddenly saw Mina come running out of the woods, seemingly oblivious to his vehicle.

"Mina!" he yelled.

Ignoring him, she jumped in her car and before he knew it, she was recklessly driving away. Jesse shook his head. She had to have seen or heard him. He followed her. What would compel her to start a damn fire? If she had done this, he was beyond disappointed in her.

Swerving carelessly, Mina drove like a drunkard. Jesse followed her in the same reckless manner, wanting to know why she had done it and to see if she was okay.

Mina finally pulled off to a gas station. She emerged from her car wearing a black sweatshirt with a hood covering her face. She went directly to a pay phone. Jesse followed her over to it. When he got to her, he realized what she was there to do. She was already talking by the time he reached her.

"Yes, I saw a fire burning out of control at the Homolovi Ruins State Park," she said.

Jesse stood beside her quietly. She pretended he wasn't there.

"I don't know anything else, I just saw the fire. You have to put it out before it spreads more!" she yelled.

Angrily, she hung up the phone.

Quickly turning, she began to walk away from Jesse. But Jesse stood directly in front of her, stopping her in her tracks.

She didn't look at him.

"What?" she asked.

"You know what. Why did you do that?" he asked.

"It's a long story and it's too bright here," she said.

She pushed past him, moving towards her car. There was no patience in his voice.

"Meet me at my house or I'm turning you in," he said.

Mina stopped but didn't turn to face him.

"You wouldn't..." she whispered.

"I would," he said, "Meet me there. You have no other choice."

"Fine," she said.

She got in her car, quickly speeding away. Jesse followed behind her.

Outside his house, he studied her. But she wouldn't look up and she wouldn't hold his gaze. He noticed she was dirty from her venture in the woods. She reeked of smoke. It was obvious that she had been around fire and it was very incriminating.

"Follow me. Fast," Jesse demanded.

Marching up the stairs to his room, Jesse was glad his parents were enjoying a movie in the living room. At the top of the stairs, he pointed towards his bedroom. She complied. He followed closely behind. Walking over to his closet, he spoke.

"You're dirty and you smell. You need to take a shower," he demanded.

He retrieved a towel from his closet and threw it at her. Mina stared at him with her eyes open wide in disbelief.

"I thought you were turning me in," she said.

"Go take a shower. Do you want to walk around full of evidence?" he asked.

Mina turned away, walking slowly down the hall to the bathroom. She was still in partial shock at what she had done. In the bathroom, she locked the door, staring at herself in the mirror in silence. Her visage had taken on a crazy, ghostly look. Like Brandon, she was just like him now. Only she just killed a forest, not herself. But she was too numb to cry.

Taking off her soiled clothes, she set the water in the shower to mostly cold. She felt like she was overheating, burning from her inside core to her outer shell. Stepping in, the cold water felt good against her skin. It almost cooled her down but instead she felt too numb all of a sudden.

In his bedroom, Jesse grabbed Mina's keys from his dresser. He was glad she always set them there. He hurried out to her car. He didn't know how long she would be in the shower, but hopefully long enough for him to find the remnants of her crime. Unfortunately, he was going to help her cover this up.

***

Bobby drove on. His destination was still many hours away. And Mina had absolutely no clue that he was coming. Wouldn't she be surprised?

The monotony of the highway tired him more than he had expected. He left a couple hours after she hung up on him, somewhere around noon. The hours all blended together by now. He sort of wished he had another driver. He wasn't used to this at all anymore.

But Bobby knew that Mina wanted him there. He wanted to help her find this beast. And after their night in the woods, he decided he wasn't scared anymore.

Bobby's clock read 9 PM.

He should drive at least halfway before getting a hotel, if he did. He had a little bit of money stashed away for a long time, for a time when this day would come. He knew that eventually he would leave the solitude of his home.

Yawning, Bobby drove on endlessly for what seemed like an eternity.

***

Scott sped the darkened highway reaching up to 100 miles per hour. It had only been half an hour or more since he talked to Jesse. Hell, he didn't know anymore. All he knew was that he was glad the highways were nearly barren at this time. He never reached this high of a speed before. Then again, he never really had to.

"What the hell is she up to?" he asked.

Somehow, he knew what she was up to; he just didn't want to admit it. After all the lecturing he had given her about not becoming obsessed. Though he should have known from the beginning what steps she would take to achieve results. Just like Brandon...

Mina was never the type of girl to sit around and wait for information. She always brought the results to herself.

***

Jesse found the bag with supplies in Mina's car. Just the smell of it showed she had been in those fiery woods. The only thing left in the bag was her digital camera. Locking up her car, Scott unlocked her trunk. Small fragments of wood chippings were visible within the carpeting.

"Yup, she stole wood," he said aloud, "She can clean that up."

He shut the trunk and carried her bag into the house.

***

Mina stepped out of the shower, dripping wet, cold and shivering. Her mind tumbled between what she just did, her research and how she hadn't seen the demon. Goose bumps framed her shivering body, though she was oblivious to it. She was in an entirely different existence. Mindlessly wiping her body with the towel, she looked at the dirty clothes in a pile by the floor. Picking up her shirt, she smelled it. The pungent scent burned her nostrils.

"Smoke," she said.

That scent was a wake-up call.

She had committed a crime.

She committed a crime that could get her in a lot of trouble. It finally registered in her brain, the importance of what she had done. And for nothing, absolutely nothing. All those memories, those camping memories, sadly, she thought to herself. Burned, all burned. Mina dropped her shirt back into the pile.

With her towel wrapped around her, she opened the bathroom door. She poked her head out to make sure no one was coming. Running to Jesse's room, she heard footsteps coming up the stairs. Hurriedly, she ran into his room, pushing the door almost shut. Jesse came through it seconds later, carrying the bag from her car.

Staring in disbelief, eyes open wide, Mina looked over Jesse.

"You went through my car?"

Jesse's face formed into the meanest smirk she had ever seen. His obnoxiousness was raked over by his anger. And even then she could tell he was restraining himself.

"Okay," Jesse began, "I don't know about you Mina, but if I were in your situation, I'd be thanking me for doing this. But I guess you're too crazy to comprehend anything right now. Now where are your clothes?"

"In the bathroom," she said, still in disbelief.

She had never seen Jesse so serious before.

Jesse went to his closet again. This time, he pulled out a button down shirt and sweatpants. He threw them on the bed.

"These might be too big for you, but you need something," he said.

Jesse walked towards the door.

Mina hurriedly looked up.

"Jesse," she began, waiting until he stopped and then pausing for just another moment, "Thank you."

Jesse never turned around. He walked away.

He was helping his friend cover up a crime. He didn't really want to be thanked. Really he didn't want to be involved at all. Now it was too late. He couldn't change that and had taken on the responsibility when he found her.

Grabbing her clothes out of the bathroom, Jesse made his way to the basement. He never did laundry. He barely knew how. Luckily, he had watched his mother a few times.

Gently taking the camera out of the bag, Jesse set it on a folding table next to the dryer. Then, he threw her clothes and the bag into the washing machine. Deciding it was a really strong scent of smoke and fire, he put two cups of detergent in with the small load. He put the temperature on hot, started it up and then headed back upstairs.

In his room, Mina had dressed and was sitting quietly on his bed. She had the look of a child ready to be punished across her face.

Jesse said nothing. Mina stared at him until he spoke.

"Why?" he asked.

Mina said nothing. Her eyes dropped to stare at the floor.

Jesse grew impatient.

"Okay," he tried again, "Why did you steal our wood? We would have given you some, had you asked."

"No one could know," she whispered.

Jesse scoffed.

"So where is Scott?" he asked.

She fidgeted.

"He's away," she said.

"I fucking know he's away, but where is he and what is he doing? Why the fuck did he call me to check up on you?" he asked.

Apparently, the two were entangled in some mess they had hidden from him and Ryan.

"So he knew?" she asked quietly, "He figured it out, why I didn't go."

She nervously intertwined her fingers.

"Obviously he knew something, something I don't know, or Ryan," he started, "But you said he was sick. Hmph. Well he did say he'd tell me when he got back, so why don't you start off?"

Mina didn't look up at him as she spoke.

"It was just a case that went too far. I learned my lesson. I know better now," she said.

"You better, after you burned our camping spot to the fucking ground!" he shouted.

Mina realized that her task affected the others as well. Her guilt suddenly became a heavier burden. Jesse's anger multiplied.

"Just like fucking...you know who, you get too fucking caught up in shit, then you cause destruction. You could have been killed. Then you would have done the same thing as your little best friend. How many times have we warned you? How many more times do we have to?" he scolded.

Mina sat in silence, taking what she deserved.

She blinked furiously before she began to speak, to tell him all that occurred.

"We took on the case, the first one, the missing people, the fire deaths. But these weren't fully fire deaths, there was a demon in the fire," she started.

Jesse stared at her in disbelief.

"You're crazy," he said, "You're seriously crazy."

"Just listen Jesse!" Mina shouted, "It's true. Scott and I talked to people about their experiences and it's true. They saw it. Even Bobby, this nice guy I met, it ruined their lives. They saw something so intangible, something we all have nightmares about. It hurt them. I wanted to find it and tape it and show these people that they're not crazy, that it exists. I wanted to see the supernatural, in its whole form. But it just didn't come."

The disappointment in her voice was thick. Jesse shook his head.

"So you lit the fire, now a forest fire, as a project of research to see a demon that only a few people saw?" Jesse asked.

"Yes," she admitted.

"Something you have never seen before and you took people's word on it?" Jesse questioned her.

"No," she said, "Scott and I both saw it along the side of the road. I don't know what made me turn around that day, but I did. A woman's car caught fire and the demon seemed to rise from the smoke. The fog settled in, then it was extinguished," she said.

Her eyes drifted back to that day, the early hours of that morning.

Jesse shook his head, unbelieving.

"I think you need some rest until Scott comes back," he said.

"Do you think Scott would have gone over five hours away if he didn't believe too?" she asked.

"I suppose not, but, knowing how you've been acting lately, you could have tricked him and probably did," he said.

Hurt filled her eyes, though tears did not.

In that moment, Jesse hated talking to her that way, but she was reckless. She used her intelligence in a much more dangerous manner than any of them, even him.

"Take a nap, I have your car keys. When Scott gets back, I'm sure he'll call or stop by," Jesse said.

He turned out the lights before leaving the room.

Wandering into the living room, he plopped in front of the television with his parents as if nothing had happened at all.

***

193

Scott constantly checked his watch for the time. Looking at his cell phone, he noticed he had no messages. Either Jesse couldn't find her, it was too late, or she was ok. Damn him for being so stupid. He knew she was up to something, he just didn't know what.

Scott glanced at the clock again. Nearly another half an hour had gone by and he was on the fast track home. He estimated he would be home around 12:30 or 1 AM. The sooner the better.

***

In Jesse's room, Mina was too wide awake with adrenaline and her constantly rambling thoughts to sleep. She considered jogging to her house. It wasn't far away, but it would look suspicious with her car out here and her at home. She dreaded having to tell Jesse everything, though knew it would have to happen eventually.

She laid there in the darkness with nothing to do but stare at the sparse street light that glimmered in through the window. Somehow, her mind inevitably let go of the case, of her friends, of the demon and the fire. Mina finally drifted off into a nightmare-plagued sleep.

Tossing and turning, Mina woke up several times within the next few hours. Drenched in sweat, the demon was now in her dreams. She hadn't seen it in reality again, but it seemed to want to forever haunt her at night.

***

Jesse watched another movie to pass the time. His parents had gone to bed and he enjoyed the time alone.

Around midnight, Jesse decided to call Scott to see where he was.

***

Nearly lost in the boringness of the night, Scott almost drifted off into a deep sleep as he drove. Not even noticing the time, or that he was back in range with his phone, he felt his brain giving in to the monotony of the drive. Constantly, he tried to force himself awake, though it was becoming more and more difficult. His eyes fluttered, his brain trying to shut him down completely.

Ring...ring...

Scott's phone acted almost like an alarm clock. He was suddenly alerted, grasping on the passenger seat for the phone. Observing that it was Jesse, he anxiously answered it.

"What's going on? Did you find her?" Scott asked.

"Yeah, I found her causing trouble," Jesse said.

Scott read the tone of his voice. Nervous tension rose in his chest, clutching him with stress. Dread followed along, pulling at the corners of his fears.

"What did she do?" he asked.

"I'll tell you when you get here," Jesse replied.

Dread built up even further within Scott. Based on Jesse's tone, he knew it was bad.

"All right," Scott said, swallowing hard.

Silence intermingled between them for a moment.

"Scott?" Jesse asked, "Did you see some demon or something?"

Scott paused, unsure how to answer.

"I'm not sure what I saw, but it wasn't right. It wasn't normal at all," he said.

"Okay," Jesse said, "When will you be here?"

"Probably about an hour," he responded.

Silence grappled them again. Scott felt his inner guilt grow talons that captured him and then began to feast upon his insides.

"Hey Jesse," he paused, "thanks a lot man."

"Yeah," Jesse replied.

Scott understood his bitter tone.

"If it makes you feel better, you just saved my life," he said, "I nearly fell asleep at 100 miles an hour."

"Be careful," Jesse replied.

Another blunt response. The coldness in Jesse's voice only grew with each word. It only made Scott feel more vulnerable.

"I'm guessing you saved two lives today," Scott said.

It flattered Jesse to hear such compliments from a friend he respected, but he was too pissed off at their secrecy and subtle lies to accept it.

"Yup," Jesse said.

He hung up the phone. Scott drove on.

It wouldn't be long before he was in his hometown.

***

Bobby was exceptionally tired. He debated pulling off the side of the road to sleep, to save money on a hotel room. Cops would stop and bother him though, especially with his long hair.

But his tiredness caused him not to care.

"Fuck it," he said.

He needed some sleep. He pulled his car off the highway, quickly finding a back road.

Using a white sock from his bag, he rolled his window down just enough to push the sock halfway through. Then he rolled it back up to clutch the sock and keep it in place. That way, they would assume the car had broken down and the owner would pick it up the next day.

Moving down in his seat, Bobby leaned his head over to the passenger side. His arms acted as a second pillow to his head, besides the bag that joined him on the passenger seat. Looking up, he made sure no one could see him in passing.

Just a few hours, he thought to himself, before he quickly drifted off into a deep sleep.

It was midnight when the dreams overtook him. The demon came back for him, only this time it haunted his sleeping self. In just an hour's time, he was sweating profusely.

***

Mina tossed and turned between sleep and consciousness. Her nightmares were more vivid than they had ever been, more scary, more haunting. She slept between intervals of fear, provoked by the demon and the guilt within her mind.

***

Scott arrived at Jesse's an hour later. He rushed up the stairs, finding hidden adrenaline despite his stiffened body. The door opened before he reached the top of the porch. Jesse stood there, a stern look across his face, one of which Scott had rarely seen on him in all those years.

"She started a fire," he said.

Scott shook his head.

"Damn it. I knew it," he said.

"Let's wake her up," Jesse said.

Together, they quietly marched up the stairs to his room. Jesse opened the door and turned on the light. But Scott and Jesse stopped in their tracks, staring at Mina. She was violently tossing her head. Her face was drenched with sweat.

"Mina," Scott said, rushing over to the bed, "Did she get hurt?"

"Just mentally," Jesse responded.

Contaminated coldness was contained in his voice.

Mina's head rolled as though she was in a trance of some sort.

"Mina," Scott repeated.

He shook her, trying to awaken her. But her nightmare continued to take hold.

"Damn it Mina! Wake the fuck up!" Scott shouted.

No dream could be that intense. Mina's eyes bolted open as she awakened and sat up with a sudden jump. Her eyes jumped from Scott to Jesse. Those innocent eyes had a new, crazily deepened fear in them. Jesse and Scott stared back at the disoriented person in front of them. The fear in her eyes was so great that it burdened each of them, in separate ways.

"Mina are you okay?" Scott asked.

Breathing heavily, she replied, "Yeah."

"What happened tonight?" Scott asked.

Mina dropped back onto the bed again. Looking at the ceiling, she remained quiet for a moment before responding. Reaching up, she wiped her hand across her forehead, feeling the dampness of sweat caused by her fear.

"I wanted to test the theory. We had completed every other step and the last one was to test it, so I did. And nothing happened," she said.

"You should have talked to me about it first," Scott said.

The scolding, the anger in his voice was unmistakable.

"You would have stopped me. It was better this way," she replied.

"Better?" Scott asked, "Huh."

He paced the space around the bed. Scott shook his head as he moved back and forth.

"I never should have helped. I thought I could help you," Scott said.

Jesse scoffed.

"No one had enough trust to involve me, I take it," Jesse said.

Mina shook her head.

"You wouldn't have believed, you or Ryan. Scott only involved himself because he didn't want me to get hurt. I'm the only one who ever truly believed," she said.

"Like Santa Claus," Jesse remarked.

Scott gave him a dirty look, "Let's not make this worse."

Jesse's nostrils seemed to flare.

"How can it get worse than this? She stole my wood, started a fire, tried to avoid me and I just washed her evidence. I think I deserve to say what I want," he replied.

"Where was the fire?" Scott asked.

The resentment in Jesse's voice grew stronger.

"Our spot. Where we go camping every year. Who knows how badly it has burned by now," Jesse commented.

The hurt in his voice overlapped the resentment. Mina shook her head.

"No. I didn't do it in our exact spot. I called the cops to put it out," Mina rationalized.

Jesse shook his head.

"Yeah, well do you know how long it takes to put out a forest fire? You could have been killed. This is crazy; you've been acting just like him. The only difference is you didn't start a fire for some dark higher power. You did it for yourself. You could have killed yourself too," he said, "You're seriously crazy enough that you should be locked away."

Mina blinked harshly, growing smaller and smaller with every word. Despite what she had done, Scott felt bad for her.

"No. Jesse, that's seriously enough. Look, I'm extremely tired. Mina looks that way too. Let's talk about this tomorrow afternoon when everyone settles down. There's no sense in ripping each other apart right now. We'll just go home like nothing happened, so it doesn't look suspicious," Scott said.

Scott always solved things in a pacifist manner and though Jesse was still angry he agreed to it. Jesse threw Mina's bag with her clothes at her, which he had even dried in the middle of his movie.

Mina went to the bathroom to change. Jesse and Scott remained in silence.

"Tomorrow, at noon, is that good Jesse?" Scott asked.

"Yeah," he muttered.

Mina returned to the room.

"Mina, be here at noon tomorrow," he said.

"Yeah," she responded drearily.

"I'll call Ryan tomorrow. He might as well know what's going on too," Scott said.

Mina and Scott left the house in silence. Outside, the smell of fire and smoke was growing thick in the air. A cloudy fog had drifted into the town. A mist dampened their vehicles. Although Scott worried for Mina, they parted ways, each going home to rest away an awful day.

Tomorrow, the whole pointless story would come to a head.

***

Bobby's nightmares seemed to resurge even stronger as he slept in his car. He tossed slightly, though it would have been more, had he more room.

Around 4AM, he awakened suddenly.

Looking around with initial disorientation, he remembered where he was. His dreams were so intense, he thought, wiping the sweat from above his eyes.

Sitting up to driving position, he stretched himself out. Although he was still tired, he decided he had had more than enough sleep. It was time to get back on the road. Starting up his car, he would just stop at the next rest station to get some caffeine.

Not counting anywhere else he might stop, his drive was approximately eight or more hours away.

CHAPTER 17:
BREWING UNKNOWN

Mina observed that the morning day was dark and dreary as she peered through the blinds of her window. She had put off looking outside for a while. But curiosity was a killer. Wanting to know what happened with the fire, she switched on the local news. It was only 11:10. She had almost an hour before she would face the group.

A far too cheery female news announcer stood in front of the park. Mina gasped. Fire burned endlessly in the background. This one had spun out of control beyond what she expected. She watched in stunned silence as the newscaster spoke.

"A fire started near the Homolovi Ruins State Park still burns this morning. Investigators said the blaze started between the hours of 8 and 9 last night, when an anonymous call was made to 911 from a local gas station to report it. So far, the fire has consumed countless acres of the woods. A thick mixture of smoke and fog has covered the city. It is suspected this fire was committed intentionally… we will bring you more news as it develops on this awful and tragic situation…"

Mina turned off the female announcer.

"Ohhh," Mina groaned.

Guilt became a higher priority burden, sinking her back into her bed. She buried her face in her hands.

"I thought it would be out by now," she whispered.

Mina pulled herself up and began to get ready, taking her time this time. She was in no hurry to discuss what she had done. Every piece of her dreaded the wrath of her accusers. She even blew dry her above shoulder length hair. When she was done, reluctantly, she was finally ready to leave.

Once she stepped outside, her nose burned with the scent of burning wood. She understood what the announcer meant of the fog. It was dangerously thick, thick enough to make it hard to see when driving. Still, she jumped in her car. The others would be there by now and waiting for her.

When she arrived at Jesse's, she noticed that his mother's car wasn't there so she let herself in. Scott, Ryan and Jesse sat in his room in silence, which was maintained even as Mina walked in.

Eyes glanced over her, all full of cold emotion. Anger, disappointment, guilt- all of those she read in their eyes. She wanted to get it over with as soon as possible, so she pulled out all of her research notes and journal, starting from beginning to end. Before anyone could intervene, she began explaining the case.

By the time she finished talking, telling them all that her case consisted of, it was after 12:30.

***

Bobby was almost there.

The difficult part would be finding her actual home. He had directions but he had no idea of the structure of the town. He stopped at the next rest stop, washed up, changed into fresh clothes and grabbed snacks for the rest of the trip.

***

When she was finished, Mina studied the group.

"Wow," Ryan said.

Jesse shook his head. Scott said nothing. Mina continued to study the boys.

"Yeah, that's it," Mina replied.

"And you didn't trust us enough to help?" Ryan asked.

He was obviously offended.

"I didn't think you'd be interested. You guys are so against the supernatural, ever since Brandon's unrealistic..." she trailed off.

"Whoa, I haven't heard anyone refer to him in a long time," Ryan said.

Jesse scoffed.

"Yeah, we're noticing some of his personality in her," Jesse said.

202

"Enough insults," Scott said, "Just stop before they start."

"Huh," Jesse said, "Well, it was a useless waste of intelligence. You didn't even get to see what you wanted to. All you did was kill another forest and cover our town in fog with an unnecessary fire which can't even be put out yet."

"Jesse," Scott began.

"No Scott. She needs to hear this," Jesse said.

Defiance trickled into Mina.

"I didn't know you were such a tree hugger," she muttered.

Jesse's face turned red with rage.

"I should have turned you in!" he shouted.

"Enough! Enough already!" Scott shouted.

Mina's face turned into a pout.

"And how do you know anything Jesse?" she began, "Maybe the demon just didn't get me. Maybe I didn't wait long enough."

"Well maybe you should go back," Jesse said.

Mina made a face. Scott stepped forward this time. Anger flashed across his usually calm face.

"Okay, stop. Enough!" he scolded.

Everyone quieted for a moment.

"Now just cool down and listen to me," he said.

Scott began to tell them the story he hadn't had the chance to tell, of the woman he had spoken with the day before. He assured Mina that it should have gotten her, since she was the manipulator of the fire, just like it attacked the woman's husband, Mike.

"But then again…" Scott started, "Maybe it really doesn't exist."

"But we saw it!" Mina shrieked, "We heard about it! It's real! You were there."

The conviction in her voice was paramount. Scott shook his head though.

"Yes, we heard about it from others, but did we really see it?" he asked, "Can we be sure we weren't delirious from driving and lack of sleep? We were so excited to have an adventure; maybe we made more of it than there was. It's like making something out of the fire instead of staring at a cloud to find a shape. It's something we don't really see. We create the images we see in the clouds. I've heard of cases like this in my Psychology class before where the mind does this, creates something that isn't there," Scott reasoned.

"Bullshit," Mina said, "We saw it."

The conviction never left her voice.

"But Mina think about it," Scott began, "Why would a demon come out of a fire, a small car fire but not a fire in the woods, and not get you when yours was of a far grander scale?" he asked.

Mina said nothing.

She didn't understand why it hadn't emerged. All she knew was now no one believed in her or her research. She achieved the opposite effect. She was truly disappointed she hadn't solved the case. Deep down she wondered if this monster or demon truly didn't exist. Stubbornly, she hid these thoughts from the group, knowing she had to have believed enough to start the fire in the first place.

"It exists," she said.

Jesse's nostrils flared at her indignation.

"That's it," Jesse said grabbing Mina's arm, "Let's go!"

Shocked, Mina said, "What? Where?"

He dragged her from the room by her arm.

Scott and Ryan followed behind them without stopping him. Jesse put his face close to Mina's, talking to her like she was a rotten spoiled child.

"We discussed this, and we think it is important that you go to the place and see what you have done. We drove by there earlier. It's a mess. It's ugly. You need to see it yourself, so you can be hit with reality," Jesse said

He continued pulling her along.

Mina didn't argue. She deserved to see what she had done.

"Guys, follow us," Jesse said.

Scott and Ryan boarded Scott's car.

***

Bobby felt refreshed now that he had made it to the town. He was excited to see Mina. Strangely though, the town appeared to be clouded in a mixture of smoke and fog. The overwhelming grayness made him nearly rear-end several drivers whose vehicles he could barely see. The fog had somehow snuck up on him. He hadn't seen any the entire drive there from Nevada. He suddenly remembered that night long ago. It crept up on him like a bad headache right before an important speech. He pushed the thought away not allowing it to surface.

Traffic of some sort had stopped all cars going into the town. He was stuck in one place, unmoving. Looking to his right, he saw the cause immediately. A great fire slashed through the woods. He hadn't seen it at first; his concentration had been on the cars in front of him. But the fire, that's where the fog came from, just like that night.

A flashback vision struck him suddenly; taking him back to the night that changed him. The fog surrounded him through the windshield...just like now.

"Oh shit," he said.

The memory subsided but suddenly he realized something.

"Please tell me you didn't do it Mina," he whispered.

Suddenly, traffic began moving again and he edged forward slowly. But he kept glancing uneasily at the fire.

Fear, seared with flash flames cut into him at the thought and visual of fire.

***

Jesse drove slowly, carefully through the thick cloud over the town. Cars in front of him were near invisible.

"Who created this mess? Sure wasn't Mother Nature," Jesse remarked, "I thought she was in charge of the environment. But I guess not when people like you take it into their own hands."

Mina gritted her teeth.

"I've had enough of your comments," she said.

"And I've had enough of your craziness," he said.

Jesse became quiet as he slowly drove. As he approached the park, numerous firefighters and police crowded the area, holding up traffic.

At a standstill, Jesse flipped on the local news radio station.

"Traffic is backed up near the Homolovi Ruins State Park leading from the highway and areas of the town. The road remains open for now, but authorities have debated shutting it down if the fire continues out of control. The smoke and fog from the fire have clouded over the town as the battle rages to get the fire under control. So far, there are no known casualties; though one firefighter received mild burns..." the male announcer claimed through the radio.

Jesse kept his silence, wanting her to see and learn on her own. They watched the road ahead of them and kept their silence.

Ten minutes later, they were in the same place. Traffic wasn't moving at all now.

"Come on," Jesse said.

Scott and Ryan sat in the car behind Jesse and Mina, listening to the news reports.

"Why is traffic so bad? I mean we're not driving into the woods. It's just the road past it," Ryan commented.

"I don't even know. Rubberneckers? Maybe there's an accident," Scott suggested.

"Probably," Ryan said.

He rested his head against the window.

***

Finally Bobby was making his way down the ramp into the town. Unfortunately, though he didn't want to, he knew he was going to pass closely by the fire. It appeared to be the only road and possibility to her house.

Bobby turned on the local news and was thankful to hear there were no casualties.

***

Car horns blared incessantly all around them. Jesse looked over at Mina, who observed the surroundings. She noticed that a wind had picked up. Unfortunately, the wind would spread the fire. Looking behind the car, Mina saw that beyond Scott and Ryan, another line of traffic had formed.

"Damn, this traffic is really heavy. I wonder what is going on," she said.

Slowly, dreamily she opened her car door.

"Mina what are you doing?" Jesse asked.

"I'm going to see what's wrong since I'm the only one with balls in this group," she said.

Quickly, she jumped from the car, slamming the door behind her. Jesse called her name. Mina walked through the thick cloud of fog and smoke, between cars to see what the problem was.

Immediately Scott noticed Mina get out of the car.

"What the fuck is she doing?" he asked.

"She's not thinking coherently," Ryan replied.

"Not coherent at all," Scott said.

He watched her walk through the fog of smoke.

Scott noticed that the wind picked up. Some of the surrounding unharmed trees swirled desperately in the breeze as if trying to escape their rooted places. The wind blew just like the woman told him last night, he remembered. Just like she described last night, the thought hit him again.

"Oh shit. The wind," Scott exclaimed.

"What are you talking about?" Ryan asked.

"Remember the woman, last night I talked to that woman. She described a hellacious wind before it came. Maybe it's on its way," Scott said frantically.

"Calm down Scott, it doesn't exist. This creature doesn't exist, it is merely a myth, one in which the two of you created," he said.

"I don't know," Scott said.

He looked forward at the fog, which made Mina disappear as she marched forward.

***

Bobby was getting closer to the town; he was nearing the road where the fire moved. Suddenly he noticed the strong wind beginning to blow. Images of the night his friends died came back to him again, swirling through his mindscape. It had become terribly windy then too.

He began to rock himself back and forth.

"Shut up, Bobby, you're just paranoid since you haven't left the house in so long," he said.

He shook his head trying to comfort himself. Suddenly ahead, not far from his car, he saw the outline, a figure of a woman who looked just like Mina. But the fog made it hard for him to be certain.

No, it can't be her so close, he thought.

***

Mina continued walking forward.

The fog was still blinding, though visibility was not impossible. She glanced back and forth at the people in their cars, walking on to see what the problem was which kept traffic still. Low beams were lit by most cars for better visibility in the gloom.

As far as she could tell, nothing was wrong to cause such traffic, besides the caution of driving in the fog. Mina assumed many were rubbernecking to get a good look at the flames.

The closer she moved forward, the greater the scent of smoke stained her nostrils, irritating her eyes. Getting a better glance at her destruction though, she saw how horribly out of control it had become. Her heart thudded with an even deeper understanding, the tearful revelation of what she had done. A tear began to slip free from her face. Rustling winds suddenly blew her off balance as she nearly fell into a blue Pontiac on her right. She steadied herself straight.

She continued walking forward.

Behind her, she heard someone call her name.

Suddenly, ahead of her, another voice yelled out for her.

Turning around, she saw Scott running up to her. She turned forward again to see a man with shoulder length black hair yelling to her. It was Bobby, his head hanging out the window of his car. It made her happy to see his face. Sudden excitement flushed her at seeing his image. Joyful turmoil boiled within her as the winds beat against her and her clothing.

She chose to continue forward. But before she made it to Bobby, traffic began moving again. Still hanging out of his car window, he got out, swiftly shutting the door. He walked to her. As the rest of traffic kept moving, the obnoxious horns were now aimed at Bobby for leaving his car in the middle of the road.

Suddenly, the sound of an airplane taking flight filled the sky. Mina looked up. Just a few feet before reaching each other, a fiery swirl unexpectedly evolved from the woods, shooting into the sky like a meteor. The darkened color, along with tinges of fire made it evident to Mina and the others what it was. It was the demon.

Fear pressed itself against her insides like a fearful child stuck between hiding inside of herself or breaking free from a restrictive wall. A screeching hell-fury sound erupted in the air. Her heart beat faster than any human's should.

As the monster ascended into the sky, another greater burst of wind flew up. Firefighters and policemen backed away from their position against the fire, fearing it would catch and cling onto them. The air seemed to scream even louder. A noise similar to the release of imprisoned, tortured souls erupted with a fury.

Mina stood frozen. Scott and Bobby froze as well, each individually frightened by the appearance of the beast. The creature let out another yell, making Mina swallow hard. She knew it was coming for her.

In just a blink, she realized the beast was descending quickly, aiming directly for her. The demon became larger as it forced itself down, seeing easily through the fog. To Mina, the image was blurry at first, becoming more and more detailed with its descent. Instead of running, she stood there, waiting to get a better look at what she had conjured up within those woods.

At the same instant, Scott noticed its planned destination. Running faster than he's ever pushed before, he quickly grabbed Mina, pulling her off to the right and rolling onto the ground as the demon continued down its path. Bobby, stunned, stopped where he was, in Mina's former space. The sight of the demon caused another deepened fear within him. Unable to move, he just simply stared at the beast as it came closer.

"Bobby!" Mina shouted.

Panic burst within her heart. He didn't hear her. He was mesmerized. He was frozen in fear. Mina struggled against Scott, trying to get up and away but he held tightly onto her.

"No!" she shouted, "Let me go! Bobby move!"

But he seemed unable to react, making Mina's desperation grow stronger. She fought against Scott but he held her too tightly. Bobby managed to turn his head to look at her with endless shock draping over him.

"Move!" she yelled.

But it was too late. Though the initial aim had been Mina, the demon did not care as it continued. With a stone face of gray, a long, sharp nose, slanted dark eyes and pointed ears, the demon looked like the devil, the true master of evil. A muscular near transparent form, almost humanlike arms and upper body stood out as a long stream of fire made up the rest of the body.

The demon took its path showing no understanding of mercy on the human before him. The mouth opened wide, a long stream of fire shooting down from its evil jaws.

"NOOOOOOOOOOOOOOOO!" Mina shouted.

Panic tortured her with the inability to act upon her inner frenzy. Bobby stood quietly, looking up as the flame came down on him. The demon swirled through the sky as it breathed, hovering in the air, shooting its devouring flames over Bobby. His body charred instantly to the blackened color of coal. His ashen statue form stood there only for a moment before it finally it fell into a pile, similar to the color of the asphalt paved onto the road.

Tears burst from Mina's face. Scott pulled her quickly to her feet, forcing her to run to the right with him.

Loud smashes of cars rear-ending each other nearly overlapped the noise of the screeching hell beast, though not fully. Those who saw the demon and the ashen man jumped from their cars and ran like a mass hysteria of people trapped in a burning building. Fleeing their own ultimate demise, the mob of people was unconcerned with who fell in the process.

The demon paused where it had just caused its first death. Hovering in the sky but moving slowly in a circle, observing its surroundings, it seemed to be calculating its next victim.

Instead of acting upon its course, from the fiery edges of the beast, smaller flames shot out, like flaming meteors. In every direction, these intangible balls of fire seemed to spit from its body, though none of the balls took aim to hit anything. Instead, the flame balls floated above the ground, hovering in the same manner as the larger beast and as if he silently instructed their actions.

People trampled each other, trying to get out of the way. A middle-aged couple was knocked to the ground in the crowd. Instead of running with the others, they rolled underneath a car to hide from the demon. Screaming men, women and children ran like swarms of mice through the cars, trying to find a place to hide. Woods were on the left side, houses far away to the right. The first few people besides Scott and Mina to reach the houses banged on doors to be let in, though residents of these homes had been evacuated hours prior and were not there to open up.

Mina turned around as she ran, and then stopped where she was to watch. Scott couldn't help but stop and watch what was happening as well. Their curiosities were stirred against their fear.

The darkened face of a gothic gargoyle encased in flame moved quickly through the line of cars. Each car in its path became ash as flames coated in red, yellow and orange shot out of the demon's mouth in fury. Car after car disappeared into ash, as though it never even existed.

As the main demon marked his path, the smaller balls of flame grew with fire, widening in size, though never reaching the size of the first demon. Each one had the same darkened face of the large demon though, only small features differentiated the creatures from one another. These smaller demons moved on, chasing the hoards of people.

Small wails of screeching fury mixing with flames erupted from their mouths. Without discrimination, they chased the people, instilling fear and destruction all around.

An athletic man ran as one of the smaller demons chased behind him. He looked back and then fell, expecting to die. Lying on the dirt, face to the ground; he peeked out the right side and then turned his head to the left, just to see the demon hovering face to face with him.

Breathing heavily now, the anguish of fear exhilarated the ugly face of the monster. His features crinkled, scrunching together like wrinkled clay, turning with the utmost interest as it watched the man.

But the demon, seeming bored that there was no chase, moved away from his face.

The young man lay there for a moment, hoping to hide from the others. Thinking he was safe, he slowly flipped over, staying as close to the ground as possible. As he turned, the man saw that the demon still hovered there behind him. It had been watching him, waiting for his next move. The man watched it in horror, wondering of its next tricky move. The ugly face seemed to smile as it quickly moved forward without hesitation. The man screamed half a scream just as his flesh was devoured in flame. Ashen fragments of his former body remained whole for just a moment before it spread like fertilizer over the earth.

Another man turned to look just in time to see the charred death. He fell to the ground in a mass of pity, uncaring if he was next. He wept tears of shock and sorrow as the demons passed him by, like a bear that only enjoyed live prey.

The larger demon kept working through the cars as though it was looking for someone specific. Through its wrath, nearly forty cars diminished into ash in a matter of minutes. Within the center of the cars, a large space had been opened up, now filled with more black sands of fertilizing ash. In front and behind the parking lot in the middle of the road, many other cars were left unharmed.

Scott grabbed Mina's arm. Since they had run before the hoards of people, they were closer to the homes than the others and the furthest from the fire.

Scott wanted to get Mina out of there and far away as soon as possible, in case it still wanted her. As he grabbed her, the demon slowly turned its head. Its beady black eyes were now staring directly at her. Though it was nearly a hundred feet away, it let out a large burst of fire that tried desperately to reach their faces. Scott forced Mina forward. They broke into a run. Heat lashed out behind them. It would not give up. And they wouldn't make it much farther.

In a split second, Scott made a decision. He jumped on Mina, tackling her to the ground. They rolled underneath the porch of the closest house. Their hearts raced deep panic as the only noise in their silence. Their curious eyes peeked out from underneath the porch.

The demon floated around, searching. Its face snarled, lifting its hideous nose into the air.

The creature stopped, directly where the two of them had fallen under. Moving closer, staring directly at them, it seemed to be playing a game of intimidation. Scott's heart beat faster with fear; his body trembled with the heat of intense sweat. He pulled Mina further under the porch with him. There was nowhere else they could go and nothing they could do to stop this monster's wrath. There was no escape.

The demon roared again, looking around with its dark, though now reddening eyes. The eyes changed as they watched- a fiber optic pyrotechnical glory of kaleidoscopic colors glided through those eyes. Those hues changed from dark to red in showing the fury within, as it seemed to be studying the house. Mina knew it had come for her, but wondered why it hesitated to get her.

Suddenly, the demon slowly drifted away, calmly as if floating on a serene tide.

Scott and Mina wondered of its plot. Silently, they lay there, waiting for its next move. Breathing heavily, they knew that at any minute they could die. Still, they laid there unmoving- knowing what it meant to be paralyzed by fear.

Meanwhile, the demon circled the house, moving out of their sight. He was studying the home as though it had never seen one before. It studied every part of the house. Suddenly, the demon flew up over the house, coming sharply down, exactly in the same spot it had left in the first place.

Roaring like an angry lion unable to find food, the demon moved closer to the space where Mina and Scott laid. Its eyes shone bright red, as the flames around its body seared brighter with anger. For what seemed like forever, the demon stared at Mina. She couldn't look at it anymore but she couldn't look away either. Wondering when it would attack, she tried to keep calm, though her heart was ready to explode with fear.

Scott began to silently pray. He had never been fully religious, but hoped something could help. The demon knew where they were, Mina was its whole aim and they were there under the porch together. He imagined his inevitable death.

"It's made of wood," Mina said, her voice shaking.

The demon was so angry, Mina realized, hoping she was right, but it wouldn't destroy the same material it had originated from. It was part of the wood, the woods- that was where it had come from.

Scott didn't understand what she meant at first, and then realized her hypothesis.

Still Scott was scared. Mina wasn't always a reliable source and he didn't know what extreme the demon would go to, to get her for her carelessness in starting the fire in the first place.

Mina pulled up the sleeve of her shirt. She slowly, subtly began to wiggle out of Scott's grip. He was too afraid to realize her movement.

The demon stared, its wrinkly skin scrunching up as it noticed. The fiery tail changed colors, similar to the style of fiber optic lights. Red, yellow and orange streamed through it, periodically changing place of the colors. It was actually quite beautiful despite its harsh appearance.

In a heightened state of shock and fear, mixed with a hope that Mina was right, Scott still didn't notice Mina's slight movement. All he could do was watch the demon, almost hypnotized by the moving colors, wondering what it would do next. It seemed calmer now, he observed and that frightened him even more. Its calmness made him think it was planning an intelligent attack.

Moving quickly, Mina rolled closer to the edge of the porch, near the demon.

"Mina!" Scott yelled.

Her sudden movement interrupted his train of contemplative thought.

"Take it!" Mina shouted.

She jutted her arm out from underneath the porch. The demon stared at her with blood red eyes. Scott grabbed her shirt from behind, trying to pull her back under, but she back kicked him between his legs. Scott let go, shrieking out in pain.

"I owe him this," she said, explaining her actions.

"Take it!" she yelled to the demon.

Hesitantly, the demon moved closer to her, though kept its distance from the wooden structure of the porch. Instead of shooting out a flame, the demon opened its mouth, the inside widening like an endless tunnel pit almost as if it was ready to swallow her whole. The structure of the mouth initially seemed human in size, but when it opened, the whole jaw seemed to give way, allowing the mouth to open wide enough to swallow a human body. The interior of the demon was the same gray, darkened color of its dry face and appeared to be the same texture, like that of a crocodile deprived of water.

From within its wide mouth, an initially unseen tongue slowly emerged. The shape and structure was abnormal. Instead of fully long and straight, the end of the tongue was rounded and appeared to have an actual shape to it, though Mina couldn't make out what it was.

Mina wondered if it was a trick, if it intended to pull her with the tongue, swallowing her into its mouth like food. Deep down, she wanted to pull her arm back in and hide, but knew that after what she had done, she deserved its wrath. It was her who had caused the loss to the demon, now she must face a vital loss of her own, her own arm.

The demon's tongue moved closer to her arm. Scott looked back up, just in time to see the demon's tongue descending onto Mina's arm. Expecting that it would take her, he shouted out.

"No!" he shrieked.

Just as Scott yelled, the demon wrapped its tongue around the middle of the inside of Mina's arm.

"AhhhhhHHHHHHHH!!!!" Mina screamed.

Stinging burning pain seared through her arm as the smoke began to rise from the burn. The demon's tongue continued to stain her with its flame. Her scream continued at the burning pain on her arm. Bubbling flesh deteriorated, penetrating the first couple layers of her skin. The scent of burning flesh stung her nostrils as she took her eyes off of the sizzling arm. Seconds later, the demon removed its tongue, just as Scott grabbed Mina, pulling her back under the porch.

Mina pulled the burned part of her arm against her chest. Still sizzling, it began to burn a hole in the front of her shirt. Pulling it away quickly, to avoid more burns, instant tears dropped from her eyes as she cried with pain.

The demon lingered there. Slowly, still staring with intimidation at Mina, it pulled its tongue back into its mouth, slurping with pleasure.

Mina continued to cry endless tears, as the demon almost seemed to smile, satisfied by her pain. It was almost as if she felt his own pain. She rocked back and forth violently crying. Scott's ability to empathize only made him feel a torrent of emotions. Sorrow, anger and countless others mixed together inside of him. He looked at the demon with all of those emotions in his eyes.

"Fuck you!" he shouted.

He pulled off his shirt, and then pulled Mina's arm out, wrapping it around her burn.

The demon smiled again, seeming to nod its head in approval as if it were a human. This mocking enraged Scott.

"Fuck you! Fuck you! Fuck you! Fuck you!" Scott continued to yell, almost crazily.

But he knew there was nothing he could do to get this demon, which had hurt his friend. Looking at Mina as she cried, he realized he had never seen her strength broken like that. He was filled with so much rage he didn't know how to begin to send it away from his body. Her tears were endless. Even though she had offered the demon her arm, he couldn't accept her pain.

Finally satisfied with his torture, the demon sprayed upward again, quickly moving back to where the cars had been incinerated. Mina, pained, though unable to contain her curiosity at what would happen next, jumped up, rolling out from under the house.

"Mina, no," Scott said, grabbing her good arm, "It might still want you."

Mina struggled against his hand, but knew he was stronger than her, especially since she was wounded. Instead, she kneeled on the ground from under the porch, holding her wounded arm against her chest as Scott tightened his grip on her good arm.

The demon hovered high above, in the center of the destruction it had caused, seeming to watch as though videotaping the event to memory. As it watched, the smaller fire balls reluctantly joined back into its body. As they joined together, a bright ray of orange-ish red light shone outwards from the demon, similar to the way the sun casts its light when it is time to set. The light spread horizontally across the sky with another ray spreading vertically, almost like a force field. More flashing spikes of this light filled the sky and area, almost like the standing feathers of a peacock.

Scott slowly, cautiously moved out from the porch, just enough to watch as well. He held tightly to Mina, not knowing if she would spontaneously get up and run towards it. They intently watched the sky.

After all of the smaller beings had been reunited in the sky, the demon looked one more time across the land at Mina, as though in warning. Her heart jumped in fear. She figured it was stronger now than it had just been and could take her out ever so quickly, easily.

Mina continued to kneel, frozen on the ground.

"Oh shit," Scott said.

He pulled hard on Mina's right arm. Fighting him with her good arm, he quit pulling. Together, they sat there and said nothing.

The demon let out one last screeching, wailing gasp of fury as they watched it, watching them.

The sound seemed to say, "Never again." Almost.

Finally, the creature shot upwards into the sky.

Mina stayed where she was. She didn't know if it intended to come for her again, but she did know she deserved her death if that was its motive.

Watching the demon, it hovered in the sky again, above the spot it had taken, staring directly at Mina. She bowed her head in respect. If it did attack, she didn't want to see it descend again, not like how it had taken Bobby.

Again, Scott tightened his grip on her wrist. He didn't care how fast that thing was, she was going with him under the porch, not into the ground with the demon.

Suddenly, the monster shot backwards into the flames in the woods, joining with the fire. Almost as suddenly as it disappeared, the winds stopped. The forest fire died down more than it had in the past day. A great rain began, helping put the fire down. Rain hadn't even been forecast that day, from Mina's recollection of the news.

Scott moved out fully from underneath the porch, finally letting Mina's arm free.

Standing, Mina slowly walked forward towards the wreckage and ash that once filled the heavily populated street with traffic. She continued on, hoping Ryan and Jesse had not gotten hurt. But she did not look for them. Instead, she walked alone to the large piles of ash.

"Mina!" Scott hollered from behind.

He couldn't be sure if the demon was fully gone, or if this was a trap.

Mina did not answer him, instead, continuing on.

"What the hell is she doing?" he grumbled.

Scott kept an eye on her from where he stood, but he was sick of chasing after her.

Mina walked until she found her first case of an incinerated pile of ashes from the demon. Kneeling down, she reached into her pocket, taking out her wallet. Within one of the pockets, she took a sample of the ashes to study.

Now, she had another mission to prove, since there was no solid video of the events that just occurred.

Mina stood again, looking around slowly, and then continued walking towards the woods.

Her arm was throbbing from the burn, though the cool water from the rain soaked through the shirt, making it feel better. Unwrapping Scott's shirt, she studied the burn. It was in the shape of a bracelet around her arm. Directly in the center was a figure, a figure perhaps of a Buddhist design or some sort of wiccan figure. It was a man, or figure of one, with what appeared to be smoke or fog above it. She had seen this image before in old books. It had no definition to it and she had briefly been intrigued by it for that reason. Covering her wound back up, she continued walking.

"So this wasn't really a demon at all, was it?" she asked herself, "It is a protector of Mother Nature. It is not simply fueled by fire, it is fueled by revenge, to teach a lesson to those who want to harm her," she said, looking around.

Some of the people had gotten away, unharmed. Their bodies lied, uncharred on the grass and ground of the area. Many cried over the loss of loved ones while others sat in the trauma of shock, rocking themselves back and forth.

Mina studied the scene, the emotions and the damage. Her technical brain spoke.

"It leaves survivors, so that they can learn from the errors of human ways. Negligence in the world we live in. Like the gothic gargoyle once built upon churches, for protection. She only attacks when she is cornered and then only to protect those whom she loves-the woods, the ground, the seas. All of which we coldly destroy. She has developed a guardian," Mina continued talking to herself.

Scott continued to yell to Mina with every step closer she moved to the woods, but she tuned him out of her mind.

"The whole time, I thought it to be evil, necessary to stop. But our people were traumatized, only because she was," the thought suddenly hit her.

More voices behind her called her name, it sounded like Jesse and Ryan, but Mina continued to walk as the fog slowly faded away, "She wants to show us her power," she said, "her strength, what she could do to us."

Mina passed the woods.

She would have preferred to go into them, into the dying fire, but for some reason, she knew it wasn't her time. Instead, she took a back route to her house, cutting through yards of houses nearby.

Finally home, she lay in her bed, scribbling a picture she had once seen in a book of legends of the earth. The picture was of a Buddha type of figure, holding a bowl with red within it. Around the head swirled an aura of gray. The figure itself was black. From what she remembered, the bowl symbolized fire as a protector. This picture was now the same ideogram that was burned upon her flesh.

"That picture was not a legend, but a part of Mother Nature that no one figured out until now," Mina said with the whitened expression of a ghost, "And now I'm marked by it. It wants me to figure it out, to tell everyone so the fires can stop."

Her phone rang, surprising her, though she managed to ignore it after the initial ring.

Going to her window, she opened it, staring at what she could see of the town.

Using her remote from the window, she turned on the news:

"We have reports of a major fender bender on the roadways where the traffic had originated due to the fog. Conflicting reports say meteors of some sort,

swooped down from the sky, causing more fire damage. As of now, the fire has *died down though; stay tuned for more news as it breaks…"* the woman announcer said.

Smiling, Mina shook her head at the fictitious words.

Mina flipped the television off.

"As many people as there were, witnesses and still they will all be brainwashed to see something that wasn't nearly as true as what they saw," she said, "A mother, protecting her children, the land, the trees, the seas," she continued.

Mina patted her pocket to make sure the wallet was still in there. All of those years in Biology will hopefully pay off now, she thought, as she knew she must study the ashes to find any type of sign, any clue as to where the being originated.

"But," she said, moving over to her mirror with cold blank eyes and studying her face, "I still have a lot of work to finish."

The phone continued to ring obsessively as she lay down on her bed. A knock came at the door and she ignored that too.

"You need to go to the hospital," Scott said.

Thankfully, she had locked the door. The phone rang again. She wondered why Bobby never left messages. She shrugged. Instead of answering it, she drifted off to sleep. The days were going to become long from here on out.

Her mission wasn't over. It was just beginning.

DEDICATIONS

As always, exceptional thanks to my parents, Shirley and John for bringing me into this world and better yet, for putting up with me!

Special thanks to those who are oftentimes there in my life; my siblings, aunts, uncles, cousins and many more who are sporadically displaced around the globe.

Super special thanks go out to my very first editor, Christie Johnson, for her time and care in the editing of this book.

Even more special thanks go out to the wonderful *A Chemical Skyline* crew, where my introduction to acting re-inspired and fueled my written artistry even greater. All of those involved, particularly the members of E-nertia Global Systems, LLC. and Veltri Talent Management deserve applause and thanks. In particular, I would like to thank Matthew T. Veltri and Jason T. Swinchock for putting their trust in me during the inception of two separate projects, *Final Moon* and *A Chemical Skyline*.

Lastly, I thank you, my dear friends, old and new, for listening to my babble and reading my books. I greatly appreciate the new fans I've acquired as well. I'd make a list of my thanks but it would be longer than this book.

Just know that you mean the world to me!

Christine Soltis

About the Author

Christine Marie Soltis was born and raised in Washington, Pennsylvania. For the past eight years, she has been avidly and passionately writing fiction. At this time, she has created ten novels, co-authored a screenplay, released two poetry books and a short story compilation. Of those written works, the previously published titles are displayed on the next page.

Just recently, Christine made her acting debut in E-nertia Global's production of *A Chemical Skyline*. Currently, she is a contributor to *Verdure Magazine*. She attended Point Park College until 2003, pursuing a degree in Broadcasting with a minor in Psychology. She has worked in the news radio business in Pittsburgh, PA since 2002.

Visit her website at http://darkwriters.tripod.com
Email at: inalandofhatred@gmail.com
Check out: www.enertiaglobal.com

Previous Publications

July 2008

December 2008

April 2009

August 2009

August 2009

November 2009

CPSIA information can be obtained
at www.ICGtesting.com
Printed in the USA
FSHW04n0704020418
46441FS

9 780557 631889